OWNED BY THE BRATVA
AN AGE GAP, FORCED MARRIAGE ROMANCE

K.C. CROWNE

Copyright © 2023 by K.C. Crowne

All rights reserved.

No part of this book may be reproduced in any form or by any electronic or mechanical means, including information storage and retrieval systems, without written permission from the author, except for the use of brief quotations in a book review.

❋ Created with Vellum

DESCRIPTION

"Let's get this over with."
His voice rumbling through the chapel like thunder.

No wedding bells.
No blushing bride.
I have no idea who this stranger before me is.
Towering over me, at least a foot and a half taller...
All I know about this intimidating man is a family history of cold-hearted criminals.

My plan: find any possible way out of this cage of horrors.

But a plot twist stops me in my tracks.
And the man I've been running from becomes my only possible hope of freedom.
And when he finds out I'm pregnant with his baby,
He becomes something completely new:
A husband who'll turn the whole world into ash before he lets his newfound family burn.

This is Pyotr Antonov's story and a fully standalone romance in the Bratva Billionaire Series. Follow the Antonov brothers as they rule their city and the hearts of their woman. If you enjoy billionaire, boss, Bratva romance suspense with unexpected twists and turns you're sure to love the Antonov brothers.

CHAPTER 1

ALINA

Today is my wedding day... and I have no idea who my husband is.

I'd heard whispers of my upcoming nuptials, but I didn't think Mother would actually go through with it. As the youngest of four siblings, I genuinely thought there were no more strategic marriages for her to deviously carry out.

I foolishly believed that maybe I wouldn't be shipped off to wed some slimy French politician like my eldest sister, Oksana, or a sketchy arms dealer from Colombia like Nikita, or a shady Russian banker engaging in one too many inside trades like Yasemin.

The news of my marriage hit me from out of nowhere. I woke up this morning fully expecting to go for a leisurely ride on my mare, Polina, through the endless grass fields behind our summer home in the countryside. Imagine my surprise when Mother stormed in, ripped off my covers, and all but dragged me out of bed by the ear.

"Stop crying," she snaps at me, roughly wiping a ruined tissue over my face. Mother clicks her tongue in disapproval. "Look what you've done, Alina. You've smudged your mascara!"

My stomach churns as I look around the space. We've come

straight to a judge's chambers, which tells me two things: this was a last-minute match, and, unlike my sisters, I will not be getting a grand wedding ceremony. Everything about this screams rushed and secretive, and I'm not going to lie, that stings.

Maybe it's because Mother doesn't think I'm worth it. I've never been her favorite daughter, and her using me as a throwaway bargaining chip doesn't exactly convince me otherwise. Unlike Oksana, Nikita, and Yasemin, I get no time to prepare. Probably because Mother knew I'd try to run away at the first opportunity.

"Such a mess," Mother grumbles as she roughly combs her fingers through my brunette hair. My shoulder-length locks are still tangled and flat on one-side from sleep. That's how fresh to this horrible situation I am.

I'm definitely not the stunning image of a bride-to-be right now.

"I want to go home," I plead with her. "Please, Mother, I'll be good. I don't want to get married!"

Mother shushes me harshly, exhaling through clenched teeth. "Enough, Alina. The Antonovs are already on their way."

I blanche, my heart sinking into the pit of my stomach. "The Antonovs?" I rasp. "You're marrying me off to an *Antonov*?"

To be fair, Mother doesn't seem all too pleased, either. The Antonov Bratva has been a thorn in my family's side for years. A powerhouse in Moscow, both ruthless and exceedingly business savvy, they've managed to snap up the lion's share of control in the city—and have butted heads with my family, the Salkov Bratva, on more than one occasion. Our coexistence is reluctant at best, but from what little I've been able to glean listening in on Mother's phone conversations, our run-ins with the Antonovs have taken a more disagreeable turn of late.

Mother doesn't tell me much about the family business. I don't think she ever had any intention of bringing my sisters or me into the fold. What I *do* know is the Antonovs are not to be fucked with. They're highly resourceful, have a seemingly endless network of powerful contacts, and they're not above keeping prisoners in their rumored Pit. So why is she marrying me to one?

When I begin to tremble, Mother grips my shoulders tight, digging her perfectly manicured nails into my flesh. "Alina, for the love of God, quit your whimpering!"

"I don't understand," I say around a soft sob. "Why are you doing this to me?"

"For peace," Mother says cryptically.

I frown. Does she mean peace of mind? Literal peace? I don't think I'll ever understand this woman.

"Who am I even marrying? One of their lieutenants?"

"No. One of the brothers."

I feel faint. I know precious little about the Antonov brothers, but what I *do* know isn't pleasant. There are four of them, I think. Tight knit, incredibly loyal to one another, and deadly. If you cross one, you cross them all. That's what I've heard, anyway. Dread claws through my lungs and leaves them ribboned and bloody.

"You'd have me marry one of those monsters?" I rasp. "Haven't you heard the rumors? They imprisoned their own uncle!"

"Alina," Mother hisses, a warning.

"You can't make me do this."

"Yes, I can." Mother glares at me, her dark black eyes cold and dead like a shark. I've never known an ounce of kindness from this woman, but this is the first time I've ever truly feared her. "If you don't do as I ask, I'll sell that beloved horse of yours."

I hold my breath, tears stinging my eyes. "Leave Polina out of this."

"You dare take that tone with me? How did I raise such a spoiled girl?"

I'm not spoiled, I want to snap. *I just refuse to lie down and let you walk all over me like you did with my sisters.*

"I know of a few butchers who've been looking to sell horse meat," Mother continues. "Keep pushing your luck. We'll see if that stupid creature survives the night."

My stomach bottoms out. Mother knows how much that horse means to me. Polina was a foal when she was gifted to me by my father before his passing. When my sisters were married off one by one, Polina was the only one I could turn to for company. I can't tell if Mother is serious, but I'm not willing to tempt fate. As the head of the Salkov Bratva, I know for a fact she's capable of unspeakable cruelty.

"Mother, *please*, I—"

"Silence Alina! They're here."

I turn slowly, every breath I draw thin and dry. Three men enter without pomp or circumstance. They're all dressed in sharp business suits, like it's a uniform. If I had to venture a guess, I'd say they're all in their late thirties or early forties—almost double my age. Brothers, judging by the similarity of their features. They all have dark brown hair and deep brown eyes to match. At first glance, there's a rugged handsomeness to all of them, a poise in their posture that only comes with confidence and power. They walk in like they own this room.

And that makes me nervous.

My eyes scan over each of their faces. Which one of them am I supposed to marry against my will?

"Violetta," the first man says. He has a deep, commanding voice.

"Mikhail," Mother replies tersely.

The second man in line sticks his hand out to shake. He has a crooked grin and an easy charm. When Mother provides her hand, he smoothly presses his lips to the back of her fingers. "A pleasure to finally meet you, Mrs. Salkov."

Mother's lip curls into a sneer, contrasting her polite words. "Likewise, Dimitri."

The third brother catches my eye. He stands in front of us, looming like a stone sentry, his gaze raking over me from head to toe as if in appraisal. His natural intensity makes my heart stutter. I'm fascinated by the hard line of his jaw, the sharp slope of his nose, and the firm press of his lips. If I'm being honest, he's incredibly handsome. Beautiful in his severity.

He doesn't speak, makes no effort to introduce himself. He just... *stares* at me. I can't tell if he's glaring or admiring. Either way, his scrutiny makes me squirm.

Dimitri pats him on the shoulder. "Don't be shy, Pyotr," he teases lightly. How he can be so cavalier at a time like this is beyond me. "Say hello to the lovely lady."

Pyotr does no such thing. He tears his eyes away and starts toward the judge, who's been patiently waiting off to the side. "Let's get this over with," he grumbles, his voice rumbling like distant thunder.

This is who I'm supposed to marry?

I don't bother giving Mother a pleading look. Instead, my eyes flit toward the door. Should I make a break for it? If I'm fast enough, maybe I can escape this place and never look back. My fight or flight instincts kick in, but I accidentally trip into a third option—I freeze. Why is this happening to me?

Mother gives me a hard shove toward Pyotr, who stands in front of the judge with his arms crossed over his wide chest. I can make out the hard lines of muscles beneath the fabric of his suit jacket. His clothes are not ill-fitting, it's just that he's already so big, the slightest flex puts undue stress on his seams.

With a shaky step, I take my place beside him, casting my eyes to the polished tile floors. The tips of my fingers and toes tingle, but the rest of my body is numb. I can't believe this is happening. If this is a nightmare, I'd really like to wake up.

"Let's cut straight to the chase," Mother tells the judge.

The man nods, casting us all with a wary look. I'm pretty sure he's on my mother's payroll, otherwise he would have objected to this very obvious marriage-under-duress. He dutifully clears his throat and begins.

"We are gathered here today to join Pyotr Antonov and Alina Salkov in matrimony. Will there be an exchanging of vows, or..."

"No," Pyotr says sharply.

A sticky lump is lodged in the back of my throat. He towers over me, at least a foot and a half taller than myself. I have to fight the instinct to shrink into a small ball and disappear.

"Right," the judge says slowly. "If that's the case, do you, Pyotr, take Alina to be your lawfully wedded wife?"

"Yes." He speaks like a gunshot: clear, blunt, and devastating.

"And do you, Alina, take Pyotr to be your lawfully wedded husband?"

I glance at Mother over my shoulder, desperation dripping from my every pore. I don't know why I turn to her for help. She's the reason I'm in this mess to begin with. When I take too long to answer, Mother discretely drags the tip of her thumb across her open throat, a threat. At this point, I don't know if she's promising to kill Polina or me. Regardless of her meaning, I know I have no choice.

I suck in a sharp breath. "I do."

Two simple words, yet their finality weighs heavily on my shoulders. Just like that, I'm married to a man I know nothing about.

The judge nods. "Then with the power vested in me, I now pronounce you husband and wife. You may kiss the—"

"No."

A quiet, bitter laugh rushes out of my lungs. What a *dick*. I mean, it's not like I want to kiss him, either, but his harsh rejection is more than I can handle right now. Am I really going to have to spend the rest of my days with this jerk? I don't care if he's easy on the eyes. If Pyotr is going to keep being this abrasive, I can kiss any hope of a mildly content marriage out the window.

The judge has us sign our names on an official certificate. Pyotr signs it quickly while I take my sweet time. If only I had a longer name, maybe I could have prolonged the inevitable.

Behind me, Mother and Mikhail shake hands like this whole thing was a run-of-the-mill business transaction. Maybe it is. That's the way it was for Oksana, Nikita, and Yasemin. I shouldn't have expected anything different for myself.

Before we leave, Mother pulls me into a tight hug. It's not exactly affectionate, more of a crushing vice grip. She presses her lips to my ear and hisses, "Be a good wife. Do as he says. Don't fuck this up."

I glare at her when she finally releases me. Father used to say that most blessings come disguised, but today, I'm not so sure. For all I know, I could be trading the clutches of one monster for another.

"You."

I look around and find Pyotr staring at me again. His eyes burrow into me, so focused and intent I can't help but feel exposed. His face is impassable. I don't know what he wants with me.

Pyotr tosses his chin in the direction of the door. "Let's go," he orders simply before heading out first.

I clench my hands into tight fists and grit my teeth.

Do as he says. Don't fuck this up.

I make zero promises.

CHAPTER 2

PYOTR

F*uck.* She's so beautiful I want to claw my fucking eyes out. I'm pretty sure I've already freaked her out with all the staring. I swear it was an accident. I just couldn't look away from that cute button nose, those gorgeous green doe eyes, and those lips... So soft and plush and *frowning.*

I never would have agreed to this, but my eldest brother is incredibly convincing when he wants to be. Mikhail explained the situation, the stakes. The Salkov Bratva aren't to be trifled with. They have a large army of loyal men to rival the Antonovs. They're resourceful, rich, and well-connected. For the past few years or so, they've been encroaching on Antonov territory in Moscow, minor border skirmishes here and there.

War would have been inevitable—and bloody.

I understand Mikhail's logic. An alliance through marriage is the simplest way of keeping the peace. The only problem is that Mikhail and Dimitri are already married. Their own children, my beloved nieces and nephews, are all much too young to be arranged. And I honestly don't think my brothers would ever think to use them as pawns. They love them far too much. I suppose Mikhail could have asked Luka, but knowing our youngest brother, he would never have agreed to such a thing.

The only viable option left was me.

I'm not interested in the Antonov Bratva's business. Mikhail and Dimitri... They've grown accustomed to this life. This kingdom promised to us as young boys doesn't hold any sway over me. If we hadn't been run out of Russia all those years ago, there's a good chance I would have grown up to lead at their side, but that's not how it played out. I have a life in New York, a company to run. So, while I'm loyal to my brothers, I do my best to keep out of their affairs.

Running a multi-million-dollar cybersecurity company whilst having affiliations with organized crime... It's not ideal. So I keep my distance—both figuratively and literally.

But when Mikhail told me about the Salkovs, the threat they posed, and the army they've slowly been gathering right on our doorstep... I knew I had to help. Not out of the goodness of my heart, but out of duty to my family. Conflict with the Salkov Bratva would have spelled disaster for my brothers. If I can ensure peace and prosperity by signing a marriage certificate, then so be it. It's just a piece of paper.

At least, that's what I told myself. I forgot there's a living, breathing woman involved in this equation—a woman who's now trembling beside me in the backseat of my car, sheepishly glancing at me out of the corner of her eye. Our driver pulls into traffic, headed downtown.

"What?"

It comes out as a grumble. *Fuck.* I'm not good at this sort of thing. Friendly conversations, easy jokes, welcoming smiles—that's my twin brother's thing. Dimitri has always had a knack for making friends, putting people at ease. He got all the charm, while I have enough charisma to impress a gnat.

It's not my intention to make her uncomfortable, but given the circumstances, I think it was inevitable. I hold no ill will toward her, but I'm not exactly eager to get to know her, either. We're strangers bound together in the eyes of the law and nothing more.

"Where are we going?" she asks, her voice so soft and sweet the roaring car engine almost drowns her out. I have to turn my left ear toward her to get a clearer sound, but it just makes me look like I'm facing away.

"New York," I answer flatly. Again, not because I'm trying to be an asshole. That's just the way I talk. Concise and to the point. In the business world, time is money, and I'd rather not waste it on meaningless pleasantries and flowery language.

Alina shifts in her seat. She smells like a field of lavender. It's... nice. Certainly not unpleasant. "New York?" she echoes quietly. "I, um…"

"What is it?"

Her eyes flit down to her lap and remain glued there. She can't look at me. I don't blame her. I wouldn't be at all surprised if she hates me.

"I don't have my passport," she answers with a shaky exhale. "I didn't have a chance to pack any of my things. My mother didn't give me very much time to prepare."

I pity this poor woman. At least Mikhail did me the courtesy of discussing the details. Apparently, Violetta Salkov was nowhere near as accommodating for her daughter. It's difficult for me to ignore Alina's glassy eyes, smudged makeup, and blotchy cheeks. Hell, she still looks half asleep. I'm sure she'd rather be anywhere but here with me.

"Your mother has already given me your necessary travel documents," I inform her. "Everything else will be purchased for you upon our arrival."

The silence that follows is tense. Thick. It's difficult to breathe.

She picks at her fingernails, pulls at a loose thread on the sleeve of her white cashmere sweater. "When do we leave?"

I almost don't hear her again. She's sitting to my left, which is my good ear, but her words are still a distant muffle at best.

"First thing in the morning. A chartered flight."

Alina nods slowly, almost as if in a trance. "Do you, um... Does this mean we're staying the night?"

"At a hotel," I answer.

She fiddles with a lock of her hair, her nerves plain to see. I may be stunted where conversation is concerned, but I'm not an idiot. I can sense her unease. Is she worried about what's going to happen once we're alone together?

We arrive at the hotel in record time. Alina fidgets as we ride the elevator up to the executive suite. I arrived yesterday evening, my small carry-on suitcase resting at the end of the bed.

The *singular* bed.

She keeps her distance, remaining by the door as I venture into the room and shrug off my suit jacket, tossing it over the back of a chair. Alina still hasn't budged from the doorway. She's my wife. I suppose I should try to make some effort in making her feel comfortable—I just don't know how.

"Sit," I tell her.

Alina glares at her me, her emerald green eyes no longer frightened and lost. She looks pissed more than anything. "You don't need to be so rude," she snaps, a hint of her fire crackling through.

It looks like there's more to this timid girl than I first thought.

I exhale. "*Sit.*"

With a disgruntled *hmph*, Alina plops down in the wingback chair near the window. I wonder if it's a strategic choice on her part. She could have taken the loveseat, but that would have left room for me to join her.

"This is what's going to happen," I say, because it frankly needs to be said. "Neither of us wants this marriage, but what's done is done. When we get to New York, we will have an interview scheduled with an immigration officer to make your citizenship permanent."

Alina listens in absolute silence. She's either taking diligent mental notes or ignoring me entirely as she glares a hole into the center of my forehead.

"We didn't exchange vows before, but I will now. I vow never to touch you or do anything against your will. You will be my wife in name only. While you're required to live with me, you're free to live your own life as long as it doesn't interfere with mine. I will make sure you are provided for financially. You will want for nothing."

She huffs. "How romantic."

I set my jaw. If today is any indication, the next few weeks are going to be rough as fuck. I'm already exhausted. "Do you have any questions?"

"Just one," she murmurs.

"Ask."

"What do you get out of this?" Alina leans back and crosses her legs. She looks like a queen upon her throne, eyeing me with nothing but suspicion. "What did they threaten you with?"

"Threaten?"

"Your brothers. What are they holding against you?"

"What makes you think they'd do such a thing?"

"Why else would you agree to marry someone you don't know?" Alina asks, arching a brow. "My mother threatened to kill my horse. And then me." She says this with a sad smile, like she knows how fucked up it is yet has no choice but to accept it.

I frown. I wasn't aware of this, though I can't say I'm surprised. I agreed to this marriage out of duty for my family, but Alina had her arm twisted behind her back. I can't think of a response. There *is* no response. Any attempt I make to comfort her would only come across as disingenuous, not that I'd know how to comfort her in the first place.

After a moment, Alina sighs. She stands up and glances at the doors leading to the ensuite bathroom. "Is it okay if I take a shower? Mother dragged me out of bed and took me straight to the judge, so I didn't get a chance to freshen up."

Dragged out of bed? She's having a rougher day than I.

I gesture to the bathroom, silently giving her my permission. Alina walks past me, giving me a wide berth, before disappearing around the corner and locking the door firmly. When I hear the muffled sound of the shower running, I finally allow myself to take a deep breath.

The guilt is starting to get to me. This situation isn't technically my fault, but I *do* feel bad for Alina. She's young. Too young. She probably thought she had her whole life ahead of her. Now she's stuck with me, and she didn't even get a say in the matter. I suppose the least I can do is try to be a little nicer.

But first, I call my brother.

"How's the honeymoon going?" Dimitri asks with a hearty laugh.

I scoff. "Shut up, that's not funny."

On the other end of the line, my brother sighs. "No, you're right. I'm sorry it had to be this way, Pyotr."

"I don't know what to do, Dima. I don't think this is going to work."

"You've only been married for an hour, little brother. Have you thought about—oh, I don't know—getting to know her?"

"She can barely even look me in the eye."

"That's because you're intimidating as fuck. Would it kill you to smile?"

"It might."

"Did you just make a joke? Oh my God, it's a Christmas miracle."

"It's June," I point out flatly.

He sighs. "The safety of both our families is riding on this arrangement," Dimitri says seriously.

"You're starting to sound like Mikhail."

Dimitri ignores me. "The two of you just need to adjust, that's all."

"Easy for you to say. *You* married for love."

"Let's not forget that Natalya literally tried to blow me up with a car bomb."

I shove my fingers through my hair, exasperated. "I don't know how to talk to her," I grumble.

"Just start small, Pyotr. And be patient. Maybe take her out to dinner or something. Talk about your interests."

"I sincerely doubt she's willing to listen to me go on and on about the ups and downs of the stock market."

Dimitri laughs. "Oh, I forgot. You're the boring twin."

"Fuck off."

"You've got this, Pyotr. And besides, no one said you had to stay married to her forever. Just until Mikhail and I can figure out how to keep the Salkovs from being a threat. This was supposed to be a temporary solution. Some tape over a leaky pipe."

"You two better figure it out fast. I'll make sure to have my divorce lawyer on standby."

"*Oh.*"

I look up, startled by the sound of Alina's soft gasp. I hadn't noticed her approach. She's fresh out of the shower, bundled up in one of the hotel's complimentary bathrobes with her hair damp and dripping over her shoulders. There's no doubt about it—she heard me.

"I have to go," I tell Dimitri.

"Good lu—" I hang up before my brother has the chance to finish.

Alina worries her bottom lip with her teeth. Even at this distance, I can smell the hotel's floral shampoo and body wash wafting off her hair and skin. She stands in the doorway to the bathroom, just as hesitant as she was when she first arrived.

"I want to take a nap. I had an early morning." She eyes me up and down cautiously. There's no trust here. Understandable. Perhaps it's best if I make myself scarce for now.

"You take the bed," I say. "I'll be downstairs making a few phone calls."

"With your divorce lawyer?" she asks pointedly.

I deserved that.

Alina doesn't crawl into bed until I'm halfway out the door. She pulls the soft blankets around her and creates her own little fortress, tucked away from the rest of the world. I consider asking her if she wants anything to eat. I'm sure I can trouble the hotel staff to send some food up. The second her head hits the pillow, the sound of her soft snores just barely reach my ears. Out like a light. I decide to leave her be and head downstairs to the lobby.

I spend the next half an hour productively. Just because I'm in a different country doesn't mean there isn't work to do. My inbox is full of forwarded emails from my personal assistant and secretary, Merrybell, the most important ones flagged for me.

I rub my temples with a heavy sigh. So much to do, so little time. I already had enough on my plate planning the corporate takeover of PrismLock, my company's biggest rival in the cybersecurity space, and now this?

Just start small, Pyotr. And be patient.

My brother's voice echoes inside my skull.

Patience... Yeah, I can do that.

I make my way back to the hotel room, entering quietly in case Alina is still asleep. I don't hear any snoring, though there is a big mound beneath the bed covers.

Maybe a little *too* big.

Suspicious, I walk over and pull the covers down and discover that Alina has piled up a bunch of towels and spare pillows from around the room to look like her.

Fuck.

It looks like my new wife is on the run.

CHAPTER 3

ALINA

Holy crap, I did it!

I was worried Pyotr would notice me sneaking out the front lobby, but I was thankfully able to hide behind a fully loaded luggage cart and waltz straight out the door. Pyotr was so involved with whatever he was doing on his phone he didn't even look up once.

Now I'm free.

I just have two problems: I have no money, and I have nowhere to go.

Returning home isn't an option. Mother will surely have my head. I bet it'd be a swift death, but if she's feeling particularly cruel, Mother will allow me to watch as my horse is slaughtered, then return me to Pyotr and I'll be right back where I started.

Right now, I need to focus on getting out of Moscow. The farther I get, the farther from my mother's influence. The Salkovs have eyes and ears all over the city, and now that I'm technically an Antonov, too, I'm sure there's a whole network of people ready to snatch me up and return me to my ever-scowling, eager-to-divorce husband.

Husband.

God, I can't believe I'm married. It doesn't feel official in any capacity whatsoever, yet the word has drilled itself into the deepest crevices of my brain. No wedding, no ring, not even a kiss after the *I do*. I never expected to have a fairytale ending but *come on*.

With nothing but the clothes on my back, I make my way through downtown. I'm thankful it's the middle of summer because I forgot my jacket. Russian winters are unforgiving and ruthless, so at least I have the seasons on my side.

I ignore the grumble of my stomach as I pass a local coffee house. It suddenly dawns on me that I haven't had a chance to eat yet. Mother was so determined to get me to the judge she didn't spare me any time for breakfast. Despite the hunger, I keep walking. I tell myself this is nothing. I can deal with a little hunger.

What I *can't* deal with is the thought of being trapped in a loveless marriage.

I make it another ten blocks before I'm thoroughly exhausted and lost. The hotel is far behind me, leaving plenty of distance between Pyotr and me. I'm sure he's realized by now that I've run away. Here's hoping this head start will keep me out of his grasp forever.

As luck would have it, I happen upon a large supermarket. Perfect. It's high time I found something to eat.

I walk in like I'm any other customer. The employees certainly don't suspect anything, and they won't as long as I don't give them a reason to. I make my way to the hot lunch section of the supermarket, picking up a small sandwich I can mostly hide against my palm. I shuffle up and down the aisles, making sure to keep out of sight as I rip into the package. Do I feel bad about stealing? Of course.

But a girl's gotta do what a girl's gotta do.

There's no time to actually enjoy the food. I scarf the whole thing down in four or five bites, afraid someone might catch me with my stolen sustenance. After finishing, I throw the wrapped into an empty shopping cart and keep walking. I leave the store directly behind a woman and her child, staying close enough to seem like I'm leaving with them and their full cart, but not so close

I cause them concern. Once I'm out, I continue my trek through the city.

I'm not sure how far I'm going to get, but I'm as determined as ever. Mother has kept me relatively isolated, but that doesn't mean I'm without allies here in the city. I haven't spoken to my sister, Yasemin, in a few months, but I'm sure she'd be willing to help me in my time of need. Yasemin, too, knows what it's like to be arranged in a marriage she doesn't want.

It takes me longer than I want to find her home. I've only got my memory to work with here. She lives in an impressive apartment complex on the richer side of Moscow. I don't hesitate to walk straight up to the building's front door and press the buzzer. The electric *brrr* rattles my eardrums as I impatiently shift my weight from foot to foot, shooting a cautionary look over my shoulder. Still no sign of Pyotr or Mother. I might be able to escape the two of them, after all.

"Hello?" my sister's voice crackles over the speakers.

"Yasemin! Yasemin, it's me!"

"Alina? Oh my God, come on up!"

The moment the front doors unlock, I whip them open on their hinges and race inside. I take the elevator to the top floor and practically sprint down the hall to her door. It's been a while since I've visited her in person, but I still remember the red-brown carpet, beige walls, and art deco-inspired sconces of the hallway. Yasemin must have heard my heavy footfalls approaching because her apartment door swings open before I even have the chance to knock.

"Alina!" she gasps, throwing her arms around me in a tight embrace. "Oh my God, it's so good to see you!"

I hug her back, relief flooding my veins. The tears come next. I've been holding them back all day, and now there's no stopping them. "Yasemin, something terrible's happened. I really need your help."

"I know," she says with a pitiful smile, leading me into the apartment. It smells like she was in the middle of making sugar cookies. "I'm so sorry, dear sister."

Something in her tone makes the hairs on the back of neck stand on end. "You... You know? But how?"

My sister takes my hand, her grip uncomfortably tight. She guides me into the kitchen, complete with floral backsplash, stainless steel appliances, and a kitchen island with a white granite counter. Seated on one of the island bar stools is a man I recognize. He's impossible to miss with his mountainous shoulders and back wide enough to rival a billboard. I'd know this monster anywhere.

Pyotr doesn't even bother turning to look at me, instead helping himself to a cup of tea Yasemin no doubt brewed for him. "Did you enjoy your walk, wife?" he asks gruffly.

Wife. He makes it sound like an insult.

My legs are two seconds away from buckling. "How did you find me?"

"Traffic cameras."

I furrow my brows. "What?"

"We Antonovs have a talented hacker in our pocket. He can hack into the traffic cameras around the city. We use the footage to keep track of our enemies... Or runaway brides."

I gulp. No wonder the Antonov Bratva is one of the most respected—and feared. If what Pyotr is saying is true, it would explain his family's ability to rapidly expand. There's no need to worry about running into rival gangsters or the police who might thwart your plans if you know exactly where they are at all times. I'd be impressed if it weren't for the fact that I'm *so* fucked right now.

"You only have one family member in the city," Pyotr continues. "It was simply a matter of asking Violetta for your sister's address."

I hold my breath. For some reason, I'm more horrified at the thought of Mother knowing what I've done than being caught by Pyotr. He may be a big, burly man, but I don't think he'd ever harm me physically. Mother, on the other hand, isn't above punishing slaps across the face and worse. I learned that the hard way growing up, fearing those thick gold rings she wears on her fingers like a bejeweled brass knuckle.

Pyotr rises from his seat, his expression unreadable. I'm starting to think he doesn't have facial muscles. It's like staring at a blank wall. "I'm going to give you two options," he says. Now that I've heard him speak more than a word at a time, I'm notice his Russian, while fluent, is tinted with an American accent.

I fold my arms across my chest, indignant. "Well?"

"You can either walk out of here with me of your own volition, or I can throw you over my shoulder and carry you out."

I scoff. "Throw me over your shoulder? What are you, a caveman?"

"No. I'm an impatient man dealing with an impertinent wife."

"*Impertinent?*" I seethe. "You'll have to forgive me for not falling head over heels for you."

Pyotr sighs. "Thank you for the tea," he says to my sister before moving in to do exactly as he promised.

With speed that could rival a cheetah, Pyotr takes three long strides and closes the gap between us. He moves surprisingly fast for someone with so much mass. I barely have a chance to blink before he bends down, wraps his thick arms around my thighs, and slings me over his right shoulder.

I kick and I scream, flailing helplessly. "Let me go, you giant ogre!"

"Don't be rude."

"Yasemin!" I look to my sister for support. "Yasemin, please. You have to help me!"

She shakes her head. "I'm sorry, Alina. This is Mother's will."

"Screw her!" I roar, red hot anger flooding my veins. The betrayal blindsides me, steals my breath.

I scream for my sister as Pyotr carries me out. I scream as we exit the building. I scream when he drops me in the backseat of a waiting car. Eventually, my voice breaks. I'm out of steam. My anger quickly dissolves into unbridled sorrow. None of this is fair and I'm helpless to stop it.

Beside me, Pyotr doesn't say a word. Instead, he nods at the driver using the reflection of the rearview mirror.

We don't go back to the hotel. Instead, we head straight to a private landing strip on the outskirts of the city. A private jet is waiting on the tarmac by the time we pull up, engines already roaring and ready for takeoff.

"I th-thought you said we weren't l-leaving until tomorrow," I say around shaky sobs.

Pyotr doesn't reply, though it isn't difficult for me to figure it out on my own. My little escape attempt probably convinced him to move up our timeline out of fear of my trying again. Once he gets me on the plane...

There's nothing I can do.

He knows it. I know he knows it.

And that's why I hate him with every fiber of my being.

"Are you going to board the plane?" he asks. "Or am I going to have to throw you over my shoulder again?"

I glare daggers at him. "You've already broken your vow."

"Did I?"

"Touch me again and I'll claw your fucking face off."

I expect him to get angry, to lash out. It's what Mother always did in the face of my stubbornness.

Imagine my surprise when he *grins*.

Smug bastard.

He leans in slightly, his eyes roaming over my face before settling on my lips. All the air is sucked out of the car. This is the first time he's looked at me with anything other than obvious indifference. I swear to God there's an almost intrigued glint hiding behind his dark eyes. Up close, I breathe in the rich, deep scent of his earthy cologne. He smells so much like the warm grassy fields that Polina and I ride through.

"Should I expect more of your insolent behavior when we get to New York?" he asks me, his voice so low the vibrations seem to rattle my bones.

I refuse to back down. Mother tried her best to break my spirit, but I won't give Pyotr the satisfaction. If he was expecting an obedient, well-mannered wife, then he's got another thing coming.

"It's my turn to make my vows," I tell him through gritted teeth. "I vow to keep running away. No matter how many times you try to stop me, I'll never give up until I'm finally free of you."

"You make it sound like a game."

I sneer at Pyotr. I wonder if I look even half as intimidating as my mother. Father used to say I got all my looks from her, after all. "Don't patronize me."

"Or what? You'll claw my face off?"

Ooh, how I loathe this man.

Pyotr huffs. "Get on the plane, Alina. I don't want a word out of you for the duration of the flight."

My nostrils flare. For that little comment, I'm going to talk his damn ear off.

CHAPTER 4

PYOTR

I should have known better than to goad her. We're four hours into our ten-hour flight and she hasn't stopped talking. The loud roar of the jet engines makes it next to impossible to hear her, so I have to pay extra attention to the movement of her lips to try and piece together what she's saying.

"I like pastel colors," she drones on. Alina's words are empty, an endless stream of consciousness filtered through her mouth for the sake of making noise. "I like playing the piano, too. I don't get to practice very much anymore because Mother says it gives her a headache, but then again, I'm pretty sure my breathing too loud gives her a headache. I like to think I'm a pretty good player, though. I used to dream about attending Julliard, but Mother would never have allowed it.

"Let's see, what else... Oh, I know! I haven't really told you about my horse. Her name's Polina and she's a grey Trakehner. She loves eating sliced apples and carrot sticks. She's a bit on the heavier side because I have a bad habit of feeding her too many treats. I was training her to become a show horse, but Mother said it was a waste of time. I really hope Mother doesn't actually sell Polina to the butchers to be turned into horse meat."

For a moment, Alina trails off. She's sitting across from me in the spacious beige leather seat next to the jet's mini bar. There's nothing but quiet sadness in her eyes.

"Do you think she will?" I ask. I'm not sure why I do. I don't feel like entertaining her and her ramblings, but for some reason, it bothers me to see her so upset.

Alina shrugs jerkily, glaring out the window. There are five of them on either side of the cabin, nothing but a sea of fluffy white clouds below. I wonder if she was so caught up in her private self-talk that she forgot I was even here.

"So what do *you* do?" she asks bitterly, tucking her knees up to her chest. Alina wraps her arms around herself, resting her chin on her knees. "For fun, I mean."

"I'm an adult. I don't have fun."

She rolls her eyes. "How old are you?"

"Old enough," I grumble, scrolling through the emails on my phone.

"Just tell me. I'm going to have to know it for the immigration interview or whatever, right? You might as well just spit it out."

Hm. She has a point, but I'm not going to fool myself into thinking she's actually interested in getting to know me for *me*. Alina's probably just bored.

"Forty-one," I answer.

She stares at me, her lips pressed into a thin line. She fiddles with the remote control attached to her seat's armrest. "Wow."

"Save your snide comments."

"I wasn't going to say anything."

"Mm-hmm." I set my phone down and study her for a moment. I count my blessings she's calmed down a bit. Maybe it's the high altitude. "What about you?"

Alina nibbles on her bottom lip, a habit, I'm starting to realize, when she's apprehensive. "Twenty-one."

I knew she was young, but *dammit*. Twenty years between us? That's another full-grown adult, an entire generation. I silently curse Mikhail for turning me into one of *those* men. Technically my elder brothers' wives are younger than themselves as well, but we don't share the same taste in women.

I prefer someone in my age range, someone mature and thoughtful... Not that it matters because I'm basically married to my work. I don't have time to date. Were it not for this arranged marriage, I likely would have died alone.

Being alone is safe. Secure. I prefer it.

Especially after everything that happened with Eileen.

Alina squirms in her seat. "So...what happens if we fail this interrogation?"

"Interview," I correct.

"You know what I mean."

"If you fail, you'll be deported and likely returned to Violetta."

Alina visibly shudders, hugging herself tighter. What's with this reaction? All I did was say her mother's name, and now she looks like she's about to be sick all over the cabin floor.

What did that woman do to her?

Something... protective sparks deep within my core. I tell myself it's nothing. Just a fleeting sensation. I swallow the feeling and bury it deep. It's pretty obvious Alina has enough fire of her own to protect herself. Besides, I'm already taking her thousands of miles away. Whatever horrible treatment she endured under her mother's roof won't happen on my watch.

"I'll have my personal assistant put together some study material," I say after a moment too long sitting in silence.

"You have a personal assistant? What do you do?"

"Business."

"Could you be any more vague? Just tell me and save your personal assistant the time."

I sigh. "I'm the CEO of CyberFort."

Alina's pretty green eyes widen. She's no doubt heard of the company my brothers and I built from scratch. Practically every computer in the world comes with our antivirus program pre-installed. Our product is kind of synonymous with internet security, the same way Elvis is synonymous with rock and roll.

"Seriously? Is that why Mother forced me to marry you? She wanted your money?"

I arch a brow. She thinks we were arranged for financial reasons? Violetta *really* kept this poor girl in the dark. "No, that's—"

"I can't believe her!" she grumbles, standing up from her seat. "I should have known. She did the exact same thing to my sisters."

"Where do you think you're going?"

"To the bathroom. Is that okay with you?" Alina grumbles bitterly.

She's just about to brush past me when the plane suddenly shakes. It's a nasty bout of turbulence that takes us both by surprise. Alina is thrown off balance, flailing with a squeaky yelp as she falls backward. My body reacts purely on instinct, my hand flying out to grab her and pull her toward me. The momentum causes her to stumble, falling directly onto my lap.

Alina clings to me, squeezing her eyes shut as the plane continues to shake. It feels like it lasts forever. It takes a lot to make me freak out, but I'll admit this turbulence is violent enough to make my throat tighten in mild panic.

"Is s-something wrong with the plane?" Alina stutters. She's starting to hyperventilate, on the verge of a full-on freak out.

"Keep your eyes on me."

"B-but—"

"*Eyes. On. Me.*"

It takes her a moment, but Alina finally musters up the courage to open her eyes again. When she does, her gaze locks on to mine. I can see the fear, the trepidation, but she does as I ask and looks nowhere else.

"Just breathe," I tell her as calmly as I can. "Keep your eyes on me and breathe. In and out, just like that. Repeat after me: everything's fine."

"E-everything's f-fine..."

"You're doing great. This will pass."

Alina nods slowly, transfixed. We're close. So dangerously close, but some small part of my brain likes the way she holds on to me for dear life. I could kiss her if I wanted to, those plush, tantalizing lips of hers well within range. I wonder if she'd let me.

The tremors eventually subside. I hold my breath, half-expecting for the plane to start shaking again. It's only when the captain buzzes in over the jet's speakers that I allow myself to relax.

"Sorry about that, Mr. Antonov. We hit a series of unexpected air pockets. I've taken us to a higher cruising altitude, so it should be a smooth flight from here on out."

"Carry on," I say clearly.

Seriously, can this day get any worse? First, I had to get married, then I had to hunt down my escape artist wife—the same wife who's *still holding onto me*.

Alina sits across my lap, her whole body trembling uncontrollably. She's balled up my dress shirt in her small hands, grip so tight I'm worried she might tear straight through the cotton. She weighs next to nothing in my arms, her frame petite and easy to hold.

"Are you alright?" I ask her as gently as possible—which isn't that gentle at all.

Her cheeks and the tips of her ears quickly turn a bright pink. She makes no effort to move away. I don't exactly rush her, either. The enchanting scent of her lavender perfume makes my head spin and my throat tight. I can see now that Alina's eyes aren't just green; there are specs of gold around the rims of her irises. Dazzling.

"I've broken my vow again," I say.

"S-sorry," she mumbles, carefully shuffling off my lap. "Are there any sleep aids on this thing?"

This private jet belongs to me, so I know for a fact there are. I've instructed my small on-call crew to keep it stocked with all manner of amenities. I toss my chin toward the cupboards across from the bathroom stall in the back of the jet. I say nothing as Alina shakily makes her way over, rifling through the cabinet above the sink to find a small bottle of pills.

"One is enough," I tell her, speaking from experience. The dosage is strong enough to make a man my size more than a little drowsy.

She takes two, swallowing them dry, before returning to her seat. Alina works silently, shutting the window visor, popping on her seatbelt, and reclining the seat so she can lie flat. She curls in on herself and closes her eyes, but she's not fooling me. I know she's only pretending to sleep right now. I guess she's tired of talking my good ear off.

Deep down, I know this isn't going to work out. I'm never going to love this woman, and I doubt she'll ever love me. We're too different. She's a wild child, full of fire I don't have the energy to tame. On the opposite end of the spectrum, I'm the stick in the mud. All work and no play makes Pyotr a dull boy. Alina would sooner die of boredom.

Just start small, Pyotr.

I sigh. Maybe there's no need to love each other. Plenty of marriages have functioned on less. Going forward, I'll take my twin's advice and practice patience and understanding. Hopefully Alina and I can find a middle ground, one where we can passably tolerate the other without being absolutely miserable.

Shrugging off my suit jacket, I rise from my seat and drape it over Alina's smaller frame. She snores softly, my clue that she's *actually* asleep. Those pills worked like a charm, and I'm sure she's endured more than her fair share of emotional drain.

I sit back down and sink into my chair, returning my attention to my phone.

There's still five hours remaining of our ten-hour flight.

CHAPTER 5

ALINA

I'm excited to be in New York, but I'm too exhausted to let it show. I've read about the city that never sleeps in plenty of books. I've seen the skyline in a thousand different movies and television shows. But actually getting to be here in person is a different sort of thrill.

The air smells different. I don't know what it is, but I welcome the change. There's so much to take in that my brain has trouble processing it all. Car exhaust, rainwater, a salty fish smell coming from the Hudson River. The mouthwatering scent of dollar hotdogs from food trucks parked on the curb, the passing waft of cigarette smoke, and the strong colognes of passing businessmen.

"This way," Pyotr says gruffly. His large hand hovers over the small of my back, but he doesn't touch me. He's been taking this whole vow thing very seriously ever since our incident on the plane.

My heart stutters at the memory. The hard press of his body beneath mine was almost unbelievable. Pyotr's size is the most obvious thing about him, but to *feel* the rolling muscles hidden beneath his stuffy suit... I couldn't believe how solid he was, how sturdy and strong. It makes my cheeks warm and the butterflies in my stomach flutter.

Not to mention how badly I wanted to kiss him. The thought leaves me torn. I don't want to like this man, but in that moment, all I craved was his comfort. His voice was hypnotizing and soothing beyond description. The way he helped me calm down... For a second, I got to see a glimpse of the man beneath his icy facade.

And to top it all off, I woke up a few minutes before landing to find he'd covered me with his jacket. I wasn't expecting him to do something so kind. He hasn't mentioned it, and I don't know if I should bring it up. We've settled for a strange, unspoken understanding. I suppose it's better than butting heads every chance we get.

The building is impressive, an architectural marvel. Constructed of seemingly endless sheets of glass, it reminds me of a shiny crystal sprouting up out of the ground, stretching all the way to the highest reaches of the skies.

A uniformed doorman greets us with a big smile, opening the door with a flourish of the hand. "Mr. Antonov," he greets warmly. "And who might this lovely young lady be?" There's something almost flirtatious in the way the doorman smiles.

As he holds the glass door open, his jacket lifts ever so slightly. I catch a peak of the gun holster he has hidden just beneath. No, this is no doorman. This is one of Pyotr's bodyguards.

"Watch it, Ben," Pyotr grumbles. "This is my wife you're talking to."

Ben quickly corrects his smile and gives me a humble bow of the head, a sudden chill in the air. "Mrs. Antonov. Welcome."

"Thank you," I say in English. It's been a while since I've had to speak the language, so it feels strange against my tongue.

The lobby is just as grand as the outside. Everything's polished and clean. A mosaic is designed into the floor, a gorgeous sweeping pattern of flowers in white and blue pieces set beneath shiny resin. There's even an indoor water feature, complete with a front desk manned by a concierge. Pyotr guides me toward a set of elevators.

Once we're inside, he scans a key fob to the reader attached to the elevator panel. It beeps, a little red light flashing green.

"I'll have my personal assistant get you a copy," he says. "You'll need your own to access the building."

"Fancy," I say, genuinely impressed. This place is so high-tech, it's enough to make my head spin. I suppose I should expect nothing less from the CEO of a cybersecurity company.

Pyotr and I ride to the top floor, the elevator opening directly into his living room. My eyebrows shoot up when I see the sheer size of the place. His home is palatial, fit for a king. Mother's summer home, which she touted as her own personal mansion, can't even compare.

I step into the living room, my jaw dropping. I'm surrounded by warm brown walls and soft beige carpeting. The windows facing south extend from floor to ceiling, offering a gorgeous view of Central Park. To my left, there's a massive shelf filled to the brim with books, complete with a rolling ladder made of brass to reach the texts on the highest shelves. A large electric fireplace across from an off-white L-sectional is big enough to fit at least ten people.

What captures my attention, though, is the beautiful grand piano set off to the side. A Steinway. Its lid is closed, its keys covered. While this place is relatively spotless, I can still see the faint buildup of dust blanketing its surface. I'm not sure if Pyotr actually plays or if the instrument is of a more decorative nature.

While I roam the space and take in my new surroundings, I'm more than a little aware of the weight of his gaze. He stands off to the side, his arms crossed, but he says nothing. He doesn't hurry me along; neither does he ask for my opinions.

I decide to speak first. "Your home is lovely."

"This whole bottom floor is yours to use as you see fit."

I gawk. "You mean there's more to this place?"

"Three levels. I live on the top floor. The bottom one is yours."

"And the middle?" I ask dryly. "Do you need that much of a buffer zone?"

Pyotr shakes his head. "No, that's where my brother lives. Luka.

I'm sure you'll meet him eventually. He's effectively nocturnal, so you might not see him much."

"Your brother lives with you?" I ask, genuinely curious.

"More like he's too lazy to find his own place, so he's decided to crash mine indefinitely."

"I see."

"He won't be a bother, though." Pyotr steps towards the narrow hallway table just to his left and pulls open its drawer. He reaches in and pulls out a pristine white box. "This is your new cell phone," he says, setting it on the table's surface without looking at me. "Again, yours to do with as you see fit. My assistant is currently in the process of setting up your new bank accounts and—"

"Bank accounts?" I echo in surprise.

"I meant what I said. Now that you're my wife, it's my responsibility to provide for you. All I ask is you don't cause me any more trouble."

I stare at him, caught between disbelief, disappointment, and anger. I'm none too pleased with the idea of this marriage, but holy hell does he have to be so clinical about it? It's obvious he's a businessman through and through. Even his marriage is a deal to be negotiated and agreed upon.

"Ground rules," he continues flatly. "You're to use English from here on out. I was assured you speak fluently, correct?"

I cross my arms and mirror his posture. "*Da, no pochemu?*" *Yes, but why*, I ask in Russian, just because I like seeing the vein at his temple throb.

"Because you speak too fast for me to read..."

I strain to hear him. "What?"

Pyotr gives me a hard look. "It's for the benefit of the interview. The easier it is to communicate with the immigration officer—"

"Fine," I snip.

He sighs. "Second, you are free to go wherever you like—"

My ears perk up at this. "Seriously?" *Even after my escape attempt?* goes unsaid.

"But you must take one of my bodyguards with you as an escort."

I deflate. Getting away from here is going to be ten times harder with a guard breathing down my neck, though I suppose it's better than being locked in like a princess in a high tower.

"Anything else?" I ask with a huff. "Let me guess, is the next rule to not cause trouble?"

Pyotr watches my lips with a heated intensity, the notch in his brow almost crescent shaped. Again with the staring. I'm not uncomfortable, per se, just caught off guard. Heat climbs up the back of my neck and pools in my cheeks. The deep brown color of his eyes is honestly disarming.

"You're not to mention the Bratva," he says sternly. "Not the Antonovs, not the Salkovs, not any other family. My position in the company means I cannot be openly associated."

I tilt my head to the side. Interesting. "Fine," I say eventually. "It's not like I have anyone to talk to anyway."

He takes a single step forward, his eyes still glued to my lips. There's something new in the way he watches me, something that wasn't there before. It's dark and heady and electric. I hold my breath as he approaches like a jaguar, strong and ready to pounce.

Pyotr reaches into his pocket and pulls out something silver.

A ring.

"Give me your hand," he orders.

My heart thuds in my chest. I'm half tempted to run, but there's nowhere to go. Besides, it's just a wedding ring. He's not going to hurt me.

Slowly, I lift my hand, which he promptly takes in his own. His palms are deliciously rough and warm, so large his fingers easily envelop mine. Pyotr slides the ring onto my finger and stares at it for a moment, his jaw clenched, and brows knitted together into a steep frown.

A part of me wants to cry. Why does this feel so cruel? I'm already chained to him—and now I have a physical token to remind me of the fact. At least Pyotr has the base-level decency to look guilty about it.

"You'll learn to forgive me," he mutters.

My anger flares, but I manage to swallow the worst of it. "Don't count on it."

Whatever trace of warmth I thought I saw melts away from his face. He's once again made of ice, impossible to decipher.

"Your room is around the corner there," he says before turning away. Pyotr ascends the stairs and eventually disappears, the sounds of his heavy footsteps fading as the distance between us grows.

My room is just as lovely as the rest of the first floor of the penthouse suite, but it doesn't really feel like *mine*. The decor isn't to my taste—too dark and sophisticated. There's a four-post bed made of mahogany, the bedsheets a deep maroon with gold embroidery. I'm definitely going to give this place a makeover. It would look great with a splash of color and—

The thought gives me pause.

A makeover?

No. No, I'm not going to be staying long enough to worry about that sort of thing. Pyotr might have caught me once, but I'm no quitter. I'll figure out how to escape him and this marriage, even if it's the last thing I do.

All I want is my freedom. I want a life that's *mine*. My mistakes, my triumphs... Now that I'm far from Mother's influence, it's about time I start to do things for myself.

My first escape attempt was made out of desperation. If there's one thing I'm good at, it's learning from my mistakes. I'll bide my time, wait for the perfect opportunity to escape him for good. I'll fly under the radar. And just when Pyotr lowers his guard...

I'll be long gone.

CHAPTER 6

PYOTR

8:00 a.m.
I'm already up, showered, and dressed for work. When I go downstairs to the kitchen, I'm not at all surprised to find my little brother seated at the kitchen island with a cold glass of water. He's dressed in a pair of grey sweatpants and an oversized black hoodie. The dark circles under his eyes would be alarming to most people, but I know Luka always looks like this.

"Did you just get up?" I ask him as I adjust my silver cufflinks.

"No, I'm just going to bed."

He's the family's computer wunderkind who stays up all night while chain chugging Red Bulls to stay alert. I keep warning him that one of these days, his lifestyle is going to catch up to him, but does he listen? Of course not.

I roll my eyes. "Your sleep schedule is concerning."

Luka shrugs. "I'm a night owl, so sue me." He takes a sip of his water and gives me a suspicious glance. "So... are we going to talk about the elephant in the room?"

"I don't know what you're talking about," I grumble as I make my way over to the coffee.

"The new *wife*," Luka clarifies. "I heard her shuffling around all night. I still can't believe Mikhail bullied you into it."

"What are we, eight? He didn't bully me. I agreed of my own volition."

"That's fucking nuts."

"Yes, I still remember the whole speech you gave me before I got on the plane."

Luka snorts. "Whatever. It's your life to screw up."

"Love you too, jackass." As I prepare my morning coffee, I ask, "Did she set off any of the alarms last night trying to get out?"

"Nope," Luka says easily. "None of the home security cameras in the living room were triggered. I think she stayed in her room the whole night."

Hm.

I'd take this as a good sign were it not for the fact that I don't trust Alina one bit. Only a fool mistakes quiet for peace.

"Keep an eye on her while I'm out," I say.

"What? Why me?"

"Because I have to go to work and deal with Richard."

"That asshole's still being a pain in the ass?"

"Always."

"You don't *have* to go straight back to work, you know," Luka says, getting up from the kitchen island. "I'm no expert, but I'm pretty sure you should use this time to get to know the missus."

"The day I take relationship advice from you is the day hell freezes over, little brother."

"Now *you're* being the jackass."

"It must run in the family."

With that, I leave Luka to his dinner-breakfast and start toward Alina's room.

All is calm and still. I normally wouldn't find this suspicious given the early morning hours, but in the short time I've known Alina, I've learned it's better to err on the side of caution. She's too sharp for her own good, and with those disarming eyes of hers, it's all too easy to let my guard down.

I knock on her door. Once, twice. No response.

There's a chance she's asleep, but that's exactly what I thought at the hotel in Moscow. The windows in my penthouse don't open wide enough to allow a person through, and though I know she's unhappy, I sincerely doubt she'd hurl herself a hundred stories to her death. Regardless, I open her door a crack just to double check—

Alina stands directly in front of me, her hand outstretched as if reaching for the doorknob. She stares up at me, her hair messy from sleep and her eyes puffy from crying.

"Oh," she breathes, seeming just as surprised as I am. "What do you want?" There's no heat behind her words, just resigned exhaustion. I don't know why, but I have to fight the urge to rub my thumb over the crease in her brow.

"I'm going to work," I tell her. "While I'm gone, I want you to—"

"I'm not going to cause trouble," she says, interrupting me.

I stare a little while longer, taking in the way she worries her bottom lip and the way she tries to hide a sniffle. I don't know what to say, just that I should say *something*.

"Your anger is misplaced. I'm not your enemy."

Alina looks up at me. "You don't mean that."

"Yes, I do. You forget that I, too, am trapped in this arrangement."

"Then call it off."

"I can't."

"Why *not?*"

I take a deep breath. "Do you honestly not know?"

"Just tell me, Pyotr!"

The sound of my name rolling off her tongue makes my chest tighten. It sounds *good*. I'm pretty sure it's the first time she's ever said it. Is it wrong that I think she's sexy when she's all angry and frustrated with me?

Probably.

"The reason we got married was because—"

My phone starts buzzing. When I pull it out of my pocket, I see a series of messages from Merrybell.

Richard Eaton Jones is here.
  He barged right past me.
  He's in your office.
  Should I call security?

"That son of a bitch," I grumble.

"What were you going to say?" Alina asks.

"I'll tell you later. I have to get going."

She puts her hands on her hips. "When are you going to be home?"

"I don't know. Some time tonight."

"And what am I supposed to do until then?"

"Whatever you want," I say, already turning to leave. "I'm not your boss."

"You're not my husband, either," she grumbles.

I whip back around and step into her space, dipping down so I can look her square in the eye. There's barely an inch between us, the surrounding air suddenly hot and thin. She smells delicious, but what fascinates me more is the way her breaths quicken and her lips part just so.

"You have a bad attitude, young lady. If you're smart, you'll mind your tongue."

"Really? I was going to say the exact same thing to you."

There's a challenge in her tone. It's as infuriating as it is sexy. The more I stare at her lips, the more I want to consume them. If I claim them, then maybe she'll finally quit with the sass.

"Be careful what you say to me," I warn.

"Or *what?*"

We're so close I can feel her words ghost across my lips. This is dangerous. I'm not used to feeling so out of sorts. I need to put distance between us, can't let her get under my skin. There's no doubt in my mind Alina's doing this on purpose. She wants to see me riled up, but I'm not going to give in that easily.

"I'm a reasonable man," I go on. "But even reasonable men have their limits."

"Tell me, *husband*," she bites out the word like a curse, "tell me what happens when you cross that line?"

"You really want to know?"

I lean in as close as I dare, my hands braced on either side of the door frame. I'm so close my mouth brushes against her earlobe, her warm breath stuttering across my cheek and down my neck.

"You're right, I'm not your husband. Not really. Because if I was, I'd keep you in my bed where I'd fuck you day in and day out like all good husbands should."

Alina's breath hitches. It's an intoxicating sound. "Why are you telling me this?" she rasps. I adore the way goosebumps break out down the back of her neck and along her slim shoulders.

"I'm telling you this because getting along with me comes with perks. I don't *need* a wife, Alina—"

Her eyes flick over to me, entranced by the sound of her name ripping from my lungs. I don't think I've ever called her by her name before, but now that I have, it feels like magic on my tongue.

"I don't want a wife," I repeat, "but I can treat you like one in all the ways that matter. Your life could be easy with me. Even pleasurable. Wouldn't that be so much nicer than fighting me all the time?"

"Is your ego really so big?" she scoffs.

I pause. I don't know what's come over me. How the fuck did we get here? Wasn't I just irritated with her? When did things take such a heated turn?

My phone buzzes in my pocket.

Right. Richard Eaton Jones—the rat bastard. I've got to deal with him sooner rather than later. I'm not pleased with the fact that he's allowed himself into my office. He won't find anything of use because

I keep all my important documents under lock and key, but still. If he thinks he can walk into my office like he owns the damn place, he's got another thing coming.

I'm going to have to put this strange head-to-head with Alina aside for now. I have more important matters to take care of.

When I step back, Alina is a sight to behold. She doesn't look offended or startled. If anything, she looks like she's about to melt into a puddle. Her whole face is red, her breathing ragged, her pupils wide. I didn't mean to tease her. Or maybe I did, I really don't know. I was so concerned about her getting under my skin that I subconsciously felt the need to get under hers first.

I took things too far. Those words should never have come out of my mouth. I don't know what it is about Alina that makes me so desperately out of control.

I turn without another word, leaving her standing there alone.

This woman can't get the better of me.

CHAPTER 7

PYOTR

Richard Eaton Jones is the scummiest man you will ever have the misfortune of meeting.

He calls himself a tech entrepreneur, rivaling innovators like Gates, Jobs, Zuckerberg, or my brothers and me when we all worked for CyberFort. In actuality, he's nothing more than a rat.

Nobody has any proof, but I have it on good authority he's stolen a patent or three, added a little sprinkle of showmanship, and sold his "inventions" at exorbitant prices. Now all he does is swoop in with his millions, buying out little tech startups here and there and selling them when he feels they're no longer profitable. He's the corporate world's version of a house flipper.

I have zero respect for what he does. The man is without a sliver of intellect. The lights may be on, but no one's home. He thinks if he can flash his cash, show up at exclusive press events, and be the loudest man in the room, that somehow means he's the most important.

He couldn't be more wrong. It's as the old saying goes, confidence is quiet.

I find Richard in my office, leaning back leisurely in my executive chair with his feet up on my desk. He's a greasy fellow, and I don't mean that in a slimeball kind of way—though he *is* a slimeball. He's literally greasy. His thinning black hair is coated in disgusting globs of gel. His combover is fooling no one, and his goatee is clearly dyed. He's dressed in an Armani suit coupled with the fat gold chain around his neck. He looks like he belongs in a seventies gangster movie smoking a cigar.

"Get out," I snap.

Richard hits me with a wide smile. His teeth are yellow from years of smoking. There's a small piece of something caught between his front teeth, but I don't bother telling him.

"Peter, my old friend!" he says, boisterous as ever. He sounds like a choking crow when he talks, much too dry and abrasive.

"Pyotr," I correct. "And I'm not your friend."

"Come now, Peter. Don't be like that! I know we're business rivals, but that doesn't mean we have to be hostile."

"You have ten seconds to tell me what you're doing here."

Richard sits up, my chair creaking under his generous weight. He better pray he didn't mess with the lumbar settings.

"I'm here to talk business," he says.

"Then make an appointment. Merrybell will help you find time in my schedule."

"I'm a busy man, Peter. And so are you. Besides, I've been trying to make an appointment, but that sweet old lady outside keeps telling me you won't be free for another four months."

This isn't entirely untrue. As CEO, I've got a lot of people depending on me. I have endless meetings with investors, my own staff, potential business partners, and so on. People have to schedule with me well in advance if they want even a minute of my time, Richard included. Though I may or may not have told Merrybell to come up with whatever excuse she saw fit to keep this bastard away from me at all costs. He has a nasty habit of stinking up the air just by breathing.

"Get out of my chair," I tell him, my patience wearing thin.

Between dealing with him and Alina this morning, I'm fresh out of fucks.

Richard rises, his knees cracking as he does so. His expression darkens, the over-the-top smile he wears slipping. "I'll make it quick," he says. "I want to buy out CyberFort."

"No."

"I'll give you an excellent price for it."

"I said *no*."

Richard clicks his tongue, chuckling as he shoves his meaty hands into his suit pockets. He moseys on over to the window and takes in the view of downtown New York. "I've seen your quarterly reports. CyberFort has barely been making a profit year-over-year."

"Growth is still growth," I reply.

"Yes, but in my hands, it could be exponential."

I fight the urge to snort. *Yeah, right.*

"CyberFort isn't for sale, and it never will be." I make my way over to my seat and settle in, logging into my desktop computer. I've got too much shit to do and wasting my time on Richard isn't on today's docket.

"Peter, let's talk numbers, hm? I'll pay you thirty billion to hand over the reins."

"Are you trying to insult me? My company is worth five hundred billion." I press the little red button on my phone's intercom. When it beeps, I say, "Merrybell?"

"Yes, Mr. Antonov?" her little voice squeaks over the speakers.

"Have security see Mr. Jones out."

"Right away, sir."

Richard laughs like I've just landed a killer punchline at the comedy club. "Alright, alright. I'll get going. No need to cause a ruckus."

I don't bother looking at him as he saunters out the door. My nose curls in disgust. Richard left the awful scent of cigarette smoke lingering in his wake. Here's hoping it doesn't take too long for the odor to clear out.

Merrybell knocks on the door, stepping in with a nervous smile. She's dressed in a modest black dress that falls to her shins, her graying hair pulled up into a tight bun. "I'm sorry about that, Mr. Antonov. I tried to get him to leave, but he wouldn't take no for an answer."

"It's not your fault. I know how he can be. Next time he tries a stunt like that, don't hesitate to have the security guards throw him out."

"Of course, sir."

My personal assistant lingers for a little longer than usual. Merrybell is usually quick to get back to work. She's been working for CyberFort since we started. In fact, she used to be Mikhail's personal assistant and secretary when he was CEO. She knows how this whole place runs, and if it weren't for her, I'd frankly be a disorganized mess. She's always on top of my emails, my calendar, *everything*. Merrybell is practically a loafer-wearing miracle.

"Did you need something?" I ask her, sending an email to the development department about requiring last month's expense report.

"I want to hear all about her," she says excitedly. "Tell me all about your new wife!"

I hush her quickly. "Remember what we talked about? Nobody needs to know."

"Right, sorry. I don't understand all the need for secrecy, though."

I set my jaw. "It's complicated. She, uh, likes her privacy. As do I."

While Merrybell may know I took time off to return to Russia to get married, she doesn't understand *why*. As far as I'm concerned, it'll stay that way. Since Mikhail stepped down and I took his place as CEO, we've been exceedingly careful about keeping the link between CyberFort and the Antonov Bratva a secret from the general public. From most people, actually.

If word ever got out that I'm from a long line of Russian gangsters, I'd be crucified by the media. Not to mention CyberFort's stock value would likely plummet overnight. Merrybell and all our other staff believe Mikhail and Dimitri took an early retirement and went home to Russia to be with their families—and that will remain the official party line.

"I bet she's beautiful. Oh, please tell me I can meet her soon."

"Don't worry, you will. In fact, I'm going to send you over right now."

"Really?"

"Alina needs new clothes, new everything. Take her shopping for me."

"On the company card, or is this a personal expense?"

"Personal, of course. I don't need to give auditors any ammunition to use against me. Head on over to the penthouse. I'm sure she'd love some company."

Merrybell frowns. "Shouldn't you be enjoying your honeymoon?"

I sigh, pinching the bridge of my nose. "Why does everyone keep telling me that? No, work comes first."

Merrybell frowns, her disapproval obvious, but she doesn't say anything. If she has a snarky comment to make, she does the wise thing and keeps it to herself.

"Do you need anything before I go?"

"I'm good. Have fun shopping."

Merrybell smiles wide. "Oh, I plan to."

"Oh, and one more thing."

"Yes, Mr. Antonov?"

"Don't let her out of your sight."

CHAPTER 8

ALINA

If Pyotr thinks he was being slick about the security cameras in the living room and by the elevator entrance, he was wrong. I noticed them when I first arrived, and I've been trying to plot my way around them ever since.

If I'm going to make a break for it, it will have to be while I'm already outside and in the clear. Pyotr said I'm free to go wherever I want as long as a guard goes with me, but I doubt I'll get very far with them keeping close.

Unfortunately, I'm bored within minutes of him leaving. He's been gone for hours, and I have nothing better to do than explore the entirety of the penthouse. It's *our* home, as he said. I don't feel the need to confine myself to the bottom floor when there's still so much to see.

There's no sight of Pyotr's elusive younger brother anywhere. The second floor looks almost exactly like the first, but darker. The curtains are drawn and all is quiet. It feels sort of like I've got an unseen vampire roommate lurking about. Since there isn't much to see here, I continue to climb the stairs to venture into Pyotr's territory.

The view up here is arguably the best in the entire city. We're well above the rest of the concrete jungle. Cars and people look like nothing more than tiny ants from on high. Central Park is a large swathe of vibrant green, the tops of the trees lush and soft. It's breathtaking…

And lonely.

I can easily imagine Pyotr up here all by himself, looking upon New York like a king surveying his lands. But everything about this place screams isolation. He may have a castle in the sky, but does one man really need all this space? Maybe I'm just projecting here. That's how *I* would feel were I in his shoes.

Once I've had my fill of the view, I continue snooping. I find a strange sort of amusement trying to glean what little I can from his worldly possessions. It's like playing detective, piecing together small aspects of his life to try and get a greater picture of the whole. Something tells me Pyotr isn't exactly eager to open up about himself, so if I want to learn more about him, I'll have to take matters into my own hands.

Unfortunately, the man doesn't seem to have very many personal effects. No trinkets from vacations past, no photographs, no useless knickknacks on the coffee table. It's like he lifted this place straight out of a catalog; every piece of furniture elegant, every piece of art beautiful, but without any personality or history behind it. Flare without substance.

His office at the end of the hall is as sterile as it comes. Cold and unwelcoming. His walls are lined with books, but it doesn't look like he's read any of them in a long time. They're all business-related nonfiction. *Boring*. His bedroom is more of the same. Dark color palette, curtains drawn. Maybe I was wrong. Maybe *he's* the vampire of the family.

Do I feel bad about sneaking around his space? No, not at all. Weird, maybe, but in a way it feels like I've stepped into an alternate reality. Being in his room honestly doesn't feel real. Getting to see how Pyotr lives, where he rests his head... It's intriguing. A clue into his psyche.

I poke through his closet—nothing but impressive suits ranging from black to even darker black. How shocking.

I rifle through his dresser next, pulling open the top drawer. Socks, all of them neatly folded like a shop display. I'm starting to get the sense that Pyotr's a bit of a control freak. The only thing that surprises me is the fat wad of bills I find in the far back corner, hidden amongst his socks.

I immediately reach for the money. My heart leaps into my throat. This is at least five thousand dollars in cold hard cash! This should honestly be kept safe in a bank somewhere, but maybe Pyotr's one of those weirdos who doesn't trust the banks. Whatever the reason, it works in my favor. This might be enough to get me out of the state and start somewhere new.

I shove the money into my back pocket and pull out the brand-new phone Pyotr got for me. I open an incognito internet browser—I'm not stupid enough to think my cybersecurity expert husband won't be keeping tabs on my search history—and quickly pull up a list of buses out of New York. How far would I get if I left right this minute? There are buses to Ohio, Indiana, north to Maine... The farthest I'm seeing so far is all the way down to Florida.

The gears in my mind start turning. If I can figure out a way to get to Florida, maybe I can charter a flight to Colombia and see my sister, Nikita. Would she put me up for a while? Or will she turn me in just like Yasemin did?

I grit my teeth. My elder sisters all fear Mother's retaliation. It sucks that I can't trust my own family to help. I'll just have to think of something else, but so far, getting to Florida might be my best bet.

I keep poking through his drawers. Who knows what else I might find? I make my way over to his peek into his bedside table drawer—

And I freeze.

Only three items are inside: an old book, its spine cracked from multiple reads and a few of its pages falling out; a Makarov pistol, fully loaded with the safety on; and most surprising of all, a hearing aid.

I pick up the hearing aid first, cradling it gently in my palm. This obviously belongs to Pyotr—why else would it be here? —but I've never seen him wear it. Does he have trouble hearing?

Because you speak too fast for me to read…

Did he mean read my lips? Now that I think about it, he *does* stare at my mouth a lot. I'm not too sure what to do with this information, so I set the small device back down carefully.

I pay the gun no mind. I may be the daughter of a Bratva head, but I never adopted Mother's cruel heart and indifference for violence. While my elder sisters had to endure shooting lessons at an early age, I instead poured myself into my piano and riding lessons.

I'm tempted to ignore the book, but I happen to catch a glimpse of something sticking out from within its pages. Curiosity takes over. Carefully, I pick the brittle book up and pull out what I now realize is an old photo. I stare at it for a moment, quietly marveling at what I see.

The picture is of Pyotr and a woman I've never seen before. He's at least twenty years younger, around my age. He's *smiling* in the picture, so bright and brilliant I can hardly wrap my head around the fact that it's really him. The hard edges I've come to know are nowhere to be seen. In this picture, he's youthful and brimming with excitement. He's so handsome it makes my teeth ache.

The woman he has his arms wrapped around is gorgeous. A total bombshell. Full and curly red hair with dazzling hazel eyes like liquid amber. She's pressing a sloppy kiss to his cheek, but Pyotr doesn't seem to mind. They both look as happy as can be.

They look like they're in *love*.

I flip the picture over.

'*Me and Eileen, Coney Island*' is written on the back.

I wonder who she was. An old girlfriend, no doubt. Pyotr clearly still hasn't gotten over her; otherwise, he wouldn't still have her picture at his bedside. As much as I want to keep studying the image,

I hear movement downstairs. The *ding* of the elevator and the footsteps of someone entering the living room tell me my time is up. I hastily put everything back—money excluded—and quickly head downstairs.

I arrive on the bottom step just in time to see an older woman walk in. She has a sweet face and an even sweeter smile. I'm curious to know how she got into this place considering the specialized key fobs needed to activate the elevator. Could this be Pyotr's mother?

"Hello?" I greet softly, slightly timid.

The woman beams at me. "Ah, you must be Alina. It's so lovely to finally meet you. My goodness, you're beautiful!"

My cheeks warm. I wasn't expecting such kindness. "Oh, um, thank you. Sorry, but who might you be?"

"I'm Merrybell," she says, walking over to shake my hand. "I'm Pyotr's personal assistant. I do hope that boy mentioned I'd be stopping by."

I almost laugh. It feels weird hearing someone refer to Pyotr as a boy. "He might have said something about shopping."

"I can take you to a few places," Merrybell says kindly. "Pyotr is a preferred shopper at a number of establishments, so I'm sure we can get you a whole new wardrobe. He's already given me his credit card, so we'll have free reign to have a little fun."

Merrybell's chipper personality admittedly catches me off guard. I'm not used to people being kind. Mother was cruel, Pyotr is cold and distant, and my sisters are so afraid of my mother I'd never trust them enough to get close. Merrybell is a breath of fresh air.

"I'd love to go shopping," I admit. "It certainly beats sitting around here all day."

"Between you and me," she says, leaning in, "I don't think it's right."

I arch a brow. Does she know about the arranged marriage? How much information is she privy to, exactly? "What do you mean?"

"Leaving you here all alone," she clarifies. "Pyotr has a good heart, but his skull is as thick as a rock. He shouldn't leave you here all by yourself, especially when you're so new to the country. He should be taking you to see all the sights!"

"I'm sure he has better things to do. He's a busy man, after all."

"Too busy for his new wife?" She scoffs. "I think not. Don't worry, I'll be sure to give him a proper talking to about all this."

For the first time since arriving in New York, I find myself genuinely smiling. I like Merrybell. She's got spunk. If she's able to give Pyotr even half the headache I can, then she's alright in my book.

She offers me the crook of her elbow. "Let's paint the town red, shall we?"

I find myself drawn to her warmth. I loop my arm through hers with a light giggle. "Yes, let's."

CHAPTER 9

ALINA

Merrybell has exquisite taste.

Channel. Prada. Gucci... At this rate, she's going to shop me right off my feet. That would be most unfortunate considering I'm going to need them to run away.

While Merrybell helps me pick out clothes and accessories, I've been carefully eyeing the exits to each store. Ben, the guard I mistook for a doorman the day before, accompanies us wherever we go. He seems friendly enough, perfectly polite. Just like Merrybell, he's very easy to get along with. But at the end of the day, I can't let myself forget where his loyalties lie. Ben and Merrybell both work for Pyotr, which means fully trusting them is out of the question.

Pyotr's money is stuffed into my back pocket. All I need to do now is find an opening, head to the nearest Greyhound station, and buy myself a ticket out of here. Five thousand dollars should last me a while, as long as I'm careful about being frugal.

"What do you think about this one?" Merrybell asks me, carrying over a lovely red dress. The fabric is light and flowing—perfect for the summertime heat.

"It's really lovely, but I'm not sure if it's quite my color."

"Hm, that's fair. Pyotr doesn't like red, anyway."

"I'm not dressing for him."

Merrybell laughs. "Of course not, how silly of me."

My ears perk up anyway, the question on the tip of my tongue. "Does he even have a favorite color?"

She regards me with a curious glint in her eye. "You don't know?"

I shrug, thinking nothing of it at first. "He doesn't exactly strike me as the kind of guy who likes anything, to be honest. I feel like you know him better than I do."

"I'm sure you know your husband better than you let on."

My smile falters. *Oh, right.* Merrybell doesn't know. I can't tell her about the shotgun wedding, or how he flew me to a new country under the cover of night.

You're not to mention the Bratva. Not the Antonovs, not the Salkovs, not any other family. My position in the company means I cannot be openly associated.

I fight back a bitter laugh. Seems my husband is leading quite the double life.

"Do you know when he'll be back from work?" I ask her.

"He didn't tell you?" Merrybell sighs. "Oh, what am I going to do with that man? I swear he's normally not this forgetful."

He's not forgetful, I want to tell her, *he just doesn't care about me.*

"He should be in his last meeting of the day," she informs me. "If traffic's light, he'll be back in another half an hour or so. I should have you back by then."

I hold my breath. Half an hour. Thirty minutes. That's all the time I have to make a break for it. An opportunity for escape hasn't presented itself yet, so I'll have to take matters into my own hands.

"So?" Merrybell prompts. "Tell me, how did the two of you meet? When Pyotr told me he had to return home to Russia, I assumed it was to visit family. Imagine my surprise when he informed me he'd gotten married! Was it a whirlwind romance? Pyotr's so private about his personal life. I wasn't even aware he'd been dating anyone, much less a lovely thing like you."

My face burns. "Oh, uh... A whirlwind romance? Sure. Yeah."

"How did he propose?" she asks, her whole face lighting up with excitement. "Did he get down on one knee? Did he cry? No, I can't imagine he would."

"It was..." I scratch behind my ear. I never thought to get my story straight. It's next to impossible to imagine Pyotr getting down on one knee, ring in hand, with a tear in the corner of his eye. "It was lovely," I answer vaguely. "Simple, but sweet—You know what? It can't hurt to try it on."

Merrybell hands me the dress and the store employee graciously shows me where the changing rooms are. Just when I think I might have some time to myself, Ben steps forward with an apologetic smile.

"I'm sorry, Mrs. Antonov. I have to check and make sure the area is secure first."

"Is there really any need? I'm pretty sure we're the only ones in the store right now."

"It's just protocol, ma'am. Mr. Antonov would have my head if he found out I was cutting corners."

I set my jaw and force a polite smile. "In that case, thank you for your diligence."

I wait at the entrance of the changing rooms, impatiently shifting my weight from foot to foot. When Ben returns, he gives me a nod and a big smile. "You're free to go in, ma'am. I'll stand watch right here."

My guts twist into knots. If I'm going to sneak out, it's definitely not going to be through the way I came. I slip past him, dress draped across my arms, and carefully take in my surroundings.

There isn't a whole lot to work with. No back exit—crap—and the windows in this place are high and out of reach. I'm pretty sure they don't open anyway—double crap. The only plus side is I'm alone, but I'm running out of time. I'm sure Merrybell is going to pop in at any moment with something new for me to try on, so I need to act fast.

My eyes settle on a nearby clothing rack. A number of different outfits hang from the rack, a densely packed collection of frills and ribbons and sequins. The whole contraption is on four wheel bearings, designed to be rolled around the storefront.

A store employee just happens to walk in, moving toward the rack with a few outfits for reshelving. "Is there anything I can help you with, Mrs. Antonov?" she asks me sweetly.

I think on my feet, immediately pulling out the wad of cash. "You can help me by sneaking me out of here," I say quietly and hastily, handing her five hundred American dollars.

The employee blanches at the money I've placed in her hand. "I don't understand…"

"You don't have to. Just sneak me out with these clothes, that's all I ask."

"Mrs. Antonov, I don't know… I don't want to get in trouble."

"*Please.*"

I don't know if it's the desperation in my voice or the desperation written all over my face, but after a few moments, the employee nods and gestures to the rack. She parts a few of the dresses and says, "Climb on. We have to be quick. I'm taking this to the storage room."

"Is there an exit there?"

"Yes, ma'am."

Perfect.

She wheels me out and we manage to sneak right past Ben, who's busy chatting with Merrybell from across the store. Deep down, a part of me feels bad. Pyotr's probably going to be livid when he finds out I snuck out right under their noses. Merrybell and Ben seem like perfectly nice people, but I can't stick around for them. I can only hope Pyotr won't be too harsh on them after I'm gone.

I keep low, hidden amongst the heavy fabrics, holding my breath, hoping I won't be caught. The trip from the changing room to the storage room around back feels like it takes a millennium. When the clothing rack finally comes to a stop, the employee whispers, "Okay, we're here."

I pop out and hastily look around. No Ben, no Merrybell. I'm in the clear.

I take the employee's hands and give her fingers a squeeze. "Thank you so much," I say earnestly. "Please don't tell them."

She nods, her face twisted in confusion and concern. "A-alright, Mrs. Antonov. Good luck, I guess?"

I turn and race out the back door. I run as far as my legs can carry me. New York is loud and busy and disorienting. Once I'm roughly ten blocks away, I pull out my phone to look at a map. The nearest Greyhound bus station on 42nd and 8th is a little way from here, but if I hurry, I should be able to make the next bus out to Florida.

Blending into the crowd is easy enough. I keep my head down and walk with purpose, vanishing into the sea of endless faces. Nobody pays me any mind, too busy getting to wherever they need to go to so much as glance at me. I appreciate the anonymity of the city. With any luck, I'll be able to slip on through without trouble.

My heart skips a beat when I finally make it to the bus station. It costs roughly $150 for a one-way ticket from here to Orlando, but that's a small price to pay for my freedom. The clerk behind the desk doesn't ask any prying questions, doesn't stare at me too long. He gives me my ticket and tells me the bus will be departing in twenty minutes.

I'm not too sure how much time has passed since I left Merrybell and Ben behind, but I'm sure they've probably realized I'm gone by now. I try not to let the guilt bother me. It's nothing personal.

I board the waiting bus and find a seat near the back, slumping into it with a shaky exhale. I'm almost out. I'm almost free. There's an endless world of possibilities waiting for me and I'm anxious to meet them. Once I get to Orlando, I'll have to secure food and lodging, and with a little over four thousand dollars, I'm sure I can figure out my next steps.

Ten minutes until departure.

I keep checking my phone, anxious. I just want to leave. I'm practically vibrating out of my seat, I'm so exhilarated.

Five minutes until departure.

More and more people board the bus. The seats are filling up quickly. With every person that climbs on, my heart skips a beat. I'm jumpy, on edge. I check each time someone comes into view, anxiously making sure it isn't Pyotr.

Zero minutes. We should be leaving any second now.

Except we never do.

"Sorry, folks!" the bus driver says from the front. "Looks like we're experiencing some technical difficulties. I'm going to have to ask you all to get off the bus while our technician works on the repairs."

My chest caves in. *No.* No, this can't be happening. I was so *close.*

A few of the other passengers grumble under their breath, but nonetheless vacate their seats and shuffle toward the exit. I remain where I am out of sheer stubbornness. I don't know what's going to happen to me if I step off this bus.

The sound of heavy footsteps reaches my ear. I sink into my seat, my heart railing against my ribcage.

"Well, I have to give you credit for persistence," a familiarly deep voice comments.

I look up to find Pyotr standing in the aisle, the vein at his temple pulsing. His tone may sound triumphant, but his face betrays his annoyance. He crooks a finger, beckoning me to follow.

Dammit.

It looks like he's won this round.

CHAPTER 10

PYOTR

"Are Merrybell and Ben in trouble?"

I don't bother answering. While I have control over my anger, I don't trust myself to speak. I rarely have to raise my voice—truly powerful men never have to—but Alina has a way of pushing all my buttons.

We're seated in the back of my car, the driver navigating the evening traffic rush in silence. There's a transparent divider separating us, but I still don't feel like having this conversation when others are present.

"Pyotr, I—"

"Not another word until we get home."

"Please don't take it out on them," Alina says, her brows knitted together in worry. "If you're going to punish someone, it should be me. I tricked them. It's my fault."

"Why are you so concerned about them?" I ask. "I told you before, I'm a reasonable man. I'm very aware of the fact that Merrybell and Ben aren't at fault." I cast her a glare. "*You* are."

Alina shifts uncomfortably in her seat, her hands neatly folded in her lap. The sight of her so defeated makes my stomach clench. I don't like this any more than she does. Does she think I *like* having to put my foot down? I find no amusement or pleasure in her discomfort.

"I'm not the bad guy," I grumble. "I wish you would see that."

We don't speak to one another for the rest of the ride.

The penthouse is uncomfortably quiet when we finally arrive. A stack of boxes and shopping bags are piled high on the coffee table for Alina.

"Merrybell had those delivered," I explain as Alina guiltily glances at them. "After she called me in a panic saying you'd disappeared."

Alina casts her eyes to the floor. "I didn't mean to make her worry. Is she mad?"

"I don't think Merrybell has it in her to be mad at anybody. If anything, she was concerned about your safety."

Alina sucks in a deep breath, the conflict clear in her eyes. "Look, I just—Why won't you just let me go? It's like you said, you're trapped in this arrangement, too."

"And let our families go to war? Absolutely not."

Her face drains of color, her eyes wide in shock. "War? What war?"

In this moment, everything suddenly snaps into place. "Your mother never told you," I realize aloud.

"Told me *what*?"

"About how our families were on the brink of fighting."

Alina shakes her head. "No, I... She never tells me anything. Are you being serious right now?"

"I wouldn't lie about something like this."

"I thought she married me off to you for the money!"

"Her financial gain just happened to be an added bonus. The real reason for our rushed marriage was to ensure that the Antonovs and the Salkovs didn't turn on each other and burn Moscow to ashes."

Alina's eyes are suddenly glossy with tears. "Why didn't you just tell me that?" she squeaks.

"Would you have believed me?"

"I mean..." She shrugs. "Maybe? But surely there could have been another way—"

"Your mother made open threats against us," I tell her through gritted teeth. I reach into my pocket and pull out my phone, swiping across the screen until I pull up a picture. I hold it out for Alina to see.

She squints, staring at the image through her gathering tears. "Who are these people?"

"This is my family," I tell her. "My brothers, my sisters-in-law, my nieces and nephews. The territory dispute between our families took a violent turn not two weeks ago. Violetta threatened to have each and every one of them executed."

Alina looks like she might be sick, but she doesn't question me. I have a feeling she understands her mother's cruelty better than anyone. "Even the children?"

I nod solemnly. "You know what she's capable of, don't you?"

"Mother keeps me out of Bratva affairs. I had no idea."

"But you *do* know what she's capable of."

Alina presses her lips into a thin line, her bottom lip trembling. "Yes," she whispers bitterly.

"Do you understand the predicament we're in now?" I snap, my patience officially paper-thin. "If you think this is a game, you're wrong. The only thing keeping our families from slaughtering one another is this marriage. Without it, our families will go to war."

Alina's shoulders tremble, her face stark white. "How many would..."

"How many would die? Hundreds. Possibly thousands—on *both* sides. Not to mention the innocents who would get caught in the crossfire. You and I are the only ones standing in the way of the bloodshed."

She looks like she might topple over at any given moment. Alina wanders aimlessly into the living room area and plops down on the couch, the weight of the world crushing her.

"I didn't know," she whispers.

"Now you do."

"This is so *unfair*. Why didn't Mother..." Alina wipes at her eyes with a frustrated groan. "Why didn't she tell me?"

"I doubt it would have made a difference," I confess. "Whether you knew or not, it wouldn't have mattered. We would have been married for the sake of peace, either way."

Alina is silent, likely at a loss for words. I get it. I really do. Because I'm right there with her. This *isn't* fair. We've been dragged into an agreement that neither of us wants to be a part of, but at the end of the day, our arms are twisted behind our backs.

"How did you even know to find me?" she asks, so soft and quiet I miss the first half of what she says.

Tired, I enter the living room and take a seat next to her. I'm surprised when she doesn't react, doesn't try to push me away. A respectful few inches remain between us, but Alina looks too worn out and crushed to put up a fight.

"Your phone," I explain. "It has a tracking app."

She groans, rolling her eyes at herself. "I should have known."

I shrug a shoulder. "I knew you'd try to run away again; it was just a matter of when and how."

Alina reaches into her pocket and pulls out some money. "I should probably give this back to you, then. Though it's a little less than I took."

I'll confess I'm not even angry. She's resourceful, I'll give her that much. Fast on her feet. If our situation weren't so dire, I'd probably be impressed. Besides, five thousand dollars is peanuts to me.

"Is there anything else I should know?" she grumbles.

"That's pretty much it. If this marriage doesn't work, our families will be at each other's throats."

A soft sob bubbles past her lips. Alina tries to stifle the sound in her palms, but it's too late. She begins to cry in earnest, her anguish ripping at her throat as her body tremors with the effort.

My heart twists. I can't stand to see her like this. I'm not mad at her for trying to run away again. I understand completely. We're in the same boat, she and I. Our wings have been clipped against our will.

Cautiously, I reach out, an action based purely on instinct. I want to comfort her, but I think against it, drawing my hand back. I don't want to make an already uncomfortable situation more unbearable. I'm genuinely worried that if I touch her, she might break.

"I'm sorry," I tell her as gently as I can. "Truly. Were it up to me, I'd let you go."

Alina wipes her nose with the back of her sweater sleeve and tilts her head back, closing her eyes as her lips part just so. "I'm sorry, too."

"For what?"

"For being such a pain in the ass. I swear I'm not usually like this."

"Would you blame a caged animal for lashing out?"

She snorts. "Are you comparing me to an animal?"

"The allegory works, doesn't it?"

She laughs bitterly. "Yeah, I guess."

I stare at her for a moment, settling on her worried lips. "Are you going to try and run away again?"

"And risk my mother's wrath and your brother's retaliation?" Alina huffs wearily. "No, I'm not going to run away again. I promise. I just wish you'd been honest with me from the get-go. We could have both saved ourselves a lot of trouble."

"I honestly thought you knew," I tell her. I turn slightly in my seat. "I'm going to give you my complete honesty from now on, so listen carefully."

"What?"

"This isn't what either of us wants, but we can make it work for our families' sake. Life with me doesn't have to be miserable. I said I would take care of you. And I meant what I said about wanting for nothing. Don't think of this as a marriage, but a partnership."

"A partnership?" she echoes. "You really are all business, huh?"

"We officially have less than three months left until our interview. Until then, will you work with me on this?"

"That's a funny way of asking me to get to know you."

I sigh. "Alina..."

"Okay," she says lightly. She chews on the inside of her cheek, appearing to contemplate everything I've said. Eventually she replies, "Okay. It's not like I have any other choice."

"From here on out, you'll accompany me wherever I go. To work, to business meetings, everywhere."

"So you can keep an eye on me?"

"That, and because we need to seem like a convincing couple when our interviewer finally meets with us. It'll raise red flags if we show up and can't stand to be in the same room together."

"What makes you think I can stand to be in the same room as you now?"

"Fair. You'll just have to get used to me."

"Sounds daunting."

"So, what do you say? Truce?"

Alina gives me a tired smirk. She sticks her hand out to shake. "Truce, but only because you asked *so* nicely."

I shake her hand and nod. The stakes are too high. This is probably as good as I'm going to get, so I'm going to take her at her word and roll with it.

CHAPTER 11

ALINA

"A security exercise?" Merrybell shriek-whispers.

"That's right," Pyotr replies unapologetically. He types away on his computer, drafting an email. "I thought I sent you a memo. Ben's a newer member of my security team, and I needed to test his performance. I gave Alina instructions to elude him at the first given opportunity."

I pick at my fingernails, nibbling on my bottom lip. I don't feel great about lying to Merrybell, but I can't very well tell her the truth, either. What would she think if I told her I tried to run away from Pyotr? I doubt that'd go well.

"I'm sorry," I say for the millionth time. "I really didn't mean to worry you."

Merrybell gives me a soft smile, waving a hand dismissively. "Don't worry, my dear. I'm not angry with *you*." She gives Pyotr a pointed glare. "Next time, a heads up would be greatly appreciated."

"Like I said, I thought I sent you a memo."

His personal assistant huffs. I can't believe she bought his lies. I think it's because Pyotr is so strait-laced and flat on his delivery that no one would ever take him for anything except at his word.

"I have documents to photocopy," she says. "Is there anything else you need?"

"That'll be all, Merrybell. Thank you."

She exits, but she doesn't go too far. A desk of her own sits just outside the big glass walls of Pyotr's corner office.

"So, this is where you work?" I ask, though my question is redundant. "What do you do all day?"

"Boring stuff. You wouldn't be interested."

"Details, Pyotr," I remind. "I need details. What if the immigration officer asks me about your work? I need to be able to answer him."

He leans back in his executive chair, strumming his finger against the edge of his desk. "I answer emails, mostly. And attend meetings. I check in with my department heads frequently to ensure they have everything they need. I negotiate contracts with potential clients, I conduct media interviews when asked, and I'm the face of our outreach program."

My ears perk up. "Outreach program?"

"It's a coding camp, basically. For underprivileged kids. Cyber-Fort believes in providing opportunities for the next generation of computer developers. Without them spearheading the future, none of us can thrive."

"Spoken like a true CEO."

"I mean it," he says, sounding as close to defensive as I've ever heard him. "I'm not blowing smoke. I genuinely believe in the program and the kids we're helping."

I find myself smiling, the genuine passion in his voice catching me off guard. "I believe you."

Pyotr once again stares at my lips, something akin to awe in his dark eyes.

Does he… Wait, does he like it when I smile? The thought makes my cheeks warm. I'm sure I'm just imagining things.

"Is Ben going to be in trouble?" I ask after walking a loop around his office, taking in all the plaques and trophies he's been awarded over the years. *Best In Business, The American Business Awards*, and others I've never heard of. I'm sure they're all very prestigious.

"That's the second time you've asked," he says bluntly.

"Because I want to know."

"Are you worried about him?"

I chew on the inside of my cheek. "Should I be?"

"Ben should have been more diligent. What if something had happened to you? As your assigned bodyguard, he should have been protecting you, external threats or otherwise. He's already received a verbal warning."

"But his job is safe?"

"For now."

I mosey on over to his desk. He's got several documents spread out in front of him, and his ultra-wide computer monitor has at least a dozen different tabs open. There's so much happening on screen it makes my head hurt.

"How do you make sense of it all?" I mumble.

Pyotr chuckles. At least, I think it's a chuckle. That deep voice of his makes everything sound like a growl. "You get used to it."

I dare to sit on the edge of his desk, perched on the corner as I watch him work. Pyotr makes no effort to shoo me away, so I don't think he particularly minds my being here.

These waters we're trying to navigate together are uncharted and choppy. Since the revelation that our flimsy marriage is the only thing standing in the way of disaster, I've been trying to make an effort to right my wrongs.

I was so quick to hate Pytor. I haven't quite come to terms with everything that's happened. It's not like a flick of the light switch. A part of me is still disgruntled, but at least now I understand his motivations. He's not a *complete* monster like I first made him out to be. If only he'd told me sooner, maybe I wouldn't have gone through all the trouble of trying to get away. Now that the truth has been laid bare, I still feel trapped—but I don't hold any resentment toward my husband.

Husband. There's that word again.

It's still such a strange thing to me. For the sake of peace, I'd better get used to it. I think about my sisters. We're not as close as we used to be, but they're still my flesh and blood. Mother might have kept me out of most of the Bratva business, but I'm no fool. I know how dangerous and bloody it can get. They very much operate under an eye-for-an-eye philosophy.

I shudder. Sometimes I can't believe I was born into this world of guns and daggers and constant dealings. Father always used to tell me my soft heart could never survive it, and that's why Mother kept me at a distance. Father made it sound like she was doing me a favor. Now? I'm not so sure.

"So..." I say, more than a little aware of the awkwardness between us. "Do you have any hobbies?"

"I read."

I roll my eyes. God, this is painful. "Come on, Pyotr. Give me something to work with."

"What? Reading is a hobby. It exercises the mind, keeps you sharp."

"I saw your piano at home," I mention quickly. "Do you play?"

"Used to."

"Why'd you stop?"

Pyotr ignores me, tapping away at his email.

"Is it because of your hearing?" I ask on a whim.

This catches his attention. He glares at me, equal parts angry and surprised. "What?"

I bite my tongue. *Crap. That was shitty.* What if he's sensitive about it? "Nothing," I say hastily, hopping off the edge of his desk.

Before I have a chance to slip away, Pyotr grasps my hand. He's so gentle it takes me by surprise. The steady warmth of his fingers sends a delightful shiver racing up my arm and down my spine.

"You should know," he grumbles.

"You don't have to, Pyotr. It's not my place—"

"You're my wife. You of all people should know."

I swallow, a curiosity blooming across my chest as I await his response.

"I'm deaf in my right ear," he says matter-of-factly. "And I'm... losing my hearing in my left."

I can tell this is a big deal for him, judging by the crinkle of his brow and the conflict etched into his features. "How many people know?"

"Just you. Well, and my doctor."

For some reason, this revelation makes me feel... *special*.

"How did it happen?" I ask softly. "I mean, you don't have to tell me if you don't want to, but..."

"It's alright." He's still holding onto my hand, tracing the lines of my palm with the tips of his fingers. "I've never been able to hear in my right. I noticed it when I was a boy. It got harder and harder to hear, until one day, I just didn't. I never told my family because I was too young to understand it wasn't normal."

"So it's a condition? Like hereditary or something?"

"No one else in my family has a hearing problem," he says with a shrug. "When I was older, my mother realized I couldn't hear properly and took me to the doctor. I have what's called conductive hearing loss. It's irreparable." He smirks. "And I enjoyed target practice as well as loud concerts, so that didn't help."

"Seriously? You shoot?"

"Yeah. I don't take part in the Bratva business, but it was important that we all knew how to shoot." He looks into my eyes. "Have you ever shot a gun?"

"Once or twice. I'm not any good."

He nods understandingly. We're part of the same world, after all, one where danger lurks around every corner and survival is a skill taught at an early age. I never thought about it that way before, but at least we have that in common.

"Well," he says, "then you know guns are fucking loud. And the rock concerts even louder. My left started to go a few years ago."

I feel compelled to reach out. I slowly lift my hand, moved by some invisible force I can't hope to understand, and tenderly caress his left cheek. Pyotr's stubble is rough beneath my fingertips, the hard line of his jaw guiding me up to his earlobe. I am mesmerized, intrigued by our proximity. Time doesn't make sense. These precious few seconds feel as though they last an eternity, giving me the chance to truly take him in.

Is it weird that I like the strong bridge of his nose? And why do I enjoy the dip of his cupid's bow? And how did he get that light scar just above his brow? These little details fascinate me. When I first laid eyes on him, I thought he was nothing more than a statue. Now that I'm up close and personal, I can see the man hiding beneath it all.

"Your turn," he says after a moment, his voice a low rumble.

I pull my hand back and drop it in my lap. "Hm?"

"A secret for a secret. That's how we'll build trust."

"So that's how this works?"

Pyotr nods, eagerness in his eyes as he watches me. I take a moment to think. I don't have many secrets, and certainly nothing that rivals the significance of the one Pyotr just told me, but I'm sure I've got a few up my sleeve I could share with him.

"I happen to like playing the piano," I tell him. "I'm actually pretty good. I used to have dreams of attending Julliard, but…"

"But what?"

"That was a very long time ago. I haven't exactly kept up with my practice."

"Why not? Because your mother said it gave her headaches?"

I smile at him, the butterflies in my stomach fluttering. "You remember that? I didn't think you were listening."

"I was." He watches me for a moment, that strange intensity once again darkening his eyes. "Why did you stop?" he urges.

"When I was little," I start slowly. "I used to play for Father all the time. But then he… Well, it was a deal gone wrong. Mother never told me the details, but he was gunned down by a rival family."

Pyotr's brows furrow. "I'm sorry to hear that."

I chew on the inside of my cheek and try my best not to get swept up in the memory. "It was miserable in that house after Father died. Mother turned into a tyrant. I tried playing the piano at Father's wake, but Mother stomped over and slammed the lid down on my fingers in front of everyone. She broke both my pinkies and bruised all my knuckles. After that, I wasn't as eager to play anymore."

The muscles in Pyotr's jaw tick. I can't decipher the look he gives me as he takes my hand in his own and inspects my fingers, carefully brushing the pad of his thumb over my knuckles. They've long since healed, but he treats me as though the injury is fresh. Never in my wildest dreams did I expect this hulking, terrifying-at-first-glance man to have such a gentle streak. It's almost intimate, the way he touches me.

"You'll have to play for me some time," he says firmly, leaving no room for protest. "I would enjoy that immensely."

I nod slowly. "Yeah... Maybe."

Neither of us make a move to pull away. If anything, I feel myself drawn to him, pulled ever closer like a moth to a flame. The longer I stare at him, the more I start to think—would it be so bad? Would it be so bad if I leaned in and kissed him?

Two knocks vibrate the office's glass door.

Merrybell sticks her head in. "Sorry to interrupt, but I've just received an invitation to the Burcheist Gala. Would you like for me to RSVP?"

Pyotr lets go of my hand and straightens in his seat. Back to business. "Isn't the gala tomorrow? Why am I only getting an invitation now?"

"Perhaps it was lost in the mail?"

My ears perk up. "What's this about a gala?"

"It's a charity dinner," Pyotr explains, "to raise money for food banks all over the state of New York."

"He goes every year," Merrybell tells me with a wink. "He's got a soft spot for those in need."

He doesn't seem to be affected by the comment, though he does clear his throat. "Tell them I'm coming," he says. "And mark me down for a plus one."

I glance at him. His eyes have already found mine. "I get to go?"

"Like I said, wherever I go..."

CHAPTER 12

PYOTR

My bringing Alina serves two purposes. For one, she can't cause trouble if I'm keeping an eye on her. Two, it'll be good to be seen in public together. There are always hordes of photographers at events like this, and if we're going to fool Immigration, we need to give the illusion we're a happy, adoring couple. A couple of snaps of us here and there are sure to go a long way.

I'm already dressed. I've got a tuxedo on standby. The Burcheist Gala is a who's who of the New York elite. Socialites, businessmen, celebrities... They're all going to be there tonight, so dressing for the occasion is a must.

I adjust my cufflinks as I descend the stairs. Luka happens to be lounging on the second floor's living room, a Red Bull in one hand and his laptop on the coffee table. He whistles at me.

"Where are you going, fancy pants?" he teases.

"Out."

"Oh, good. And here I thought you were in your casual attire."

"You haven't been stopping by the office," I tell him, ignoring the jab.

Luka shrugs. "I can get all of my work done here. There's no need for me to go in. Too many distractions."

"I'm starting to worry that you're becoming a shut-in."

"I'm not. I work more effectively at home, you know that. Given all the, uh... *stuff* Mikhail and Dimitri have me do, it's better to have a private space to work."

"Fair point. Try not to burn the place down while I'm gone."

"No promises."

I roll my eyes and continue descending the steps to the first floor of the penthouse. Alina is nowhere in sight, though I can just barely hear music playing in her room. As I approach her door, the music gets louder. Whoever's singing has a beautiful voice. It isn't until I'm at her doorway that I realize—

It's *Alina*.

I can't make out her words, but that's not what captures my attention. Her notes are crystal clear, so sweet and angelic she has me almost hypnotized. I don't even realize I've taken a step into her room until she sees me in the reflection of her floor mirror and whips around with a gasp.

"Oh! H-how long were you standing there?"

"Not long."

"Actually, excellent timing," she says, turning away to expose the back of her open dress. Her cheeks are pink, her nervous eyes cast down to the carpeted floor. "My zipper got caught. Do you think you can help me?"

My feet carry me forward before my brain ever gets the chance to think about it. I approach her slowly, my hands moving all on their own.

Alina's in a gorgeous red dress like liquid fire, the fabric shimmering, intricate beadwork catching the room's soft light. The dress hugs her hips and dips at her delicate waste, draping over her shoulders like red rivulets. The zipper is indeed stuck, caught in its own teeth, but it gives me plenty of opportunity to gaze upon her back.

She's covered in scars.

My mouth goes dry. Something dark and angry boils in the pit of my stomach. I reach out, gingerly tracing fingers over the dull red welts upon her skin. My lips curl up into a sneer, my rage barely kept in check.

"Who did this to you?" I growl.

Alina squirms a little. "It's nothing."

"Answer me."

She looks at me using the reflection of the mirror, her eyes wide and full of bitter acceptance. "Who do you think?"

A protective instinct flares within me. There's no love lost between Violetta and me. The moment she threatened my family was the moment I wrote her off. I tolerate her at best for the sake of this peace treaty but knowing she has harmed Alina—and clearly not just once—has me seething. The rational part of my brain flies straight out the window. I have half a mind to fly back to Russia and teach her mother a lesson. Everything I learn about Violetta only solidifies my hatred for her.

"Do they still hurt?" I ask Alina through gritted teeth, tracing over the next welt I find.

She shakes her head. "Not anymore."

"How?"

Alina looks down as if ashamed. "Riding crop."

Anger licks at the nape of my neck. "Excuse me?"

"Long story short? I wanted to go riding. Mother disagreed. She thought she could beat the stubbornness out of me."

It takes a lot to make me queasy, but I think I might genuinely hurl. It's no fucking wonder Alina's been so determined to run away, why she can't bring herself to trust so easily. The one person in the world she's supposed to rely on hurt her.

"It was a long time ago," Alina mumbles. "She can't hurt me here."

I don't know what compels me to do it, but I find myself dipping down to inspect her scars even closer. My mind is on autopilot, taken over by my overwhelming need to press my lips to her back.

Alina moans softly, her breath a shudder.

I move my way up, entranced. I can't get over how soft she feels against me. I kiss a line up her spine, working my way to the back of her neck, gingerly pressing my lips to her skin. Our eyes remained locked in the mirror, our desire reflected back at us as I snake an arm around her waist. Alina tilts her head back, exposing the open column of her throat. Her mouth falls open as a breathy gasp escapes her, her hips bucking so she grinds against the growing hardness in my pants. When I reach up to squeeze her breast over the fabric of her dress, the sound of her moan damn near leaves me winded.

"Oh, Pyotr..."

The sound of my own name breaks me out of my trance. What am I doing? I didn't mean to do any of that. Why is it that where Alina is concerned, I always seem to lose my mind?

"Secret for secret?" I mutter against the crook of her neck.

"What?"

"I want to rip this dress off of you."

"Pyotr, I..."

God, I want her. I want her right here, right now. I've totally forgotten why we got all dressed up and where we were supposed to go. There's something addicting about the flush of her cheeks, the way her blush spreads all the way up to the tips of her ears. I can't stop thinking about what she might look like beneath me, pressed against the sheets with her fingers combing through my hair.

My phone buzzes.

Dammit.

I can't *not* answer. It could be business-related—CyberFort or my brothers in Russia. Both are too important to ignore, but...

"It's okay," Alina whispers, as if reading my mind. "Answer it. It might be important."

I nod. "Thank you."

It's just a text, but it nonetheless needs to be addressed.

. . .

I have the car waiting for you and Mrs. Antonov downstairs. We've got the follow car ready, too. We should arrive at the event in roughly twenty minutes if we leave now.

"We need to go," I tell her.

"Uh... My zipper?"

I mentally slap my own forehead. Oh, right. I help her do up the back of her dress without any... complications getting in the way. She really does look stunning.

"It looks good on you," I murmur.

Alina casts me a shy smile. "I was worried it might be too bold, but—"

"No, it... suits you."

Her smile widens. "Really?"

"Yeah. It makes your eyes stand out."

I bite my tongue. *Where the hell did that come from?* Not only do I lose my mind with her, but I apparently don't have a filter, either.

Thankfully, Alina giggles. The sound takes my breath away, so light and airy, like windchimes on a summer morning. For a moment, I forget every single word in both English and Russian, too stunned by her brilliant smile to form a proper thought.

Alina chuckles. "Don't we need to go?"

I clear my throat. "Right. Yes, of course."

"Blue, by the way."

"What?"

"A secret for a secret. Blue is my favorite color. Light blue, like the sky."

I suppose to most, this might be a mundane sort of fact, but coming from Alina, it feels like I've struck gold.

"Duly noted," I mutter as she slips past me.

My feet follow without hesitation.

CHAPTER 13

ALINA

I've only been to one or two events as grand as this, when Father was still alive and Mother wasn't nearly as much of a menace. Oksana's wedding reception and Nikita's eighteenth birthday. I remember there being a lot of guests and even more booze, but I was far too young to recall any faces or truly partake in festivities. But this?

This is what I'd call a party.

The Burcheist Gala is hosted at a hotel venue downtown, its grand ballroom set up for the occasion. A red carpet leads into the main area, and at least a hundred different photographers are lined up on the other side of a rope. I'm almost blinded by the flash of cameras, the roar of photographers yelling to 'look this way, please', making my ears ring.

Worry sets in. I'm not used to this level of public scrutiny. Is my makeup okay? What if I trip and fall in front of everyone? I'd not only embarrass myself, but Pyotr, too.

Yet Pyotr has a steady hand on the small of my back the entire time. He's a stable presence, a rock against the tumultuousness of the evening.

"I'm not used to having my picture taken," I confess as we approach the entrance. "Can't we just slip through?"

"Is that what you'd prefer?" he asks.

I chew on the inside of my cheek. "I mean, yes. But I know you probably need it for PR reasons, right? And for—" I look over my shoulder cautiously to make sure no one hears— "for Immigration, right?"

"They'll grab a few of us walking past," he says firmly. "We don't have to stop if you don't want to."

I let out an appreciative sigh.

"Stick close," Pyotr says, his arm circling around so he can grip me steadily by the hip.

We walk forward, the onslaught of flashes and camera clicks so overwhelming it seems surreal. People call out to us to slow down for the photo op, but Pyotr pays them no mind.

"Who's your friend?" someone shouts at him.

"Who's the lovely lady?"

"Can we get a picture of you two for The Bastion?"

"What's the hurry? Are you looking forward to the fun night?"

"Is this your daughter?" someone follows up.

At this, Pyotr stops and glares at one of the photographers. I cling to him, dizzy and unsure. "This is my *wife*," he says flatly.

The crowd suddenly bursts into a cloud of chaotic questions.

"Did he say wife?"

"I didn't know he was married."

"What's your name, sweetheart?"

"Kinda young, isn't she?"

My ears burn.

"Come along, Alina," Pyotr says, so close to my ear I feel his lips brush against the outer curve of it. "Pay them no mind."

By some miracle, we make it into the venue in one piece. It's a relief, to be sure, though it's no less crowded in here than outside. I'm surrounded by extravagance the likes of which I've never before seen.

Champagne is freely flowing, the lights are dimmed and almost golden, and there's even a chocolate fountain where a handful of guests help themselves to dipped fruit. A live band in the corner plays soft jazz, the music sweeping throughout the room. Naturally, the center of the ballroom has been cleared out, offering plenty of space for guests to dance the night away.

It's all so dazzling I can't help but stare. I feel as though I've walked straight into a dream.

"Stay close." At first, I think Pyotr is talking to me, but I look up and realize he's giving an order to Ben.

My bodyguard nods respectfully. "I'll keep an eye on her, sir."

"You're not staying with me?" I ask Pyotr.

"I have to shake some hands," he answers begrudgingly. "But I won't be long. Help yourself to some food. I'll come find you."

A strange wave of disappointment washes over me. I know this partnership of ours is new, but I was sort of hoping he'd keep me at his side all night. I don't know anyone here, after all. The idea of being by myself—Ben excluded—makes me uneasy. Nevertheless, I mosey on over to the refreshments table, Ben following hot on my heels.

"I'm sorry about the other day," I tell him.

Ben hits me with a charming smile. "Don't worry about it, Mrs. Antonov."

"No, I really must apologize."

"Seriously, it's okay. Mr. Antonov explained everything. I should have been more vigilant, so that's on me. I promise to do much better in the future."

I smile at him. Ben's sweet. He sort of reminds me of a golden retriever, determined and brave. He isn't holding my little stunt against me, thank goodness.

"Do you want anything?" I ask, gesturing to the table.

"No, ma'am. I'm not allowed to eat while on duty."

"Surely an hors d'oeuvres here or there wouldn't hurt."

"That's the rule, ma'am. Besides, if Mr. Antonov catches me slacking off... Well, I'd rather not risk it."

I pick up a small plate and help myself to tiny cakes cut into bite-sized cubes, popping one of them into my mouth. "Seems a bit excessive, doesn't it?" I whisper to him. "A charity gala to raise money for food banks, yet the money spent on this gala could have been used instead."

Ben shrugs. "You want my honest opinion?"

"Of course," I say, leaning in to listen to the gossip.

"Most of these people, they're all phonies. They're here for the photo ops and the networking opportunities. They don't actually care about feeding the poor."

I furrow my brow. "I'm sure some of that may be true, but what about Pyotr?"

"Ah, he's the exception. He comes every year and makes a massive donation matched by the event organizers. He's the real deal."

"You speak very highly of him."

Ben chuckles. "He's a good man. Rough around the edges, as I'm sure you know, but he's very honorable."

"How long have you worked for him?"

"Only about six months. My Aunt Merrybell was actually the one who landed me the interview. Mr. Antonov was kind enough to give me a shot despite not having much experience."

I raise my eyebrows. "Merrybell is your aunt?"

"I know, I know. I'm a nepo baby. Don't judge me."

I throw my head back and laugh. "I'm not going to judge you."

"I honestly didn't think Mr. Antonov would go for it, but you've met my aunt. She can be a real firecracker. Hard for anyone to say no to."

"Boy, I'll say. Did you always want to be a bodyguard?"

Ben chuckles. "I wanted to be a cop, actually, but I failed the police academy exam."

"Oh, I'm sorry."

"Nah, it's cool. Between you and me, this pays *way* better."

I laugh again, feeling light and at ease. Ben's really easy to talk to. I sincerely hope we can be good friends.

Out of nowhere, Pyotr swoops in from behind, his protective hand on the small of my back. He looks... kind of pissed, but I'm pretty sure that's just his face.

"What's so funny?" he grumbles.

"Ben was just telling me about his job—"

"Dance with me," Pyotr says quickly, taking my hand to drag me out to the dance floor. I manage to give Ben my plate before I'm whisked away.

The song the band plays is slow and romantic, the golden tones of the saxophone coming in bright and clear. Pyotr takes my hand in his, his other arm wrapping tightly around my waist. His hold is sturdy and strong. I don't really know how to dance, but he makes it easy, guiding my movements to the beat of the song. When I look up, I find him glaring in Ben's general direction.

"Oh my God," I say around a laugh. "Pyotr, are you..."

"What?"

Are you jealous, I want to ask him, but decide against it. It certainly seems like he is. Did he see me laughing and smiling with Ben from afar? Is that why he swooped in like an eagle and whisked me away?

"You're a really good dancer," I say instead.

"I'm alright."

I roll my eyes. "Take the compliment, *husband*."

"What did he say to you?" he asks, clearly still hung up on what happened before. "What did Ben say to make you laugh?"

My stomach flips. I smile, surprised by his obvious irritation. "He just made a joke, that's all."

"What did he *say*?"

"Honestly? I've already forgotten."

"It must not have been that funny, then."

As we spin around the dance floor, I can't help but notice all the eyes on us. Men in their impressive suits, women in their gorgeous dresses—we have their undivided attention.

"Why are they staring at us?" I ask Pytor, making sure to whisper on his left.

"Not us. You."

God, he's right. The attention is heavy and hot against my skin. "But why?"

"Because."

"What did I say about details, Pyotr?"

He dips down slightly, his lips ghosting along my ear. "Because you're beautiful."

My heart skips a beat, the breath knocking from my lungs. It should be illegal for him to sound this sexy. I'm weak to the deep notes of his voice, the warmth of his breath brushing against my cheek sending heat straight to my core.

"In all the years I've attended this gala, I've never brought a guest with me. They're probably interested in knowing who you are."

"Never?" I echo.

"Never."

"Well, I feel special."

The song eventually comes to an end and—much to my disappointment—so does the dance. Pyotr continues to hold onto me regardless, staring at my lips with the same intense fervor I've come to know so well. He's so close he could kiss me, or I could kiss *him*. What's stopping me? Why can't I find the courage to do it?

"Pyotr?"

"Yes, Alina?"

"I, um..." My legs are jelly, my heart a hammering drum. "Where are the bathrooms?" I ask, folding so hard I might as well be a house of cards.

Pyotr releases me, tossing his chin in the direction of the doors. "Should be down that hall there. I'll have Ben accompany you."

"N-no, that's okay. I'll be quick."

He gives me a suspicious squint. "Are you trying to run away again?"

I shake my head. "No. No, I promise."

After a moment, Pyotr nods. "Alright then."

CHAPTER 14

ALINA

I can't get my heart to slow. At this rate, I may very well pass out right here on the bathroom floor. It's blessedly empty in here, which means I can have my mini-panic attack in peace.

I don't know what's happening to me. It's all happening so fast, too fast. Where once I couldn't look Pyotr in the eye without feeling intense hatred and fear, now I'm feeling... *different*. This really *is* uncharted territory.

Only a few days ago, I thought I was marrying my enemy. Now I'm not so sure. Could it be that I'm starting to like my own husband?

I turn on the sink, splashing cold water on my face.

The ghost sensation of his hand on my back, the warm solidity of his body pressed against mine... It's enough to make me swoon if I were the swooning sort. I can't remember the last time I was this flustered. Pyotr didn't even *do* anything, yet I'm on the brink of melting into a puddle. It's definitely his eyes, so deep and dark and alluring. Combined with his undivided attention and gentle touch? How's a girl supposed to keep her composure?

I take a deep breath and study my reflection in the mirror.

Not us. You.

Because you're beautiful.

I dare say that one compliment from Pyotr feels like it's worth a thousand from any other man. Maybe it's because he doesn't talk very much that every word out of his mouth is worth its weight in gold—precious and rare, to be appreciated and not taken for granted.

Smoothing my hands over the front of my dress, I think about the way he held me in front of my own mirror back home. I still can't believe it. My core throbs with the memory of him squeezing my breast, a shiver racing down my spine when I recall the feel of his lips against my skin. The hunger in his eyes was unlike anything I'd ever seen before.

And now I want more.

The realization is daunting at first. The jolt of excitement I get when I know he's looking at me is still new, but I find myself craving it. This new footing we've found for ourselves is thrilling, but do I dare allow myself to explore?

I decide to get back to the party. If I keep Pyotr waiting any longer, he might think I've tried to pull a fast one on him again. Our newfound trust is fragile, just a seedling. Given the importance of our marriage and the shaky alliance it upholds, the last thing I want is to shatter what little we've managed to build between us.

I find a man leaning against the opposite wall when I leave the bathroom. I don't think anything of it at first. Maybe he's waiting for someone. But when he sees me, he immediately smirks—a smirk that exposes his yellow teeth and a twisted incisor.

"So, you're the belle of the ball, hm?"

I blink at him. "Excuse me?"

He approaches, taking a single step forward. I assume he is a guest because he's dressed in a sharp tuxedo, but it doesn't quite fit him right. He bulges in weird places. His shirt is a size too big and his pants are a size too small. He's *greasy*, and it's honestly uncomfortable to look at. The man sticks out his hand to shake. "The name's Richard. Richard Eaton Jones. I'm one of Peter's business partners. I'm sure you've heard of me."

I take a step back as my guts twist. This guy gives me the creeps, but if he's Pyotr's business partner, I try to be polite. "Is that so? Don't you mean Pyotr?"

He chuckles. "Yes, yes. My pronunciation has always been off."

But it's not that hard...

"I'm afraid Pyotr hasn't mentioned you, though he doesn't tell me much about his work in general."

"No? I guess we'll have to get better acquainted on our own."

His wording weirds me out. The air around him is at least two degrees colder than the rest of the hall. There's a sinking feeling in the pit of my stomach telling me to leave as soon as possible.

"I should really get back to the party," I say with a polite smile.

I try to sidestep him, but Richard puts an arm out. "Now wait a second," he says, voice thick and lips smacking. "I have to confess; I had no idea Pyotr got married. I've heard the rumors about you."

"Rumors?"

"Yes, that he rushed off to Russia in the dead of night to marry you. I'd love to hear all about it."

"Maybe some other time." I try to get around him, but he uses his body to block my path.

"What's he doing with a pretty thing like you, I wonder?" Richard goes on. "Come on, I adore a good love story."

"Oh, uh..." I'm *so* uncomfortable right now. "Were you waiting out here for me or something?" I ask him outright.

Richard laughs, scratching behind his ear. "Can you blame me? Pyotr's been hogging you all to himself. I really wanted to introduce myself."

"If you're his business partner, you could have just approached us." I frown, the alarm bells in the back of my head officially going off. "Who are you really?"

Richard's expression suddenly grows dark, his grin twisting into a sneer. "Just someone who wants to be your friend. Come on, let's get back to the party. I want the next dance."

Panic lances through me. "I don't want to."

"Don't be such a stick in the mud."

"Get the hell away from me!"

"Let's take a little walk," Richard says, ignoring me entirely. "I think you and I might be able to help each other."

"Help each other? What could I possibly want from you?"

"Please," he says. "Like I'm actually going to believe you're Peter's wife. I bet he hired you for the evening."

I shift uncomfortably, looking around for a way back to Pytor. "I don't know what you're talking about."

"Let's not play games, dollface. A pretty young thing like you? I bet you're from one of those special elite agencies. Tell me, how much are you charging him for your *services*?"

My stomach lurches. "You think I'm a prostitute?"

"Would you prefer the term 'escort'? Look, there's no way Peter has the pull to nab himself a hot babe like you. How much for a blow job?"

I shake my head in disbelief. I want to slap this man senseless. "I'm going to find Pyotr."

When Richard doesn't move out of the way, I push past him. With more speed than I thought he was capable of, Richard grabs me harshly by the wrist.

"Calm down, dollface. You scratch my back, I'll scratch yours. I'll make you come way harder than he can. I'm a good fuck. Just tell me what you charge."

I don't bother hiding the way I cringe. "I'd rather burn my hands off, thank you."

Richard's grip tightens, his fingers digging into my skin with such intensity I yelp. "Listen here, you little bitch—"

"*Pyotr!*" I scream at the top of my lungs. "*PYOTR!*"

Richard hisses. "Shut the fuck up, you stupid cu—"

I hear him before I see him. The thunderous shake of heavy footfalls reaches my ears. As soon as I see Pyotr rounding the corner, I allow myself to breathe. I've never seen him more furious. Even after I ran away—both times—Pyotr didn't look this angry. He stomps forward, wedges himself between Richard and me, and shoves the man so hard he falls flat on his ass with a pathetic whimper.

"Don't you fucking touch her, Jones!"

Richard makes a show of groaning, rocking from side to side while clutching his shoulder. Definitely an over-the-top performance, but he's drawing in quite the crowd—something I suspect he wanted from the very start.

"I... I think you broke something!" he cries. "You son of a bitch!"

Pyotr stands in front of me like a shield. Even though I can't see his face, I can *feel* his fury radiating off his back. I carefully reach out, my fingers grazing the curve of his clenched fists. He relaxes in an instant, turning to check on me.

"Are you alright?"

"I'm fine," I assure him.

"You're going to pay for this!" Richard hisses. "You all saw that, didn't you? He assaulted me!"

I grit my teeth. "He did no such thing! Pyotr was defending me from *you*!"

Richard continues to huff and wail, greasy face contorting in pain. To be fair, he did land rather hard, but his overt reaction isn't warranted at all. "I'm going to sue you! Someone call the police; I want a report filed. You'll be hearing from my lawyers, Antonov!"

A couple of event security guards approach. Just when I think they're going to help us and put an end to Richard's show, they instead turn to Pyotr.

"Mr. Antonov, we're going to have to ask you and your guest to leave."

My jaw drops. "But we didn't do anything!"

Pyotr carefully takes my hand and squeezes my fingers firmly. Is it a silent warning? Or maybe a gesture of comfort? I'm honestly too frazzled to tell the difference. He doesn't say anything, but his eyes seem to say, *Let's go.*

I hate being escorted out. I'm embarrassed and indignant as we're ushered out of the building. Whispers and judgmental glances follow us all the way out. If Pyotr's bothered by it, he does a good job of not letting it show. Thankfully, Ben has pulled the car up to the curb so we can get in without delay. Thank God for the tinted windows and soundproofed doors because I really don't want to deal with these people anymore.

"I'm so sorry," I murmur as we pull into traffic.

Pyotr sits beside me, as stoic as ever. "Did he hurt you?"

I rub my wrist, glaring at the angry red fingerprints that asshole left on my skin. Richard yanked on me so hard I can see the start of a bruise wrapping around my forearm. That's not my biggest concern right now, however. Right now, I'm worried about the fallout and the ridicule I must have caused.

"I'm sorry," I say again.

"Why are you apologizing? You did nothing wrong."

"I made a scene."

"Again, you did nothing wrong. *Richard* was the one making a scene."

"Are you mad at me?"

Pyotr gives me a flustered look. "Why would I be mad at you, Alina?"

I chew on the inside of my cheek. Mother used to always get mad at me over the littlest things. I'm so used to getting defensive, assuming those around me are seconds away from beating me down.

But Pyotr regards me with a gentleness and understanding I never would have expected. He doesn't raise his voice, and he doesn't have a hint of aggressive body language. He's different than I first thought. I was never safe around my mother, but with Pyotr... He makes me feel safer than I've ever been.

And I don't know how to feel about that.

CHAPTER 15

PYOTR

"Whoa, you two are back early," Luka says casually as Alina and I stride into the penthouse together. We must have caught him mid-trip to the kitchen for yet another Red Bull. I should seriously consider telling him to switch to sugar-free if he continues drinking that crap. "You must be the missus."

I huff. "You still haven't introduced yourself?"

"I've been busy, dude." Luka nods at Alina, offering the stiffest of smiles. "Nice to meet you. I'm the younger brother, Luka."

She manages a soft smile. She sounds more tired than anything. "Ah, the vampire I've heard so much about."

"What?"

"Nothing."

Luka frowns when he sees Alina's swollen wrist. "What happened?"

"I need you to do some research for me," I instruct, ushering Alina to the kitchen. "Richard Eaton Jones accosted her while at the gala. I want all the dirt you can find on him."

Alina casts me a suspicious look. "How?"

"I told you the Antonovs have a talented hacker in their back pocket, didn't I?"

"It's Luka?"

Luka smirks, holding his head up with pride. "I'm my brothers' secret weapon."

"We need to get ahead of him and squash this thing," I continue. "Damage control. You know the drill."

My brother nods and starts up the stairs. "I'm assuming you want a media blackout while you deal with this?"

"Naturally."

"Coming right up."

Alina appears as quizzical as ever. "What's going on? I don't understand."

"I'll explain everything after I get you an ice pack."

Her tension is almost palpable as I shift through the freezer and find a cold compress tucked away in the back. She sits at the kitchen island, anxiously worrying her bottom lip with her teeth.

This certainly wasn't how I expected the evening to turn out. Had I known Richard was on the guest list, I never would have gone, let alone brought Alina along with me. I'd bet good money he either crashed the gala or bought his invitation through a generous last-minute donation. The only question I have is *why*?

Did he come with the intention of confronting Alina? Richard may be an annoying, dramatic son of a bitch, but he's not stupid. This is a game to him, and while I'm not privy to the rules, I'm sure as hell not the kind of man who likes to lose.

I inspect Alina's wrist and ignore the bite of irritation. When I heard her scream my name, my heart nearly launched out of my chest. "I knew I should have had Ben escort you," I mutter under my breath. "I should've just seen you there myself."

"Who is that man?" she asks as I lay the compress on her arm.

"Richard Eaton Jones. My biggest business rival and giant pain in my ass." My thoughts take a bitter turn. "And now he's hurt you, so he's a dead man."

"It's not so bad."

"What did he say to you?"

Alina squirms in her seat, her eyes cast down to the floor. "He... might have called me a prostitute."

I freeze. "Might have?"

"He did."

My temper flares. "You should have kicked him in the balls."

"I thought about it."

Alina slowly reaches up and grazes the tips of her fingers over mine. Our hands are folded neatly together as she watches me work, our breathing calm and steady. The air is still, sizzling with something just shy of overwhelming. I find myself drawing closer and closer into her space, unable to look or move away.

Her gaze flits to my lips. "Pyotr..."

She tilts her chin up, pressing the softest of kisses against my mouth. It's bashful and sweet. Tentative, like Alina isn't sure how I'm going to react. She's like that with a lot of things, no doubt due to her awful upbringing. I can't imagine what it must have been like growing up with Violetta as a mother. Despite the horrors she's had to suffer through, I'm amazed by Alina's burning spirit and determination. She could be a force to be reckoned with if she wanted.

Maybe I can be her guide.

"Sorry," she whispers so quietly I almost don't hear her.

"Stop apologizing." I lean in a little closer, transfixed by the green of her eyes. "Is this what you want, Alina?"

She licks her lips, her breaths measured and tight. "Is that okay?"

"I want you to do something for me."

"What?"

"Stop asking for permission. People like you and me, we take what we want."

"People like you and me?"

"The ones they underestimate. So show me, Alina. Show me what you want."

She pauses just long enough for my words to register.

And then she pounces, every ounce ferocious and hungry and demanding.

Alina throws her arms around my neck, crashing our lips together with such force I have to take a step back. I regain my balance, meeting her with just as much need. I easily pull her into my arms, circling her waist as I lift her a few inches off the floor. She's so unbelievably soft. I can hardly believe it. Just the sight of her skin doesn't do her justice. Her body fits perfectly against mine, molding to my shape.

I'm suddenly ravenous. I need so much more than a kiss, than an embrace. I want to know the feel of her hair slipping between my fingers and the sound of her languid moans. I want to see if her blush extends further than just her cheeks. I need to know how bright the fire in her eyes can burn.

My body moves on its own, easily carrying her toward her bedroom. Alina's unlocked something within me so powerfully protective and eager it's almost a little scary. Since the day I first laid eyes on her, I knew she was special. And while our meeting was less than ideal, I think we were destined to end up in each other's arms.

I shut the door hastily, kicking it closed with my foot as I carry Alina to her bed. Her nimble hands are insatiable, combing through my hair and clawing at my tux, practically yanking off my bowtie like she's ripping off the ribbon of a birthday present. Our lips never part, our tongues dancing over one another with matched urgency.

We move in perfect synchronicity. She undoes the buttons of my shirt, exposing my chest and abs. I reach around to undo the zipper of her dress, quickly sliding her delicate straps over the smooth curves of her shoulders.

She stands before me in a matching pair of black lace panties and a bra, her skin more breathtaking than a still landscape of snow. Alina sucks in a sharp breath as I allow my hands to roam freely, savoring every inch of her body beneath my palms.

"Pyotr..." she moans, tilting her head back.

I dive in like a hawk, hungrily mouthing at her open throat. She grips my shoulders with a desperate whine, the sound of it going straight to my cock. I ignore the throbbing ache in my pants and instead pin her to the bed, settling between her spread legs as I continue to taste her skin. Alina rolls her hips against me, a maddening heat suddenly roaring to life within me.

"*Pyotr—*"

"Is this what you want?" I ask her, barely holding on to my sanity.

"Yes," she wheezes. "Yes, please... but there's something you should know."

"What is it?"

"I've never done this before."

The realization takes me by surprise, though I suppose it makes sense. Given the tight grip Violetta had on Alina her whole life, I doubt she ever had the freedom to meet many people or explore her own desires. That's all about to change. The thought of having her all to myself...

It excites me more than I thought it would.

"My sweet virgin wife," I mumble. "I'm going to take such good care of you."

CHAPTER 16

ALINA

I think my heart might be two seconds away from bursting.

My lightheadedness makes the entire room spin on its axis. The air in my lungs burns with a ferocity I've never experienced before. Every inch of my skin is so hot I swear I might catch fire if Pyotr so much as thinks about stopping.

Thank God he doesn't.

He's rough with me, delightfully so. Not once do I feel like he's going too fast or taking things too far. If anything, everything he does excites me to no end. He moves like a man on a mission, determined to claim me all for himself.

A gasp escapes me when he easily tears my lace bra off my body, the thin fabric standing no chance against his meaty hands.

The cool bedroom air brushes against the hardening peaks of my nipples, goosebumps fanning out over my delicate flesh as Pyotr dips down to devour. He mouths at the crook of my neck, works his way down to my collarbones, and finally comes to the mounds of my breasts. I moan loudly when he sucks a nipple into his mouth, gently teasing with his teeth while his free hand squeezes my other breast firmly.

I barely recognize the sound of my own voice, so squeaky and breathless and wanton I feel like I'm almost having an out of body experience. The pleasure surging through me can't possibly be my own, yet every nerve ending crackles with intense electricity.

Pyotr continues his work, moving down until he's kneeling at the side of my bed, grabbing my hips to pull me toward the edge. He makes it look so easy, like I'm a doll for him to play with. I'm pretty sure he hasn't even broken a sweat while I've been reduced to a bumbling mess of ecstasy. He throws my legs over his shoulders and immediately tears off my lace panties, tossing them to the ground without a care in the world.

My initial instinct is to close my legs, but Pyotr leaves no room to retreat. I'm not ashamed by any means, just a little shy. I've never experienced anything more erotic, more intimate. The warmth of his breath ghosting across my inner thighs, the heat of his mouth hovering just above my core... my pussy is wet and aching.

"P-Pyotr," I whimper, my hands flying to his hair. "What are you—"

He licks a stripe up my folds, his tongue practically searing. A yelp rushes past my lips as my pussy clenches around nothing, my toes curling with unbridled pleasure. Pyotr wastes no time, working with such diligence I feel like I can't catch my breath. He licks and he teases, exploratory in his ministrations. When the tip of his tongue flicks my clit, I nearly shoot straight out of bed.

"Oh, *God!*"

"Easy, wife," he mumbles. I can *feel* his smile.

"Easy?" I echo, incredulous.

"You trust me, don't you?"

I nod, the ringing in my ears so loud I can barely concentrate. "Y-yes, I do."

"Then be a good girl, lie down, and let me show you how a husband is supposed to treat his wife."

Pyotr redoubles his efforts, drawing tight, concise circles against my swollen clit. Liquid fire floods my veins, knocking all sense and reason straight out of my head. All I can do is grip the sheets, writhing beneath his attentive touch. A tight coil deep within the pit of my stomach suddenly grows brighter and hotter, growing more and more intense with every pass of his devilish tongue. My breaths come fast and shallow, my sanity balancing on a razor-thin edge.

My climax crashes into me with such force, my back arches, my hips buck, and a moan rips from my throat. Spots speckle my vision as a warm haze suddenly envelopes me. It's unlike anything I've ever experienced before—so breathtakingly beautiful and freeing. For a moment, I completely forget where I am, suspended in time and place as I slowly ride out my high. A deep satisfaction soaks into my very bones, sleep tugging at my mind.

Pyotr has other plans.

No sooner do I come back to my senses does Pyotr begin again, his tongue acting almost like a salve against my sensitive skin. His grip on my thighs is strong enough to leave light prints where his fingers dig in.

"You taste so fucking good," he grumbles, voice low and thick with the promise of sex. "Did you like that, wife?"

Wife.

He keeps calling me that, and I can't say I mind. I *am* his wife. But when he uses it as a term of endearment, it makes my heart stutter. He makes it sound so beautiful, the word laced with pride.

"It felt really good," I confess, still breathless and reeling from my orgasm.

"I'm not done with you yet."

"What—"

His mouth covers my clit again, this time with the dull press of his thick finger at my entrance. "Do you want me to keep going?"

"Yes!" I blurt out. "Anything you want."

Pyotr chuckles. "Careful, Alina. What I want is to bend you over and fuck you senseless, but tonight, we're going to go slow."

I'm not even a little ashamed of the squeak I make when he slowly presses into me. There's a burn to the stretch, but it's not unbearable. Pyotr moves with the utmost care, so tender and patient it almost takes me by surprise. He crooks his finger slowly, sweeping over a spot inside me that nearly has me shooting out of bed.

"Oh, *God!*"

My second climax is twice as brilliant, hitting me so hard and so fast I'm pretty sure I blackout for a moment. Pyotr doesn't ease up. His mouth continues its attack while he adds a second finger, and then a third. I come again and again until I'm a begging, pleading, writhing mess beneath his touch.

"P-*Pyotr!* I can't take it anymore. Please, just—"

He keeps going, eating me out like it's the only thing he knows how to do.

Pyotr is a sight to behold. His hair is a tousled mess, his lips wet with my heat. His pupils are wide, a look of utter intoxication etched into his normally unreadable features. I don't think I've ever seen a man more mystified.

I can't help but throw my head back against the sheets and laugh. "Come here."

He rises from his knees, towering over me with heated adoration. It doesn't feel like that long ago when I would have found his presence daunting. Now when I look at him, it's nothing but a thrill. I sit up quickly and get back to undressing him, my greedy hands still shaking from all the adrenaline coursing through my veins.

While he slips off his shirt, I clumsily get started on his belt. The obvious bulge in the front of his pants is... daunting, to say the least, but it makes my heart flutter. As much as I want to rush and yank him out of his clothes, I want to savor this moment, too. I don't think I've ever been more nervous. Not because I'm scared, but because of this new intimacy we've found.

I don't love Pyotr. But I don't hate him, either. In this in between, I am navigating in the dark, reaching out in some desperate hope of finding a safe harbor.

The metallic rip of his zipper rings loudly in my ear. Pyotr doesn't seem to be in as much of a hurry, leisurely combing a few strands of my hair away from my face to tuck behind my ear. My hands move on their own, gingerly brushing over the fabric of his black boxer briefs. I can feel the heat of his skin through it, throbbing beneath my touch.

"Go on," Pyotr urges gently. "Don't be shy."

I lick my lips, hooking my fingers under his waistband, pulling down slowly as if to savor every inch of new skin I expose. My breath catches in my throat when his erection finally springs free. He's deliciously thick and impressively long, the tip leaking with want.

"Can I?" I ask him, my mouth suddenly watering.

"What did I tell you about taking what you want?"

I grin.

Slipping off the edge of my bed, I get down on my knees. I'm not entirely sure what I'm supposed to do, but I have no doubt Pyotr will guide me in the right direction. He traces the pad of his thumb over my lips, prompting me to open my mouth just so. Curious, I lick the head of his cock, taking him in inch by careful inch.

I may be the one on my knees, but I've never felt more powerful. The second I wrap my lips around him, Pyotr looks absolutely *ruined*. His deep moan vibrates straight through me, his fingers curling in my hair to tug gently at the roots, his grip firm enough to hold me exactly where he pleases.

"Just like that. Feels so fucking good."

Heat pools between my legs at his praise. Minding my teeth, I hollow my cheeks and suck in earnest, allowing him to set the pace as my head bobs up and down his shaft. He is hot and heavy against my tongue, his taste mildly salty, yet wholly addicting. I can't quite take him all the way to the back of my throat, so I make it up to him by wrapping my fingers around the base of his shaft and stroke him in tandem with my mouth.

"*Fuck*, Alina... You look so fucking sexy with my cock in your mouth."

I press my knees together and moan. Why is the sound of his voice enough to send me spiraling? Every grunt and groan I pull from him only spurs me on. I want to make him feel as good as he made me feel. I know I'm getting close when I feel him thicken on my tongue, but just when I think Pyotr's going to finish—

He pulls away with a growl.

With speed and strength I don't think I'll ever get used to, Pyotr hoists me back onto the bed and hastily deposits me onto the sheets. He's on top of me in an instant, furious mouth finding mine. It's a frenzy, and I never want it to stop.

Pyotr positions himself between my legs, the hard press of his cock nudging my inner thigh. His eyes are locked onto mine, a question in his eyes. I nod, almost reading his thoughts.

"I want this," I assure him aloud. "Please, Pyotr."

"I'll be gentle," he murmurs against my lips.

The stretch momentarily knocks the air from my lungs. His fingers could never do him justice. He kisses me through the initial burn, his strong arms wrapped around me as I moan his name. He starts slowly, his pace measured and careful.

Before long, pleasure blooms within me. My walls clench around him and grip him tight, the friction utterly divine. I drag my nails through his hair, down his back, and in a moment of clarity, I realize I've pressed my lips to his left ear. I don't know if it was a conscious decision on my part or if we just wound up that way, but all I truly care about is having him hear just how much I need him.

"Pyotr, *pozhaluysta*," I whimper against him. "*Please*."

"Pretty little wife," he mumbles in Russian. "Does my pretty wife want to come on my cock?"

I'm not sure if I answer him. I'm too overwhelmed to form proper thoughts, let alone words. My whole body ignites like a firecracker, explosive and dangerous. Climax tears through me, unleashing wave after wave of ecstasy.

He isn't much further behind me. After one last hard thrust, he spills inside me, our bodies rocking together as a satisfied exhaustion finally sets in.

It isn't long before sleep drags me under, and I fall asleep in my husband's arms.

CHAPTER 17

ALINA

The golden morning sunlight filters in through the sheer curtains of my bedroom, helping me rise slowly from a lovely dream that's already slipping through my fingers. When I roll over onto my side, I find Pyotr lying next to me, facing away.

What I see stuns me.

I reach out and trace the scars on his back. Burns from cigarettes? He's covered in them. I don't think I've ever been more horrified and heartbroken.

"Who did this to you?" I ask, so angry I almost can't get the words out. My eyes sting with furious tears.

"You're not the only one who knows about cruel mothers." His voice is thick with sleep, but he slowly stirs all the same.

I shake my head in disbelief. "Your mother did this to you? But why?"

He doesn't answer me right away. At first, I think it's because he's fallen back to sleep, but then I realize he's trying to avoid the answer.

I gently press my kiss to one of the puckered scars on his back just below his left shoulder. "A secret for a secret?"

Pyotr sighs. "It's as I said. We're the ones they underestimate. The ones they care least about."

I furrow my brows. "Tell me."

Pyotr rolls over to face me, barely an inch of space between us. "My eldest brother, Mikhail... He was always the leader, so brave and strong. My twin, Dimitri, was always the charmer, the optimist. It's next to impossible to hate him. Luka... My little brother is a genius, a tech whiz in a league of his own. And then there's me. My mother always told me I was the unremarkable one. No hidden talents to be found."

"I never want to hear you say that again," I grumble. "That's *not* true. You're a CEO, for goodness' sake."

"Only because I took over for Mikhail."

"You're charming."

"I think you're the only person who thinks so."

"And I'm sure you must know a thing or two about computers! You run a cybersecurity company, after all."

Pyotr shrugs. "Not enough to be classified as a genius like Luka."

I huff in disbelief. This is the first time I've seen Pyotr so vulnerable, yet he doesn't look like he cares much what others think of him. Even his own mother. I wonder how long it took him to get to that place.

"I still don't get why your mother would do this," I say, running my hand over a burn in his shoulder.

"Catherina was angry at the world after we were run out of Russia. She needed a punching bag, so I guess using her least favorite son was her best option."

I blink up at him. "Run out of Russia?"

"It's a long story. Before your time."

I laugh softly, despite myself. "Was that an attempt at a joke?"

"Did it work?"

"Only a little."

Pyotr runs his fingers slowly through my hair. "When I was a little boy, our uncle, Konstantin, drove us out of Russia after my father betrayed him. We were on the run. If we'd been caught, it would have cost us our lives."

I'd obviously heard stories about Konstantin Antonov. He was ruthless. Bloodthirsty. Unbending and capable of the truly unspeakable. But I always took those stories with a grain of salt. Most of the time, they're more fiction than fact. This little tidbit Pyotr's offered me, however, rings true.

"I had no idea."

"It's not exactly a story we blast all over the underworld. All that matters is we made it out, eventually came back to Moscow to claim what was ours, and the Antonovs have been in control ever since. That didn't stop Catherina from being a miserable bitch and terrible mother, though."

My heart sinks. "Where is she now? Rotting in hell, I hope."

"No. She and my father live upstate. I refuse to see her. My brothers think I'm being too cold, but in truth, there's no love lost between us."

"Do they now know what she did to you?"

Pyotr shakes his head. "I suffered in silence. I was just a boy. It never occurred to me to ask for help. Even if I had, what could my brothers do?"

A heavy tear streaks down my cheeks. "I don't know," I say around a sniffle. "They could have done *something*."

"And risk Catherina's wrath? I would never have wanted that for them."

"So you took the brunt of her cruelty for them?"

"Yes."

"*Why?*"

"Because I love my brothers. I'd do anything for them. Hell, I'd do it again in a heartbeat." Pyotr wipes my eyes with the pads of his thumbs. "Don't cry, Alina."

"But—" I hiccup.

Now that I've started, I can't stop. It's no wonder Pyotr doesn't wear his heart on his sleeve. After what was undoubtedly years spent suffering at the hands of his mother, why wouldn't he turn himself into stone? I thought he was intimidating and cold by nature, but now I see it was the result of turning inward. Nobody can hurt him if he doesn't let them in.

Suddenly it all makes sense. When I first got here, I thought this penthouse—his castle in the sky—was some sort of display of power as he looked down upon the rest of the world. Now I see it for what it really is. A fortress, a safe haven where no one can hurt him.

Where no one can hurt *us*.

Pyotr wraps me in his arms and presses a kiss to my forehead. "Don't cry for me, Alina. I'm alright."

"I guess we're kindred spirits, huh?"

He hugs me a little tighter. I can hear the smile in his voice. "I guess so."

Somewhere in the room, a phone buzzes. I'm willing to bet it's Pyotr's because I frankly have no one to talk to. With a resigned groan, he reaches behind him and fumbles around on the bedside table before retrieving the device. The screen illuminates, casting his features in cold digital light.

"Dammit," he grumbles, his brows knitting together in a steep scowl.

"Something wrong?"

"I need to head into the office. Work emergency."

I don't know why I feel so disappointed when he gets out of bed. I know it's coming—it's not like we can stay in bed forever—but is it wrong to want a little more time to bask in the afterglow?

"Does it have to do with what happened at the gala last night?" I ask.

His silence as he gets dressed speaks volumes.

"Is there anything I can do to help?" I try again.

"You can help by keeping a low profile," he says, not unkindly. He comes back to my bedside and presses a single, chaste kiss to my lips. "Stay out of trouble and let me handle this. Take the day, relax.

Play some piano. I'll be back by evening. And if you try to run away again—"

"I'm not going to run away." I give him a sheepish look. "You'd just come after me."

He nods, appearing almost amused. "Damn right, I would."

"Will you at least tell me what's going on? I don't like being kept in the dark, Pyotr."

He sighs. "A couple of the photographers at the party might have snapped a few images of our... altercation with Jones. It's nothing I can't handle, though."

My ears perk up. "Is this why you asked Luka for a media blackout?"

"That's right."

"He can do that?"

"Like I said. A genius." He starts toward the door. Pyotr stops and turns, almost like he's double checking to make sure I'm really here and not a figment of his imagination. "Be good," he says with a good-natured chuckle.

For once, I decide not to challenge him.

CHAPTER 18

PYOTR

What a headache.

The pictures Luka managed to intercept were on their way to TMZ before their files were 'mysteriously' corrupted and transferred to me instead. I review the images one by one. They don't paint Alina or me in a particularly flattering light, what with Richard rolling around on the floor in apparent agony. I don't know who took these shots of us, but it's too convenient. Something smells fishy. I wouldn't be at all surprised if Richard planned the whole thing in an attempt to start a smear campaign against me and CyberFort.

To be perfectly honest, I don't want to be at work today. I'd much rather spend my time at home with Alina. Every time I try to concentrate on an email or a memo Merrybell drafted for me, my thoughts drift back to last night.

It was, in a word, *amazing*.

I can still smell traces of lavender on my skin. The softness of her body is permanently etched into the back of my brain. It wasn't my intention to sleep with her last night, but I certainly don't regret it. I'd be lying if I said the thought hadn't occurred to me before. The only reason I tried to keep my distance was because I didn't want to cross any boundaries and make her feel uncomfortable. It seems all that is officially out of the window, and I'm...

I'm strangely excited.

This is the start of something new. The next chapter to our otherwise unconventional story. I would have been perfectly content settling for an agreeable partnership, but this new territory I've found with Alina could prove as agreeable as it is pleasurable. Happy wife, happy life—as the old saying goes, and I'm certainly not complaining. I just have to be careful not to get addicted to this buzz at the base of my skull, the one making my mind wander to less than business-like thoughts.

I'm bombarded with thoughts of bending Alina over my desk, shoving into her, and railing her from behind. I think about settling between those soft thighs of hers and spending the whole afternoon eating her out. Maybe I can make good on my promise to tie her to my bed and fuck her until we both lost our minds.

Before closing out of the images, I send Luka a quick text.

I need the names of the photographers. As well as their contacts at TMZ.

I've already got them blacklisted.

Any idea who hired them?

I was searching through their inboxes earlier today. They've all been contacted by the same person, but it's a burner email.

Can't you find the IP address and the owner of the account?

. . .

That's the thing. I can't. They're quadruple encrypted, and their VPN has them pinging out of Thailand. It'd take me at least a week.

Never mind. I think I know who it is.

The answer is pretty damn obvious. I already had my suspicions that Richard was the one behind the whole fiasco, but the information my brother's provided all but confirms it. Who else has the resources to go to such lengths to hide their identity?

Burner emails, airtight encryptions, *and* a VPN? In trying to keep himself secure, Richard's made himself an obvious target. Richard's hubris will be his undoing.

Still, I can't afford to rush my next steps. There were still eyewitnesses at the party. There's no doubt in my mind word's already spread amongst various whisper networks. I have to bide my time and find a way to take Richard out quickly and quietly. Until then, he's an afterthought. I've got too much on my plate to worry about his underhanded antics.

I've got a company to run, and I won't be distracted, thoughts of Alina aside.

Three sharp knocks sound at my office door. Merrybell pokes her head in, a huge stack of folders in her arms. "This just arrived for you," she explains, walking over to drop everything on my desk.

"What is it?"

"A merger proposition from—"

"Don't say it."

"Richard Eaton Jones."

I rub my temples and sigh deeply. I can already feel a headache coming on. Richard and I don't need to exchange words. This is as obvious a threat as it's going to get. I can either sign over CyberFort like he wanted, or he'll likely follow through with his threat to sue me for assault—even though his claim is absolute bullshit.

"Shred it," I tell Merrybell. "Better yet, send it right back to him and tell him not to waste trees next time."

"Happily, Mr. Antonov. There's also a lady waiting for you in the lobby. Should I send her up?"

I frown. "I wasn't aware I had any appointments today."

"She's a drop in. Said it was rather urgent, but she wouldn't give me her name. I thought it best to ask you first before I sent her away."

This strikes me as suspicious. I personally hate it when people drop in on me unannounced, and the fact that she wouldn't give a name? Absolutely not. I should have Merrybell send her away immediately, but I get a weird feeling in the pit of my stomach. I can't tell if I should take it as a warning sign or something else entirely.

"Send her up," I say calmly.

"Right away, Mr. Antonov."

"Oh, and one more thing. I need you to contact the nearest florist and have them send my wife a dozen roses."

Even though Merrybell's already starting to turn away, I can practically hear the smile in her voice. "What a lucky girl. Will do, Mr. Antonov."

I try my best to sort through a few more emails before my unexpected guest walks into my office, her arrival announced by the sharp click of her stiletto heels on the floor. When I look up, I find a woman in her mid-thirties, dressed in a conservative black dress. I can't look away from her face. Her curly hair is shorter and darker than I remember it, but I don't think I'll ever get over those hazel eyes.

I stand on instinct, shocked onto my feet. "Eileen?"

She smiles sweetly, the corners of her eyes crinkling. "Hello, Pyotr. It's certainly been a while."

CHAPTER 19

ALINA

"Flowers? For me?"

I take the bouquet of freshly cut roses from Ben with the biggest smile on my face. I don't think I've ever been gifted flowers before. Such a small gesture, yet it makes my whole face light up with barely contained glee. The arrangement didn't come with a card, but it's pretty obvious who the sender is.

"I'll have to put these in some fresh water. Thanks for bringing them up, Ben."

"Of course," he says. "But before I go, I wanted to apologize."

I arch brow. "What for?"

He shakes his head with a huff, his eyes cast down in disappointment. "For what happened at the gala. I keep screwing up. I'm really worried Mr. Antonov is going to fire me." Ben shifts his weight uncomfortably from foot to foot as he scratches sheepishly behind his ear. "That was an oversight on my part. I shouldn't have let you leave the ballroom without me. Mr. Antonov isn't without enemies, and I honestly should have known better."

I reach out and pat his arm in a comforting manner. "Just relax, Ben. Pyotr isn't going to fire you."

"But this is my second screw up in just as many days. I really don't know what I'd do without this job. Not to mention I'd be embarrassing my aunt. I couldn't let her down like that, you know? Especially when she stuck her neck out to vouch for me."

I shake my head. "You're worrying about nothing. I promise Pyotr isn't upset in any way. Neither of you could have predicted Richard would accost me."

"See, that's the thing. I'm supposed to protect you from the unpredictable."

"That's too tall an order."

"That's the job," Ben counters gravely.

I offer him a gentle smile. "I was the one who went off to the bathroom by myself, so you're really not to blame. Besides, I would have felt weird if you were standing just outside waiting for me."

"But—"

"Let it go, Ben. I'm fine, Pyotr's not angry, and your job is still safe, okay? Nice deep breaths."

It takes him a moment, but Ben does take a breath and visibly relaxes. "Yeah, okay."

"Can you help me find a vase or something to put these flowers in?"

"Of course, Mrs. Antonov."

"Alina, please. That's way too stuffy for my taste."

Ben chuckles. "Alright, Alina."

We head into the kitchen together. I gingerly set the flowers down on the island counter while Ben sifts through the cupboards in search of a glass tall enough to house my bouquet.

"Do you think this'll do?" he asks, turning to show off a tall, far too narrow glass.

"I don't think it's big enough. Here, why don't you snip the ends off for me and I'll just..." I slip behind him, hopping up onto the counter without a second thought.

"Be careful!" he warns. "I could have just gotten it down for you."

I wave him off. "Remind me to go and buy a step ladder later." I rifle through the very top shelf and manage to find a tall, frosted vase. It's covered in dust, but it's nothing a quick rinse won't fix. I pass it to Ben and hop on down from the counter with a triumphant grin. "See? No need to freak out."

He puts a hand on his heart. "You're not making my job easy, Alina."

I laugh. I have to admit it's easy to get along with him. Growing up in a household full of sisters offered a completely different dynamic, but if I ever had a brother, I imagine Ben would fit the mold perfectly.

"Okay, okay," I tell him. "I'll be more careful starting now."

Out of the corner of my eye, I swear I see something glint through one of the penthouse's many large windows. At first, I think it's a trick of the light. Maybe the sun is refracting off a neighboring building or maybe it's one of those distant helicopters I've seen flying around New York to report on daily traffic. I'm inclined to ignore it, except—

I see it again. And this time, it's more than a glint. Something solid and fast whizzes straight past the window. My brain has trouble identifying the object. Maybe it's a bird? But what's the strange whirring sound following it wherever it goes?

"What is that?" I mutter to myself, approaching the balcony in confusion.

Ben frowns, appearing just as concerned. "Let me check it out."

He takes the lead, leaving through the large sliding door adjacent the living room that opens onto the penthouse's impressive balcony garden. I haven't spent too much time out here—I didn't realize I had such a terrible fear of heights until this exact moment—but it's nonetheless impressive. Were I not so concerned by the strange buzzing noise zipping around over our heads, I might've taken my time to appreciate the view.

"Holy shit," Ben says around a gasp as he points upward.

I squint against the bright blue sky. Above us as clear as day...

"Is that a *drone*?" I exclaim.

I'm no tech expert, but I can tell this must be an incredibly advanced model given its sleek design and speed. Its four legs are spread out in a cross pattern, its rotating blades moving so quickly they're barely even a blur.

"Luka!" I shout over my shoulder. "*Luka!*"

I hear the scramble of footsteps trudging down the steps. My brother-in-law was clearly in the middle of sleeping, his hair messy and shirt wrinkled. Luka rubs his eyes with a wide yawn.

"What the fuck's going on?" he asks, frazzled.

"Is that yours?" I reply quickly. "The drone, is it one of your little gadgets?"

Luka's eyes widen when he sees it outside. "No, it's not mine. I don't use shit like that."

A cold dread sweeps through me. If it doesn't belong to Luka, who *does* it belong to? A million and one questions hit me all at once. Is someone spying on us? What is it doing all the way up here?

"It's taking pictures of us!" I say, alarmed.

Ben moves to pull out a gun from his shoulder holster. "I'll shoot it down."

"No, wait! If you miss, someone could get hurt. And if you hit it, the drone could still crash into someone."

"Then what am I supposed to do?"

I glance at Luka. "Can you hijack the controls from here?"

"Maybe, but it might fly off before I get a chance."

Reacting purely on instinct, I shrug off my cardigan and hold it open between both my hands. "Ben, get ready to shoot it down." With a nod, he draws his weapon and aims. "Do it!" I shout.

Ben sets off a single shot, successfully hitting the drone in one of its arms. It sputters and tilts, struggling to keep itself up now that it only has three working hover blades. The drone begins to lose altitude, but I manage to lean over the balcony's high railing and catch it in my cardigan-turned-net. The blades get caught up in the yarn, effectively burning out the motor.

"Careful!" Luka shouts as he pulls me and the drone back to

safety. We both end up falling on our asses, but I'm thankfully able to keep my catch from being crushed.

My breaths come hard and my heart pounds loudly in my ear. "Wow. I didn't expect that to work."

"Are you alright?" Ben asks me as he helps me stand.

"I think so."

Luka is quick to check on the drone, doing his best to untangle the blades to get a better look. He frowns as he works, yanking off the top of the device to get a good look at its internal hardware. I'm not sure what he's able to discern, but whatever it is, it's not good.

"We need to call Pyotr," he says.

"What's wrong?"

Luka chews on the inside of his cheek as he prods through the different chips and wires. "There's no internal memory on this thing."

"And I'm supposed to be concerned because…?"

"Because if this thing was taking pictures of you, those images aren't stored here. We can't destroy the data." He points to a small receiver. "Whoever was spying on you has likely already uploaded the images to a server."

My stomach flips. An ugly, clawing worry sinks its nails beneath my skin to tear at my muscles and bones. "Why would someone do this?"

"Someone's clearly trying to watch you from afar."

A chill races down my spine. I don't think I've ever felt more violated. Even a hundred stories up in one of the tallest buildings in New York, it's clear to me there's no such thing as privacy.

"Take her inside," Luka tells Ben. "I'll take this up to my office and see what information I can pull from it."

"Come on, Alina," Ben says to me gently.

I wander back into the penthouse, alarmed and confused. What the hell is going on? Who'd go to such lengths to take a couple of pictures of me? Were they trying to catch me in a compromising situation? I don't know how long the drone was buzzing around out there, but the thought has my brain spiraling. If I was being watched this whole time, did the sicko controlling the drone happen to see me getting dressed? It's too creepy to think about.

It makes me want to close all the blinds and curl up in bed. Is there really nothing I can do? Maybe we should call the police. Isn't this a violation of my rights? At the very least, it's trespassing.

I sit down on the living room couch, the tips of my fingers numb. I can't shake this sickly feeling dripping down the nape of my neck. I don't know what to do. All I *do* know is that I want Pyotr here. Surely, he'll know what to do. And if not, at least I feel safer when I'm with him.

Reaching for my phone, I dial his number, trying to hold back my tears.

CHAPTER 20

PYOTR

"You look great," Eileen says kindly. "I'm really glad."

She sits across from me in one of the guest chairs, my desk the only thing separating the two of us. It's like the air's been sucked out of the room and I've forgotten how to breathe. It's been almost twenty years since I saw her last. She's a ghost from my past I never thought I'd see again.

"What are you doing here?" I ask, perhaps gruffer than intended. Eileen's taken me by surprise—and I *hate* surprises. Though she's certainly not an unwelcome one.

Eileen looks around my office with a twinkle in her eye. "My goodness. CEO, huh? You've done well for yourself. I still remember when CyberFort was nothing but a dream you and your brothers were trying to build out of your garage."

I chuckle. "That certainly brings back memories."

"How are they, by the way?"

"They're good. Mikhail and Dimitri both moved back to Russia. They're married now, big families."

Eileen's face lights up. "Oh, that's wonderful! And Luka?"

"Still a pain in my ass, but he's fine. He works here in the development department, actually."

"Is he here today? I'd love to drop in to say hi."

"No, he's at home. Prefers to telecommute."

"And what about you? Pretty busy, by the look of things."

I shrug, finding myself growing more and more at ease in her presence. I'd almost forgotten how easy it was to be around Eileen. It's almost enough to forget all about how she broke my heart. "I'm never bored," I answer vaguely.

"I'm sure."

"You'll have to forgive my bluntness, but what are you doing here, Eileen?"

Her smile falters, but only slightly. She takes a deep, anxious breath. "Well, I... To be honest, I'm looking for a job."

"A job?" I glance down at her hand, staring at the slim wedding band of white gold around her ring finger. "I thought you said William was going to provide for you. That's why you left me."

Eileen swallows, shifting uncomfortably. Things are officially awkward, but I won't allow myself to feel bad about it.

"Pyotr, I, um..." She fiddles with one of her loose curls, twirling her locks around her finger. "I'm surprised you remembered his name."

"He swept the woman I loved off her feet and whisked her away. It's hard to forget someone like that."

"We both decided it was for the best, Pyotr."

"No, *you* decided it was for the best."

Eileen's shoulders deflate. "I didn't come here to fight, Pyotr. The truth is, I miss my independence. William takes good care of me, it's true, but I feel like I'm going crazy without anything to do. I miss working, and I know for a fact there's an opening in your accounting department."

"So you decided to come straight to me to jump the interview line?"

"I came straight to you because I wanted to see a dear friend."

"Friend?" I echo, doing my best not to sound bitter. I thought I let go of my heartbreak ages ago, but Eileen's impromptu drop in has apparently cut open a wound I long since thought healed. "I was more than a *friend*, Eileen."

Eileen hits me with her special look—one that's somehow stern, but soft in understanding. "I would have said yes, Pyotr. You *know* I would have. But..."

"But I didn't have a penny to my name and you wanted a secure future." I lean back in my seat. "I can hardly blame you for it."

"I'm genuinely proud of everything you've accomplished." She smiles gently. It's so hard to stay mad when she smiles like that, but the more we talk, the more I realize the feelings I once had for her are long gone. There's no chemistry between us anymore.

Maybe her wanting to work here isn't such a terrible idea. We've both moved on. We can be adults about this. And from what I remember, Eileen was always excellent at crunching numbers. I'd be an idiot to miss out on hiring a stellar employee just because we had a rocky break up nearly two decades ago.

"I just need this one favor," she says. "For old time's sake? I promise not to cause any trouble. I just want to work, but I've been out of the game so long that very few places are willing to give me a shot once they see the huge time gap on my resume."

"A job in my accounting department, huh?" I ask. "Are you sure? I've been told I'm an asshole of a boss."

She sits up a bit straighter, more hopeful. "Thankfully asshole-wrangling is listed as one of the skills on my resume."

I chuckle lightly. "I'll put you in direct contact with Terry, the accounting department head. I'll put in a good word, but you'll still have to go through our usual interview process. No guarantees you'll get the job, but it's a foot in the door."

"Thank you, Pyotr. That's more than I could have asked for."

I rise from my seat and guide her to the door. "What's William up to these days, anyway? Still working for the city council?"

"He's actually running for mayor next term," she informs me with a proud smile.

My ears perk up. I never know what sorts of contacts could benefit CyberFort in the future. I can't be too obvious about it, though. Nobody likes a brownnoser. "Is that so? Good for him."

"And what about you? Anything new with you? Massively successful company aside, I mean."

"I—"

My cell phone rings in my pocket before I have the chance to finish my sentence. I pull it out, half expecting to see one of my brother's names pop up on the screen. Mikhail and Dimitri only use this number when there's a Bratva-related emergency. Imagine my surprise when I see Alina's name, instead.

"Hello?" I answer.

"*Pyotr?*" Alina squeaks. Her voice sounds shaky.

Alarm lances through me. "What's wrong?"

"There was a drone! Pictures... It took pictures and—" She's talking so fast I can barely understand her. Even though I have my phone pressed to my good ear, the high pitch of her voice makes it difficult to pick up every vowel and consonant.

"Slow down, Alina. Take a deep breath."

"Luka said the pictures are already out there."

"What pictures?"

Merrybell turns in her seat, casting me with a worried expression. "Um, Mr. Antonov?" She points at her computer screen. "You're going to want to see this."

I approach slowly, my eyes barely able to make sense of the images pulled up on Merrybell's browser. It's some sort of gossip website or some such bullshit. I normally don't pay attention to sites like this. They try to drop my name and image every now and then for the sake of clicks, but what I see disturbs me to no end.

The picture is of *Alina*. There's only a few of them, but it's clear they were taken from directly outside the penthouse windows. Suddenly Alina's ramblings about a drone make sense.

She's with Ben in the pictures. Fine. He's her bodyguard. I'd expect him to be with her around the clock.

She has the flowers I sent to her earlier today. Also fine. Knowing I'm the one who sent them to her gives me an entirely different context to what I'm seeing.

She has a hand on Ben's shoulder, smiling up at him with a glimmer in her eyes... Also fine, I try to tell myself. Maybe she's just being friendly, though it certainly *looks* flirtatious. A strange, jealous pang hits me in the chest. No matter how hard I try to ignore it, the flashy headline the site has splashed just above her pictures makes my jaw clench.

Pyotr Antonov's Flirty New Bride: Trouble In Paradise?

I ball my fists up so hard my knuckles crack. This is a problem. A *huge* problem.

One, some pervert has gone to great lengths to take pictures of my wife without her permission. Two, the same pervert has leaked said pictures onto the internet for all to see, likely making a hefty profit for themselves in the process. Three, this is going to reflect badly on not only Alina, but myself. And so soon after our run-in with Richard? I thought I could contain and control the whispers and gossip, but it seems someone is determined to undermine my efforts. Four, they're framing this whole situation to pin Alina as some young and wild cheater. If word of this gets back to Russia...

"Pyotr?" Alina mumbles in my ear. "Pyotr, please come home. I need you."

"I'm on my way."

CHAPTER 21

ALINA

Dinner is tense. To say we're all a little on edge is an understatement.

Luka has made a rare appearance tonight, crawling out of his dungeon of a bedroom to help Pyotr sort through this mess we're in. While I eat, they're both busily typing away and making important phone calls.

"I want to know who your source is," Pyotr snaps into his phone. He's on a call with the gossip website's main editor. Obviously, I'm only privy to his side of the conversation, but I get the sense things aren't going too well. "What do you mean 'anonymously provided'? Dammit, we're talking about an invasion of privacy here. Harassment! Some asshole out there is stalking my fucking *wife*."

The way he says it takes my breath away. I don't know why it gives me butterflies, but it does. Even though my nerves are fried at the moment, hearing Pyotr defend me so avidly makes my insides all gooey. Neither of us could have predicted something like this could happen, but now that he's up to bat, Pyotr sounds like he's ready to tear all of New York apart to bring the perpetrators to justice—all for me.

Luka has effectively turned the kitchen table into a workbench. The drone from earlier lies in bits and pieces, every screw, wire, and chip methodically placed out before him on a clean white towel. He labels as he goes, making sure nothing is out of place.

"What exactly are you looking for?" I ask him.

"Anything useful," he mumbles under his breath. "Serial numbers and the like. I doubt it's registered to the buyer, but you never know."

I shift in my seat, poking at my pasta. I don't really have an appetite, only having managed three or four bites since sitting down. "Do you think it's Richard? He's the only one who has any beef with me, warranted or otherwise."

Luka shrugs. "It definitely seems likely, but we can't just go around pointing fingers without proof. That'll land us in hotter water."

"For fuck's sake," Pyotr snaps. "Then put me on the line with someone in charge, dammit!" With a huff, he covers the mic of his phone with his free hand. "I made the editor cry."

Luka snorts as he checks his watch. "It took you nine minutes? You're losing your touch, big brother."

"Zamolchi." *Shut up.*

I set my fork down, ignoring the pressure that's been pounding behind my eyes all evening. I hate this. My fingers itch to do something. Pyotr and Luka are working hard to fix this. Even Ben's downstairs interviewing the front desk to see if they saw anyone suspicious. Surely, it'd be hard to miss someone with a drone control standing out front, right?

And then there's me. Sitting here, twiddling my thumbs. I can't stand it.

"Is there anything I can do to help?" I ask anxiously. I've already seen the pictures online, the way they've painted me as an unfaithful seductress. The only thing that boils my blood more is my inaction. I have to do *something*. I refuse to stand by while someone out there thinks they can tarnish not only my name, but Pyotr's as well.

"Just relax," Pyotr tells me. His voice takes a much gentler turn when he addresses me, a stark contrast to all the yelling he's been doing for the past hour and a half. "Why don't you treat yourself to a bath? Make sure all the curtains are drawn."

I nod numbly. As unproductive as a bath sounds, it does sound lovely.

It feels so strange moving about the penthouse. Every step I take is unsure. I can't make a move without wondering if someone out there is watching me. It's suffocating, the heavy weight of eyes that may or may not be there crushing down on my shoulders. Your home is supposed to be the one place you feel safe and secure, but that's all been taken from me. For what reasons, I can't be sure—and that's the truly insidious part.

I draw myself a bath and triple check to make sure there aren't any cracks in the curtains. My paranoia is through the roof. It's obvious whoever took my picture was willing to go to great lengths to get them. Who knows what other horrendous tricks they'll resort to?

I scroll through my phone as I slip out of my clothes and step into the water. It sloshes against the high sides of the clawfoot tub, the steam filling my lungs like a much-needed balm. I know it's probably not good to doom scroll, but I can't help it. My pictures are *everywhere*. No matter where I turn, people are not only talking about me, but Pyotr as well.

AnonyMouse123: lol ewww what's they're age gap??? #canceled #cyberfortisoverparty

User12304: that's what happens when u marry a floozy

IngridB420: she's hawt, i'd tap that

KirriganHorner: omg guys mind your own business!

Pipipopo69: LMAO cheating under his own roof, too. Daammmnn

NellyFan4Life: what a stupid slut hope he got a good prenup

JorpenWasHere: i'd marry for the cyberfort money too lololol

I grit my teeth. It'd be easy to get upset with random strangers on the internet, but I try not to let it consume me. They don't know what's going on, nor do they even know me. It's just words... even if they *do* hurt.

I keep scrolling, following a never-ending trail of links until I stumble upon a recent article about CyberFort itself. It's not flattering. If anything, the journalist has used this entire situation as an opportunity to tear into Pyotr's company. From its dip in profits last quarter to its product's stagnation in an ever-competitive market to complaints from independent contractors concerning low payment rates... It's a slanderous piece of work that never cites its sources, but it has almost ten thousand views and counting.

That's not what scares me the most, though. Pyotr and I still have our immigration interview to worry about. If we don't get ahead of this thing... If we give our interviewer any reason to doubt the legitimacy of our marriage, I might wind up with a one-way ticket back home. The thought of slinking back to Mother makes me shudder. I can't let that happen. I just can't.

There's a knock at my bathroom door.

"Are you alright in there?" Pyotr asks from the other side.

I fight the temptation to cover myself up. It's an unconscious reaction, but one I'm learning to overwrite all the same. I tuck my knees up to my chest. "Come in."

Pyotr enters my ensuite bathroom and closes the door, his eyes drifting down to my naked form. There's something appreciative in the way he looks at me, like he's admiring a work of art. He approaches slowly and kneels next to the tub, resting his arms on the edge. When he sees what I've been reading on my phone, his brows crinkle.

"Give it to me," he says, not unkindly.

I do as he asks. He doesn't even glance at the article, instead shutting my phone off and setting it aside on the nearest counter.

"Ignore stuff like that," he says.

"How?"

"You'll learn to grow a thick skin."

"You make it sound so easy."

"The website's taking the pictures down, but it might be too late. They won't reveal their source, either. Something about protecting their identities to promote free and fair journalism."

"What a load of horseshit," I grumble.

"That's what I said. Still, the moment I mentioned a libel suit, they took the article down quickly."

I press my lips into a thin line. "I'm so sorry—"

"Alina." He gives me a hard glare. "What did I say about always apologizing? I'm not your mother, lyubimaya. I'm far more reasonable. I know this wasn't your fault."

I nibble my bottom lip. "Call me that again."

He tilts his head to the side, reaching out to tuck a few strands of my hair behind my ear. "Lyubimaya."

"Wife... Darling... You're really spoiling me with the terms of endearment."

The corner of Pyotr's lip tugs up into a slight grin. "Should I stop?"

"No. I like it. I just feel bad."

"Why?"

"Because I don't have any for you. I can't think of anything that might suit you."

"Try me."

I curl up against the edge of the tub, closing as much space between us as possible. I take in the hard edge of his jaw, the distinguished bridge of his nose, and the ever-serious dip of his frown. I bring my hand up to caress his cheek, pleasantly surprised when he leans into my touch.

"Soltsne?" *Sun.*

Pyotr grimaces. "There's nothing sunny about me."

"Sakharok?" *Sugar.*

"Again, nothing sweet about me."

I laugh softly. "I beg to differ. I think you're *very* sweet when you want to be."

"I don't know. It's a mouthful, isn't it?"

"Then what would you prefer, husband?"

His smile widens. "That. Exactly that."

I reflect his smile, my worries suddenly melting away. God, he's gorgeous. I'm strangely protective of those smiles, like they're little secrets only I get to see.

"Alright," I murmur. "Thank you for the flowers, husband. And thank you for getting those pictures taken down."

Pyotr's face suddenly turns hard and serious. "I'm going to get to the bottom of this, Alina. I swear it. I'll protect you no matter what. Whoever's behind this... I'll see to it they pay."

A heat blooms within me, arousal pooling between my legs. As much as I love his smiles, I love it when he's all serious, too.

"I know you will, husband."

"Until then... I think you should remain at home. I'll double your security and—"

"No."

He regards me carefully. "No?"

"I don't want to hide, Pyotr." I cling to the edge of the tub, resting my cheek on his forearm. I like the warmth of his skin and the way the steam easily carries the scent of his cologne. "They're trying to paint me as unfaithful, like I'm some gold-digging opportunist. I'm not going to let whoever's behind this shame me into hiding."

"Alina..."

"I kept asking myself if there was anything I could do to help. This has damaged your reputation and could reflect on our company, too."

"You let me worry about that."

"That's the thing. You shouldn't *have* to worry about everything. You don't have to shoulder everything by yourself, Pyotr. Whether we like it or not, we're in this together now. They're trying to paint us as a marriage in trouble, so let's double down and prove them wrong. Take me to events, let's do twice the amount of good. There's no way we can stop the rumors now, but maybe we can drown them out. It's like you said—damage control, but this time, I have a say in how it happens."

Pyotr runs his finger along my cheek, drawing a circle against my skin. "Are you sure? You'd be in the spotlight. Open to even more scrutiny."

"I'm Russian, Pyotr. It's going to take a hell of a lot to scare me." I dare to tilt my chin up and press a kiss to the tip of his nose. "I won't let your reputation take a hit because of me. Let me do this for you, husband. For us. I'll play the part of the perfect wife and erase all doubt of a troubled marriage."

"Play the part, huh?" he echoes after me.

"What?"

"Nothing." After a moment, Pyotr eventually nods. He knows as well as I do what's at stake here. "Alright. There's a handful of public events coming up. I'll have Merrybell ensure you're listed as my plus one to each of them."

"Good," I say with a smile. "Now, care to join me for a bath, husband?"

His grin grows again, the corners of his eyes crinkling. "I thought you'd never ask."

I lick my lips as I watch him undress, savoring his slow but sure movements. His tie goes first, then his shirt, then his belt and everything below. I drink in the sight of him, mesmerized by the chiseled plane of his wide chest and the defined muscles of his arms. I'm a little *too* appreciative of the bite mark I might have left on his shoulder.

Pyotr gets into the tub with me, settling in on the other end. It's more than big enough to fit the two of us, but right now, I don't want any space between us. I carefully make my way over, warm water sliding over my sensitive skin as I climb onto Pyotr's lap, straddling him. I've got my hands on his chest, his own easily gripping me by the waist.

As he pulls me in for a deep kiss, I feel him hardening beneath me. Heat stirs in my core. The hard nudge of his cock against my folds sends a thrill shooting up my spine. I'm wet just thinking about him sliding into me, claiming me for his own like he did yesterday.

"Pyotr," I murmur against his ear, circling my arms around his neck so our bodies are flush against one another. "Will you help me feel good, husband?"

He hums, the vibrations of his voice so deep and delicious I feel it in my very bones. "Only because my pretty wife asked so politely. Are you sure you're not too sore from yesterday?"

In lieu of response, I reach down between us and gently grasp his cock, stroking once, twice. I bring him toward my entrance, using the buoyancy of the water to help me hover just so. My pussy clenches around nothing, my walls already fluttering in electric anticipation.

"I want you to fill me up," I say breathlessly, bringing one of his hands to my throat. Once again, he wraps his fingers around but doesn't squeeze. "Please, husband? I need to feel you inside me."

"Anything you want Alina," he grumbles before moving in for a punishing kiss. "Anything for you."

I lower myself onto his cock, moaning as the stretch knocks all sense and reason from my head. I like being on top. I get to set the pace—and it's punishing. Rolling my hips, I seek more and more of that sweet friction, adoring how well we fit together. Pyotr's arms wrap around me like a vice, his mouth trailing down toward the stiff peaks of my nipples. He sucks hard kisses against my tender skin, marking me with a ferocity that only makes me hotter.

"Fuck, you feel so good," he grunts against me. "Does my pretty wife enjoy riding my cock?"

"*Yes!*" I gasp, rising just to slam myself down again.

We're making a terrible mess of the bathroom, water splashing and spilling over the edges of the tub, but we're too enthralled with one another to care. My pussy clenches around him, my clit already throbbing and sensitive thanks to the heat of the water.

"Pyotr," I whine. "Pyotr, I'm gonna—"

"This pussy's all mine, do you understand? The only cock you're ever going to come on is mine."

I moan, his filthy words ringing in my ears. "I'm so *close—*"

Pyotr's hand slips under the water's surface, sliding between our bodies with ease. He brushes his thumb over my clit, setting off wave after wave of pleasure within me. My body trembles as I slam into my climax, my head dizzy from the combination of ecstasy and steam. He claims my mouth as I moan his name, stealing the sounds all for himself. Pyotr continues to piston in and out of me, hips snapping upward to chase his own pleasure.

"Gonna pump you so full," he murmurs against my skin. I almost don't hear what he says, too weary with satisfied exhaustion.

A squeak escapes me. *Fuck*, that's hot. Something about his unfiltered, dirty thoughts makes me ache for more.

"Do it," I rasp against his left ear. "Give me a baby, husband."

Pyotr growls, his eyes suddenly dark with lust. He slams into me even harder. "*Fuck*, Alina. How many do you want?"

"How many will you give me?"

"So many. Six, at the very least."

I can't help but laugh, breathless and dazed and feeling lighter than air. "Come on then, husband. What are you waiting for?"

He spills into me with a heated grunt, kissing me so hard I swear he might try to devour me whole. I hold onto him tight, some strange part of me too afraid to let go. This all feels like such a wonderful dream. Maybe if I hold on a little tighter, I can ignore this sinking feeling brewing in the pit of my stomach.

I've long since learned that happiness—or anything close to it—can never last. It's just a matter of waiting for the shoe to drop. It'd be best if I didn't fool myself. If I don't allow myself to believe I've stumbled into a happily ever after, I can save myself from a world full of anguish.

CHAPTER 22

PYOTR

Invitations are coming in left, right, and center, more than I usually receive. Despite my best efforts to have those pictures taken down, whispers have already spread far and wide. Events I'm usually not invited to as well as one I've gone to every year are filling my inbox and mailbox. Bad press means press coverage, and right now, we're a hot topic.

Inconvenient, but unsurprising. All RSVPs are returned with cannot attend.

Alina and I are going to have to work double time to fix our tarnished reputations—even though none of this was our fault to begin with.

"Your invitation to Gabriel Schuster's golfing weekend has arrived," Merrybell says gravely. "I already sent a no. Not that you would have gone, anyway."

"Thank you," I comment dryly.

I rub my temples and pray my headache goes away. Moments like these, I really miss my twin, Dimitri. Before he decided to follow Mikhail to Moscow to be his right-hand man, Dimitri was the head of the PR department. His charm and wit made him perfect for the role.

No crisis was too big or too small to manage. He was the go-to guy whenever CyberFort had even the tiniest smear article in the latest copy of *Business Today*. My twin had a way of getting on everyone's good side—even Richard Eaton Jones, believe it or not—but now I'm a one-man-show doing his best to put out every little fire that pops up unannounced.

Beside me, Alina scrolls through a company-issued iPad I've loaned her. Merrybell has wheeled in her own chair, at my request, giving her the left side of my desk to work on.

"What about this library fundraiser?" she asks, pointing at an old invite that almost got lost in my personal secretary's never-ending inbox. "It's scheduled for tomorrow but marked as undecided."

"We have to think of it from a branding perspective," I say firmly. "What's a cybersecurity company doing at a public library fundraiser?"

She arches a skeptical brow at me. "Oh, sure, but hitting golf balls all weekend with some guy is somehow a higher priority?"

"I never go, but Schuster is a client. It's clear why I would go."

Alina shrugs. "Still. I can think of a couple of ways you can spin it for the press."

"Go on."

"Donate two or three new computers," she suggests with a smile. "Maybe also bring attention to the outreach program you're so fond of. Public library spaces are a great free place for young minds to come and learn, championing the way forward for future tech entrepreneurs and the like."

I find myself smiling as she speaks. Damn, that's a good way to put it. "What else?" I ask, curious about what she might say next.

Alina nibbles on her bottom lip as she continues to scroll through the list of remaining events on the list. I am intrigued by the slight crinkle of her nose, a sign—I've come to learn—she's deep in thought.

"This wedding invite," she says. "John Ackerman?"

The name rings a bell. "Ackerman? I went to business school

with the guy." I glance at Merrybell. "Why didn't I know about this invitation sooner?"

"My apologies, Mr. Antonov. Some things get lost in my spam folder."

"When's the wedding?" I ask Alina.

"This Saturday."

"Probably too late to let them know we're coming. I've seen enough episodes of Bridezilla to know you should never crash a wedding."

Alina smirks. "Bridezilla?"

"It's a trashy American television show."

"Yes, I know what it is. I just didn't expect you to watch that sort of thing."

I shrug unapologetically. "Luka keeps weird hours. Sometimes I stay up late with him and we'll watch whatever's on TV."

"You don't have to show up for the ceremony or stay for the reception," Alina explains. "Just show up to shake a few hands, give this old classmate a gift, take a few pictures."

"This isn't business-related."

"It doesn't have to be," she reasons. "Not everything has to revolve around CyberFort, Pyotr. The public needs to see you as a man, not just a CEO."

I'm pretty sure I'm all-out smiling now. She's a natural at this. "Have you ever thought about studying public relations?"

Alina laughs quietly. "PR of what? The staff in my mother's oppressive house? It's never occurred to me, no."

"Think about it. I think you'd be great at it."

Merrybell clears her throat, cutting through the warm, cozy atmosphere. To be perfectly honest, I'd almost forgotten she was standing there.

"I think we should have one more event slotted for the remainder of the month," she says. "To round out the calendar now that we've refused so many because of..." She doesn't finish her sentence and reddens slightly, smiling sheepishly and shrugging.

I nod at Alina, a silent signal asking for another one of her suggestions. They've been brilliant so far. I have faith Alina will easily be able to come up with a third event for the sake of restoring our public image.

"Actually, I don't see any other viable options," she mumbles as she scrolls. "But I think I have an idea. Why don't we host our own charity event?"

I furrow my brows. "You want to put together an event in under a month?"

"Just hear me out. It can be small, but open to the public. A night of music."

I lean in, hanging on her every word. I don't know what she's thinking or where she's planning to go with this train of thought, but I'm interested in hearing the rest.

"I'm sure I can find a handful of musicians and a nice, open location to put on an evening concert. There can be drinks and some food... And tickets can be by donation. Everyone's welcome, *including* the press. And, to answer your question about how this all relates to CyberFort—the money raised can go toward your outreach program for inner city kids. I can plan the whole event if you want."

"That's an awful lot to take on," Merrybell comments. I feel the same, but I want to see Alina's reaction before I comment.

"I used to help my mother plan huge parties," she defends, her tone determined and confident. "She gave me tasks, and believe me, I knew to get it right." My gut clenches, but I don't' comment. "The last party I was in charge of food. The attendees said it was the best they'd had at one of Mother's parties."

"So you're comfortable with doing the whole thing?" I ask her, smiling so she understands I'm not doubting her.

"I know I can," she affirms, smiling brightly at me. She nods, adamant. "Besides, I've been bored out of my mind. I think... I mean, if it's alright, this project is exactly what I need."

This conversation feels strangely similar to the one I had with Eileen just yesterday. Where I was only lukewarm about the idea of giving Eileen a job, I find myself overly eager to give Alina the chance to shine. I'm excited to see what she'll do, and the fact that she's taking all of this in stride... A strange pride swirls in my chest. I like that she's getting involved with CyberFort, even if it's in an unofficial capacity.

Speaking of Eileen, though, I should probably tell Alina about her, but... then again, maybe not. It's not like Eileen has the job yet. Bringing up my ex-almost-fiancé might cause Alina more stress than she's already under. Besides, despite our whole policy on honesty, I'm not ready to talk about arguably the most painful time of my adult life.

"The project's all yours," I tell her, adoring the way her smile lights up the entire room. I turn to a beaming Merrybell and say, "Let's respond to those invites and make the necessary travel arrangements. I also want you helping Alina with anything she needs for her charity concert."

"Of course, Mr. Antonov."

I log out of my computer and rise, grabbing my suit jacket from off the back of my chair. "That concludes business today," I tell Alina.

"Really?"

"You sound almost disappointed."

"I was kind of hoping to see you in action. *'Buy! Sell! We have a deal!'*"

"Is that what you think I do?"

Alina shrugs. "Is it not?"

"No, lyubimaya... Come. We can study over lunch."

"Study?"

I chuckle. "You'll see."

CHAPTER 23

ALINA

He has a list of roughly a hundred and twenty different questions the immigration officer could potentially ask us during our interview. I feel like such a schoolgirl, sitting across from him with my hands folded neatly on my lap as we go through each and every one.

"It's about time we got around to this," he says, shifting through a few printed documents. "We need to get our story straight, and since you're so dedicated to playing the role, I figured now is as good a time as any."

Playing the role.

I'm not sure why, but the way he says this makes my stomach clench. I'm not sure what to make of his tone. Does he think I'm not taking this seriously? Why does he sound so bummed about it?

The restaurant he's chosen is a fancy one. It's surprisingly busy considering it's only noon. We're seated in the back section at a little table for two. The ambiance is lovely—breezy jazz music playing over the speakers, slender pendant lamps hanging overhead, and even a small water feature babbling near the front. The menu is impressive, too, pared down to only a few select options to make ordering easier. I've chosen the steak and fries, while Pyotr ordered the day's special.

"Okay," I say as I sip my glass of ice water. "What's the first question?"

"How did we meet?" he reads aloud.

"Under duress."

He gives me a pointed look. "Take this seriously, Alina."

I crack a smile. "I'm *joking*, Pyotr. I know that won't fly. What kind of story should we come up with?"

"Something simple. Easy to remember."

"Well, how about through a family get-together? That's feasible, right? Our families are in, uh... business together. We could have easily met over dinner."

"That's a slippery slope."

"What do you mean?"

"Tell me, what exactly does your family do?"

I hesitate, sensing his concern. We can't very well bring up the fact that we belong to two different Bratva families. It would open the door to all manner of red flags. "Okay, fine. What do you suggest?"

"We met at the grocery store. Reached for the same carton of milk, and the rest was history."

I can't help but roll my eyes. "That's so *boring*. Not to mention unbelievable."

Pyotr frowns. "What's so unbelievable about it?"

"My darling husband, do you remember who you are? Why would the CEO of a massive company like CyberFort do his own grocery shopping?"

"Okay, you have a point." He leans back in his chair and crosses his arms. "Damn."

"Let's work on a different question."

Pyotr glances down at his papers. "Who proposed?"

"You did."

"How?"

"Seriously?"

"We need as many details as possible if we're going to convince our interviewer."

I sigh. "Fine, um... We were at dinner. After dessert, you got down on one knee and popped the question."

"What was the name of the restaurant?"

I pinch the bridge of my nose and squeeze my eyes shut. "I don't remember?"

"That's not going to fly."

"Pyotr, you have to be reasonable. If we're too rehearsed, the interviewer will definitely know something's up." I nibble on my bottom lip. "Okay, fine. Let's change the story because I'm hopeless when it comes to remembering the names of places. How about we say you proposed to me at the park? We went for a walk together. It was the middle of winter, so it was snowing like crazy. After I complained about my hands being cold, you took them in your own and instead of warming them up, you slipped a ring on my finger."

Pyotr regards me quietly, something soft washing over his expression. "That... could work."

Our waiter drops off our food, so we continue to iron out the details of our supposed romance around mouthfuls of our meal.

"How many siblings do I have?" Pyotr asks me.

"Three. Mikhail, Dimitri, and Luka. How many siblings do *I* have?"

"Three, as well."

I arch a brow. "What are their names?"

Pyotr grimaces, obviously struggling to recall. "I remember Yasemin..."

"Oksana and Nikita," I prompt.

"Right, right." He continues down the list. "What size is our bed?"

"That's a question?"

"Evidently."

"I mean... We have separate beds, so I'm not sure how to answer."

"We'll say we sleep in mine."

"Okay, fine. A California King, then."

Pyotr's eyes flick up to me and I realize my mistake. "You've been in my room, have you?"

My heart stutters. Wow, I didn't expect to be caught out like this. "Uh... yeah? That's how I found the money I needed when I tried to, um..." I clear my throat, shifting uncomfortably in my seat. "When I tried to run away."

"So, you've been through my things." If he's upset by this realization, Pyotr does a good job of not letting it show. "That's how you knew about my hearing."

"I didn't mean to overstep."

"I already told you it's fine."

I swallow, my throat suddenly dry. "Can I ask you why you don't wear your hearing aid?"

Pyotr visibly bristles at my question. Neither of us were expecting to have this conversation today, but here we are. "A secret for a secret?"

I nod, leaning in. My heart is pounding; I'm so eager to learn the truth the rest of the world seems to fade away. I focus on Pyotr.

"This is going to sound stupid," Pyotr confesses.

"I'm not going to judge you."

He takes a deep breath. "I don't like to wear it because it makes me feel weak. I know it's ridiculous, but I'm strangely self-conscious about my hearing loss."

I reach across the table and take his hand. "There's no reason for you to be self-conscious about it, Pyotr."

"I know. It's a me thing. I've got an image to uphold and I'm worried..."

"Worried about what?"

"People might have some less than pleasant things to say. Comments about my age, snide remarks about my capabilities. I do a good job of drowning those voices out, but that doesn't mean they don't get to me. Nothing gets past me, Alina. I hear everything. Just because I don't respond to the hate doesn't mean it doesn't affect me.

I don't like wearing my hearing aid because I'd rather not give the public any more ammunition. I've been able to get by without it just fine. I keep telling myself I'll wear it when I have to."

I squeeze his fingers, smiling at him. I'm not entirely sure what to say, or if it's even my place to say it. Pyotr's honest vulnerability takes me by surprise. At the end of the day, I can't tell him what he should and shouldn't do. It's all up to him and I respect his decision.

I can't even tell him his worries are unfounded. I've seen first-hand how easy it is to drag his name through the mud. I've experienced it myself, had the anonymous voices on the internet call me all manner of terrible things simply because they could. I totally understand what Pyotr means about giving them unnecessary ammunition, but I don't like that he feels too ashamed to wear it, either.

"Thank you for telling me," I say gently.

His smile is small, but sweet. "Your turn. Tell me a secret about yourself."

"I'm running out of things to tell you. Even with the family I come from, my life hasn't been all that remarkable."

"Take your time. You can always tell me later."

I can't stop smiling. I like this exchange we have going on. Where once we were complete strangers, now I know Pyotr better than anyone else in my life. I didn't expect him to grow on me so quickly.

Maybe that's why his comment earlier made me so uncomfortable. The tiny voice in the back of my head doesn't want to play a role. It wants all of this to be real. The only problem is I don't know how to voice that to him. This marriage was a business agreement. Our partnership was meant to keep the peace. I didn't factor in that I might start *feeling* something more toward him.

My stomach does an uncomfortable flip.

"Are you okay?" Pyotr asks me from across the table. "You haven't touched your food in a while."

I nod numbly. "Yeah, I think all this studying has sapped the energy out of me."

"Just take it easy. We still have plenty of time to think things through. We'll go straight home after this so you can take a nap if you want."

His consideration makes my cheeks warm. The more I get to know him, the more I realize just how kind Pyotr is. It's a side of him only I have the privilege of seeing, and damn if it doesn't make me feel a little special.

Those precious smiles.

The even rarer sound of his laugh.

The way he looks at me with a warmth he'd never afford anyone else...

Holy shit, I think I'm falling in love with my husband.

CHAPTER 24

PYOTR

Ben's already texted me to inform me that the car has been pulled up in front.

I'm not entirely sure how to dress for this thing. It's nowhere near as formal as a fundraising gala, but I'm not going to show up in a pair of jeans and a Ralph Lauren polo shirt, either. I settle for a navy-blue dress shirt and black dress pants, my sleeves rolled up to just below my elbows. The public might like to kick me while I'm down, but at least I look good while they do it. All I need now is my wristwatch and I'll head downstairs to meet Alina.

My watch sits on my bedside table. Curious, I pull open the drawer to peer inside. My gun is tucked away, and my unused hearing aid sits in the middle. And in the back… I pick up the book with Eileen's picture in it, flipping through the pages until I get to it. I wonder if Alina saw this during her little snooping session. If she did, surely, she would have asked me about it by now.

I pick up the photo and study it. It's admittedly been years since I've looked at it. I'd all but forgotten it was even there. I used to look at it with a combination of bitterness and sorrow, and now… Now, I don't feel much of anything. That chapter of my life is over and done with. What I had with Eileen is in the past.

What I have with Alina...

I fold the picture and toss it into the trash bin as I exit my room, descending the steps to get to the bottom floor of the penthouse. The curtains are all drawn, which makes the room somewhat gloomy.

I hear her before I see her. The soft notes of the Steinway fill the air. I don't recognize the tune, but it's gorgeous all the same. Holding onto the railing, I strain to get a better listen. Some phrases I catch and others I don't. Deeper tones are easier to hear than the higher ones, so I'm only able to hear the base harmonies with any semblance of clarity.

Remaining perfectly still on the bottom step, I listen—enraptured.

Alina sits at the piano bench, her feet working the pedals as her hands fly over the keys. She moves with elegance and grace, fingers floating over the piano with ease and confidence unlike anything I've ever seen. Alina sways gently from side to side in time with the rhythm, just loud enough for me to hear her humming along with the melody of her right hand.

Without meaning to, I take a step closer. And then another and another, moving as quietly as possible so I don't disturb her. It's been forever and a day since anyone's played this piano. Luka doesn't know how to play and I no longer make the time. It seems rather fitting that Alina should be the one to bring it back to life.

When the song comes to an end, I surprise myself by saying, "Keep going."

Alina jolts in her seat, turning with a surprised laugh. "How long were you standing there?"

I can't answer her. I was so lost in the beauty of her playing that time stood still. "You're an excellent pianist."

Alina rubs her hands together, flexing her fingers. Her smile falters slightly, and I'm immediately overcome with a feeling of protectiveness. "It's been a while since I've practiced," she confesses.

Without thinking, I reach for her hands and bring them to my lips. I press a soft kiss to the backs of her fingers, doing my best to help her forget her mother's cruelty.

"You'll have to play for me more often," I say.

"I'd like that."

Alina smiles wide, forming cute little dimples on her cheeks. She's so strikingly beautiful my chest tightens. I don't think she's ever looked at me that way before. I want to stare at her forever, but I know we don't have the time. Still, I can't help myself. I want to claim this smile for myself, so I dip down and kiss her.

It's a slow and tender thing, but it's also perfect.

Alina tastes so sweet and every inch of her smells like lavender. When she combs her fingers through my hair, the gentle scrape of her nails over my scalp sends a delightful shiver down my spine and goosebumps trailing down my arms. I don't think I'll ever get over the sound of her soft sigh against my lips. What I wouldn't give to hear it over and over again.

Something hungry awakens in me. I grip her waist and help her stand, pulling her flush against me. I have half a mind to rip her dress right off her, throw her over my shoulder, and carry her to my bedroom. At this point, I've forgotten all about the fundraiser. Maybe I'll just send a check in the mail instead of delivering it in person. It's the thought that counts—and right now, my thoughts are of a particularly horny nature.

"Let me see what underwear you're wearing," I mumble against her lips.

Alina laughs. "Don't we have to get going? We can't afford to miss the fundraiser."

"We can settle for being fashionably late."

"*Husband*," she warns.

"Yes, wife?"

"I can't show you my underwear, Pyotr."

"Why not?" I growl, sounding almost childish in my pouting.

She grips the lapels of my shirt and pulls me down so she can whisper into my good ear. "Because I'm not wearing any."

The sound that escapes me can't be classified as human. My arousal immediately goes straight to my dick. "I'm going to bend you over this damn piano if you don't behave."

Alina gives me a coy smile and circles me, dragging her hand flirtatiously over my chest as she starts towards the elevator. "Be a good boy, Pyotr. We've got some computers to donate."

I groan. "Why did my wife have to be an absolute bombshell?"

"What did you say?" she calls back to me as the elevator doors slide open.

"Nothing," I grumble, dutifully following behind her.

The Public Libraries of New York Association hosts this fundraiser every year, but this is the first time I've actually attended. My work schedule is normally so crammed full I have no choice but to be selective about which events I can and can't go to. The event organizers seem as surprised as I am to see me here.

"Thank you so much for coming, Mr. Antonov," Charlie, the lead coordinator, says as he vigorously shakes my hand. He reminds me a bit of a hamster—chubby cheeks, fluffy light blonde hair atop his head, and a round body. He's dressed in a dull brown corduroy suit complete with elbow patches, a pair of thin spectacles sitting on the wide bridge of his nose.

"How's the new equipment working out for you?" I ask.

He keeps shaking my hand, his gratitude practically radiating from his every pore. "They're splendid, Mr. Antonov! Absolutely wonderful. Your generosity is truly appreciated. We have enough to donate at least five new units to every single branch in the city!"

"I'm very glad to hear it."

The fundraiser is alive and kicking. As far as events go, this is by far the most casual I've ever been to, but I can't exactly blame them.

Being a non-profit means there's usually very little wiggle room where their budget is concerned. The main lobby of the central branch has been done up to the best of their ability. They've sprung for a handful of colorful balloons, streamers, and a spread of several long tables hosting an assortment of different finger foods and drinks.

The turnout is great. There are plenty of parents and their children, a few members of the library board, and—most importantly—a gaggle of news reporters and journalists. Given everything that's been going on, I'm not here to make a spectacle. Just showing up and making a huge donation will no doubt do the heavy lifting for me. If I try too hard, I run the risk of playing too obvious a hand.

"Would you like to meet the rest of the board?" Charlie asks me with a wide smile. "I'm sure everyone would love to thank you personally."

"Sure, let me just check on my—"

I turn to discover that Alina is no longer by my side. I've lost her in the crowd somewhere. It's not quite panic I feel, but it's definitely a heightened sense of concern. My first and immediate thought is she's somehow managed to slip away again. It's been a hot minute since Alina made any attempt at escaping me and this marriage. For a moment, I feel stupid for letting my guard down. The trust we had been building... Was it all for show?

My thoughts immediately quiet down, however, when I see her across the library lobby with a group of children. Alina crouches down so she's eye-level with them, a handful of the kids proudly showing off the books they'd picked from the nearby shelves. I'm too far away to hear what she's saying, but I can tell she's laughing by the shake of her shoulders and the way the corners of her eyes crinkle as she smiles.

Guilt suddenly hits me in the gut. I thought she had abandoned me. I've never been happier to be proven wrong.

Thankfully, the next hour passes quickly.

Lots of hands to shake, plenty of elbows to rub. Nobody here brings up the recent scandals Alina and I have faced, though I do get a couple of pointed looks here and there. It's a good thing the guests all have enough sense not to bring it up. It wouldn't be a good idea to insult the biggest donor of the night, after all.

Alina eventually finds her way back to me. Her cheeks are rosy and her smile is contagious. She easily settles in at my side, looping one arm comfortably around my back while I rest an arm over her shoulder.

"Where have you been?" I ask lightly.

"Were you lonely without me?" she teases. "I was caught up with the kids' story time. They're so cute! I couldn't pry myself away."

I press a kiss to her temple. I'm not exactly a fan of public displays of affection, but today, I can't seem to help it. "You looked good with them," I whisper.

Her ears redden as she looks up at me in amused surprise. "Did I really?"

I hum. "Yes. Very matronly."

She nibbles her bottom lip, leaning against me a little further. "Actually... I wanted to ask you about something."

"What is it?"

"Well, it's about what you said the other day. About wanting six—"

"Mr. Antonov!" someone calls my name. I turn just in time to see Charlie shuffling on over, a photographer following close on his tail. "Mr. Antonov, would it be alright if we took a picture together? It's for the *PLNYA*'s monthly newsletter. I want all of our subscribers to know about you and your wife's generous donation."

I smile stiffly. "Sure, I'd be happy to."

I've never been a particularly photogenic person. Staring down the lens of a camera has always unnerved me, but when I feel Alina's hand on my back, my unease quickly melts. After a couple of quick flashes, the deed is done and my breathing finally returns to normal.

"Thank you again," Charlie says, still riding the high of his initial excitement. "We seriously can't thank the two of you enough for coming."

"It was our pleasure. Thank you so much for having us," Alina says with a diplomatic air about her. She really would be a great fit for the PR department if she were ever so inclined.

The night is quickly wrapping up, and while I had a good time, I'm eager to get Alina home. As I guide her toward the door, I lean down to murmur in her ear.

"I was serious," I answer her interrupted question from earlier. "A minimum of six kids."

Alina shivers against my touch, a mischievous grin stretching across her lips. I allow my hand to slip down, following the contour of her tight dress. A shot of adrenaline courses through me. I detect no panty lines whatsoever.

"Naughty girl."

"Let's go, husband. Maybe we can get a head start in the car."

I don't think I've ever been so happy to leave a party before.

CHAPTER 25

ALINA

I'm all over him, straddling his lap in the backseat of the car. Pyotr raised the solid black privacy partition so Ben can't see us, but judging by how loud I'm being, I seriously doubt he's none the wiser.

Pyotr is ravenous. Not just his kisses, but his hands. He's so nice and rough, but never in a way that frightens me. If anything, he handles me like a man possessed. Every single one of his touches tells me he *wants* me more than he could ever put into words, so he shows me through action instead.

He drags up the fabric of my dress and hikes it up to my hips, exposing my thighs and lack of underwear. Beneath me, I feel the bulge of his cock harden as he moans deeply.

"Fuck, you weren't kidding."

A manic little giggle escapes me. "Do you like what you see?"

"Fuck *yes*."

When I tilt my head to the side, he immediately dives in to mouth hungrily at my neck. I adore his needy hands, the way he grabs at me so desperately like I might slip away at any moment. So I kiss him harder, a silent reassurance that I'm not going anywhere. A languid moan rises from my chest when he reaches down between us to swipe his finger over my clit, grinning to himself as he runs his thick fingers over my slick folds.

"Gorgeous," he murmurs to himself. "So fucking beautiful."

"Pyotr!"

He hushes me gently. "We don't want to disturb our driver, now do we?"

"Oh, I'm pretty sure he already knows." I reach down and make quick work of his belt and the fly of his pants, my core throbbing for him. Even though I know the passenger windows are tinted, I still cast a quick look out at the city around us. "Are you sure nobody will see?"

He grasps my chin and drags me down for another kiss. "No one will ever harm you like that again, Alina. I swear it."

Moved by his words, I kiss the corner of his mouth sweetly, almost as if to say thanks. This man really is something else. Maybe the old saying about everything happening for a reason is right. Out of all the people Mother could have married me off to, I'm so glad it was Pyotr. Patient Pytor, sweet-only-for-me Pyotr. Of all the countless ways my life could have unfolded, I'm grateful he was the one who got roped into it.

"Ride my cock, lyubimaya. Let me see you on top."

I can no longer deny my desire. I swiftly pull him free of his boxer briefs and carefully lower myself onto his length, doing my best to bite back my moan of pleasure as he buries himself deep inside me. I'm so wet and ready for him it takes no effort at all. Every inch of my body is unbelievably sensitive, my heart hammering like a war drum with the knowledge that right outside, the rest of New York is none the wiser to our passionate affair.

I grind my hips and set the pace, taking every inch of him that I possibly can. When the head of his cock sweeps over my sweet spot, I swear I see stars bloom across my vision. It takes all my concentration and energy not to scream his name.

"Look at you," he murmurs with a satisfied grin. "You take me so well, Alina. Do you like it when I fuck you like this?"

"Yes..."

"I can tell you're getting close. Your pussy's getting so nice and tight around me. Does my wife want me to make her come?"

I laugh, a breathless, crazed sort of sound. "*Yes!*"

It's quick, but it's brilliant. A warm haze clouds my mind as pleasure washes over me. Pyotr kisses me through it, so loving and gentle it makes my heart sing.

"Beautiful," he whispers, his eyes locked into mine. "You're so beautiful, Alina."

I giggle, tracing the line of his jaw with my fingers. "You're pretty handsome yourself."

He chuckles. "I'll take your word for it."

"You *are*."

Pyotr doesn't let go of me right away, instead choosing to hold me pressed against him for the remainder of the ride. We kiss like it's no one's business. I have to admit there's something deeply satisfying about feeling him soften within me, our bodies still intertwined.

I trail my thumb over his bottom lip, smiling to myself. "So, why six? That seems like such a specific number."

He grins. "It's my lucky number."

"Oh?"

"I was born on the sixth of June at six in the evening, exactly six minutes after my brother, Dimitri."

I circle his neck with my arms, leaning forward to rest my face against the warm crook of his neck. "Sounds nice, actually. Hopefully we can teach our kids to get along."

It doesn't occur to me until the words have left my mouth what I just said. *We. Our.* When did I start getting comfortable with this arrangement? When did I start thinking about our futures as being entwined? Why does the thought of having children with Pyotr, spending our lives raising them together, bring me so much unfiltered joy?

I wink at him. "Let me guess, you're the kind of guy who already has his kids' names picked out?"

The smile he gives me is downright goofy. I drink it up like a parched woman stranded in the middle of the desert. It should honestly be illegal for anyone to look this handsome.

"I've only picked out the names for the boys," he says. "I figured I'd let my wife choose for the girls, though obviously it's all open for discussion."

"Have you always wanted a big family?"

Pyotr nods. "Yes. I've always liked the thought of a lively home. Kids to play with and clean up after. Never a dull moment."

I think about the penthouse. All that space, cold and lonely. It sort of makes sense that Pyotr wants to fill it with the exact opposite of what he now has.

"Not to mention, having children will help solidify the peace between our families."

My smile falters slightly. I slip off his lap and take my seat beside him, quickly readjusting my dress. "Oh," I mumble.

A cold pit sits heavily in my stomach, mild embarrassment washing over me. Now my mind is spiraling and won't stop. Of course Pyotr would think that. I've been so foolish. I'd almost forgotten he's a businessman through and through.

I feel so silly. Did I honestly expect him to feel anything for me? He didn't want to marry me in the first place and our union has brought him nothing but a PR nightmare so far. Having children is just the logical choice to secure the Salkov and Antonov's alliance, that's all.

"Is something wrong?" he asks me, no doubt sensing the sudden change in my mood.

Will he laugh if I tell him I'm falling in love with him and I'm allowing myself to believe this marriage is real?

"Just a little tired," I lie. "Who knew playing with kids all afternoon could be so tiring?"

Pyotr's lips press into a thin line. He nods, offering me his hand to hold. I do end up slipping my fingers through his, but we spend the remainder of the drive in silence.

What am I supposed to do when, at the end of the day, Pyotr is all I have?

CHAPTER 26

PYOTR

Things have shifted between us, and not necessarily for the better. I thought we were getting along swimmingly, but then everything changed after our conversation in the car.

Did I say something to upset her? Was my bringing up wanting children too much, too soon? Alina seemed so enthusiastic about it, too, which is why the sudden distance between us is so jarring to me.

John Ackerman's wedding is today, but Alina and I won't be stopping by until later this evening when the reception is in full swing. This means I still have a whole day at the office. Plenty of contracts to sift through, expense reports to approve... and it's damn near impossible to get done when Alina is seated on the other side of my office instead of directly next to me like usual.

She's busy working on her iPad next to Merrybell, planning the charity concert she seemed so excited about. While I'm glad she has a project to keep her busy, I'm not exactly fond of how far away she is. Yes, she's in the same room, but given that she hasn't really looked at me all day, we may as well be miles apart. Her obvious discontent has agitated me more than usual.

"So we've secured a venue," Alina says. "And I've quoted a

couple of places with regards to their catering rates... Now all I have to do is figure out who's going to play."

Merrybell hums. "Most local musicians book out weeks in advance. We might be hard pressed to find someone on such short notice."

"Why not play the piano yourself?" I suggest.

Alina glances up at me, our eyes finding one another—but only for a moment before she looks away again. She smiles down at her iPad, bashful and clearly avoidant. "That's definitely Plan B. I'm out of practice."

"Not from what I heard."

"We'll see." Her voice is soft, but her words are clipped. I don't know how to get a read on her.

Merrybell, astute as ever, catches my concerned glance. "I'll get started on the guest list," she tells Alina helpfully. "I know it's an open invitation, but we'll still want to try and invite as many big fish as possible. You never know who might bite."

Alina smiles. "Thank you. That'd be great."

"Mr. Antonov, it's just about time for lunch. I'm sure Alina would love to see the cafeteria downstairs." Merrybell pats my wife on the back of the hand. "You should see it down there, my dear. It's practically a food court! Mr. Antonov likes to make sure his employees have a healthy selection to choose from. Boosts morale and such."

Merrybell couldn't be any more obvious as she shuffles out of the office, leaving Alina and I alone for the first time since arriving at CyberFort. Nevertheless, I take the opportunity and rise from my desk.

"Lunch?" I ask her.

Alina nods. "Sure."

The entirety of the second floor is a dedicated eatery and hangout space, put together by some of New York's top interior designers to encourage the open exchange of ideas amongst employees and build a sense of community.

The area is well-lit, not only because of the massive windows overlooking New York, but because of the large lighting panels installed in the ceiling. There are plenty of live plants to add a refreshing hint of green, as well as plenty of circular tables with ample seating so my employees can sit wherever they choose. There's a wide assortment of foods, from a fresh salad bar, a sushi station, and even handmade pizza.

"What do you feel like having?" I ask Alina.

"Whatever you're having."

A flicker of annoyance licks at the nape of my neck. "Alina. Tell me what's going on."

"I don't know what you're talking about."

"You've hardly spoken to me all day."

She forces a smile. "I'm just feeling a bit under the weather."

I reach out in concern, pressing my fingers gingerly to her forehead. She's not warm, though she does look uncharacteristically weary. "Should we call it an early day, then? If you're not feeling well, maybe you shouldn't come with me to the wedding."

I relish the way Alina leans into my touch, even if it's only for a moment. Before I can suggest anything further, someone behind us clears their throat. I turn—and freeze.

"Eileen?"

She stands behind us with her classic sweet smile, the one that used to drive me up the wall crazy. Eileen is dressed in a simple dark grey pencil skirt and frilly white blouse. A blue lanyard hangs from her neck, revealing her CyberFort employee ID badge. Apparently, she got the job in the accounting department, after all. I'm admittedly surprised, though it's not like I'm in charge of overseeing every single hire.

"Fancy seeing you down here," Eileen says chipperly. "My

cubicle mates made it sound like the boss never ate amongst his people. I told them that was silly."

Beside me, Alina's eyes grow wide. "Um, hi? I'm Alina."

"I'm Eileen," she says, sticking her hand toward Alina to shake. "It's so lovely to make your acquaintance."

She smiles stiffly in return, shaking her hand with the rigidity of a marble statue. There's recognition in her eyes. "It's lovely to meet you, too," Alina manages through gritted teeth.

"I wasn't aware you hired a new assistant," Eileen says to me.

"I didn't. This is my wife."

In that moment, I swear to God the entire cafeteria suddenly goes still and all eyes are on us.

Eileen's friendly smile falters, but only for a moment before she says, "*Oh!* How lovely. I didn't see a ring on your finger when I popped in the other day, so I had no idea you'd gotten married." She turns her gaze to Alina. "Goodness you're so... young. I mean, beautiful. Please ignore me, I'm rambling."

I absentmindedly clench my fists. That's right. Our wedding ceremony had been so quick and impromptu that I'd given a ring to Alina, but not the other way around. It never occurred to me before, but now I'm hyper aware of how naked my finger feels.

"How long have you worked for CyberFort?" Alina asks.

"Only about a week," Eileen replies. "Pyotr was kind enough to put in a good word for me with the accounting apartment. I was hired on the spot, thanks to him."

"How generous of him. It sounds like you've known each other for a long time."

Eileen giggles nervously. "Well, we used to be a bit of an item."

Alina doesn't look surprised, but nonetheless says, "Oh? I had no idea."

I set my jaw. This is getting uncomfortable. I knew Eileen walking back into my life after twenty years was going to come back to bite me in the ass somehow. "It was a very long time ago," I insist.

Eileen nods in agreement. "Ancient history."

"I'd love to know more," Alina says innocently. "Pyotr has never mentioned you."

I'm not sure whether this is supposed to be a jab at me or at Eileen or both. Whatever her intentions, Alina's words are sharp and clipped—prodding a reaction out of us.

"Oh, uh..." Eileen anxiously smooths her skirt. "I'm not sure if this is an appropriate conversation for the workplace."

"Sorry, I don't mean to make you uncomfortable. I figured since it's 'ancient history,' we may as well get to know each other."

Eileen laughs uncomfortably. "We dated for about five years."

Alina's eyebrows shoot up. "Wow! Five whole years?"

"Yes, but it really was nothing."

I frown at this. "Nothing?" I echo, struggling to hold back a note of bitterness.

Alina gives me a pointed glare. "You know what? I'm sure the two of you have a lot to catch up on. All that ancient history and such." She turns on her heel to go.

"Where are you going?"

"Home."

"You shouldn't go by yourself. It's not safe—"

"I'll have Ben escort me."

"Alina, wait."

She doesn't. In the blink of an eye, she storms off, disappearing around the corner before my brain has a chance to catch up.

"Oh, goodness," Eileen mumbles, looking downright guilty. "I'm so sorry, Pytor. I shouldn't have said anything. I never meant to upset her."

"It's not your fault," I say quickly, already turning to follow Alina out. "Congrats on the job."

CHAPTER 27

ALINA

I storm into the penthouse, so angry I can barely think. Pyotr follows me in, hot on my heels.

"When were you going to tell me your ex-girlfriend of *five years* works for you?" I snap, turning so quickly he almost trips over my abrupt stop.

"How did you know who she was?" he counters with his own question.

"Um, she introduced herself," I say stubbornly.

"No, the moment you laid eyes on her, you knew exactly who she was, don't lie."

"Answer my question first."

"No, you answer *mine*."

I chew on the inside of my cheek. "I saw her picture. When I... stumbled through your things."

"You mean snooped through my things. And stole my money."

"I've already apologized for doing it. I was desperate to get out before. Can you blame me for trying to be resourceful? You, on the other hand—"

"What?" he growls.

"I thought we agreed to be honest with each other. Secrets for secrets. Knowing your old flame works for you... That's something your wife is entitled to know, isn't it?"

"Actually, no. It's like she said, we're ancient history."

I cross my arms over my chest. "If that's the case, why'd you get all pissy when she called your history nothing? Don't think I didn't notice, Pyotr. You looked like a kicked puppy when she said that."

"How would you feel if I said *we* were nothing?" he snaps.

I bite my tongue so hard I swear I taste blood. I can definitely see his point, but that doesn't make his reaction hurt any less. "Why didn't you tell me about her?"

"Because she's none of your concern."

"Of course she is. She's the ex-girlfriend!"

"Ex-fiancé, actually."

I gasp. "That's even worse!"

My heart twists in my chest. I don't know why I'm so emotional right now. One moment I'm doing alright, the next I'm angry as hell, and now all I want to do is bawl my eyes out. It's definitely not doing me any favors where arguing with Pyotr is concerned.

"You're being ridiculous," he says.

Right now, I'm so brittle and vulnerable, his words might as well be a dagger through my ribcage.

"You're not denying it, Pyotr."

"You're making this a bigger deal than it has to be."

"If I had an ex-boyfriend, ex-fiancé, ex-*whatever*—and you found out he was always within reach, how would you feel?"

"But you don't."

"That's not the point."

"This isn't some sort of competition, Alina. *You're* my wife, end of story."

"Yeah, but not the wife you wanted. Just the one you were forced to marry."

He looks at me like I've slapped him across the face. We stand there, the silence so thick I can feel the air stick to my skin.

"Alina..."

"Did you not want me to know?"

"You want the truth?"

"Always!"

"Eileen is so far in my past she's an afterthought. She came in a little while ago to ask for a job. That's all. She's married, too, by the way—though that doesn't have anything to do with this. I haven't seen the woman in twenty years. Whatever I once felt for her is long gone, Alina."

"Then why did you still have her picture?"

"I forgot it was even there," he confesses. "I've already thrown it away. She means nothing to me. You, on the other hand—"

"What about me?"

We stare at each other. His jaw ticks. It's taking way too long to get an answer out of him. With every passing second, my stomach clenches tighter and tighter until I can't breathe anymore.

I suck in a sharp breath. "Do you feel something for me, Pyotr?"

"I..." He casts his dark eyes to the floor.

"This is what I was afraid of."

"What are you talking about?"

I swallow hard, trying to dislodge the sticky lump at the back of my throat. It doesn't work. The words sit on the tip of my tongue, but I'm afraid of what's going to come after. I just need to say it, blurt it out, like ripping off a Band Aid.

"I'm falling in love with you, Pytor," I say on a breathy exhale. "I'm falling in love with you, and I'm afraid you don't feel the same way. That you'll *never* feel the same way. That all I'll ever be is a business arrangement."

Tears well up in my eyes, the sting unbearable as my vision becomes blurry. I feel so stupid for telling him. Childish, even. Seriously, what's gotten into me? To make matters even worse, Pyotr doesn't say anything. He either doesn't have an answer for me, or he doesn't *want* to answer—and I don't know which is worse.

Swiping my palms over my eyes to dry my tears, I shake my head and try to get a grip on my emotions.

"Forget I said anything. I'm going to bed."

He frowns. "But the wedding..."

"You should still go. My stomach's not feeling well. Besides, I'd rather not be around the happy couple. It'd just remind me of the fact that we're not."

Pain flashes across Pyotr's features. "Alina..."

I scurry down the hall and go straight to my room, shutting the door harder than I mean to. The sound of it slamming rings loudly in my ear. I don't think I've ever been more humiliated.

Crawling into bed seems like the only viable option I have left. Burying myself beneath my pillows and covers, I curl up and wrap my arms around my stomach. My belly really does feel awful. Queasy. Like I've been aboard a ship in the middle of a terrible storm, and I'm two seconds away from getting sick.

I'm pretty sure I hear Pyotr out in the hall, but his footfalls stop just shy of my door. He lingers out there, as if he's unsure whether he wants to come in or leave me alone. A tiny voice in the back of my brain wants him to knock. To enter and check on me. To tell me I'm not alone and he feels the exact same way.

But then he leaves, his silhouette shrinking away from the gap beneath my door.

I'm not sure which has taken a bigger hit: my heart, or my ego.

CHAPTER 28

PYOTR

I'm falling in love with you, and I'm afraid you don't feel the same way.

Alina's words echo around inside my skull. No matter what I do, I can't stop thinking about her tear-stricken face and the utter dismay in her eyes when I failed to respond. I didn't mean to leave her hanging, but her outright confession surprised me.

What was I supposed to say? That I'm falling in love with her, too? It's true I'm beginning to feel something for her, but I'm not quite where she is. We're reading the same book, but she's a few chapters ahead. Lying to her would only be a disservice. It'd be unfair to string her along when I'm not ready. I'm more than aware of the irony, that marriage is the biggest commitment of all, but I can't tell her what she wants to hear. Not yet anyways.

I head out to John Ackerman's wedding alone. The drive to the venue takes an eternity, especially when all I can do is stew in my own silence in the backseat. Regret claws through me. Maybe I should have canceled. I shouldn't have left Alina alone at home. I was trying to be courteous and give her some space, but I'm wondering if the decision was a mistake. Nothing pains me more than the thought of her cooped up in her bedroom, crying after she so bravely put her heart out on the line.

I grit my teeth. *Fuck, I'm such an asshole.* What kind of dickhead leaves his crying wife at home? How could I do that to her? I have half a mind to tell my driver to turn back, but my destination comes into view.

It's an outdoor reception at a spacious park. The warm weather makes it the perfect location for an evening party, surrounded by luscious trees and flowers in bloom. The occasional twinkle of passing fireflies adds to the ambiance, the silver glow of the moon bright and full in the sky.

The reception is well underway, a live band playing lively tune after tune. A portable dance floor has been laid out over the grass, giving guests ample space to dance and mingle. Four tall posts hold up a soft white canopy of cotton, a string of warm white light bulbs hanging from the underside to add to the romantic atmosphere.

I get out of the car and tell my driver to keep the engine running. This is going to be a quick visit. An in-and-out sort of deal. I'll shake a few hands, leave a good, friendly impression, and then…

And then I'll go back home and do what I should have done for the start—comfort my wife.

John Ackerman is dressed sharply in a black tuxedo, complete with spiffy bowtie. It's been a hot minute since I saw him last, but I easily recognize his lopsided smile and chestnut brown hair. When he sees me, his smile widens as he throws out his arms to greet me with a hug.

"As I live and breathe!" he says with a friendly laugh. "Pyotr Antonov, in the flesh. I didn't think you'd make it, old friend."

"Apologies for the late reply to your invitation."

"Oh, don't worry about it. I know you're a busy man."

"Congratulations," I tell him, slipping him an envelope with a check inside for five thousand dollars. "A little something for you and the missus."

John claps me on the shoulder. "Thanks, man. I really appreciate it." He turns and waves a woman over, his bride, dressed in a stunning white dress that hugs her hips. She's practically glowing. "Pyotr, this is Michelle."

I shake her hand. "Congratulations, Michelle."

"Thank you so much," she replies around a giggle. Her cheeks are pink and rosy, her hair done up in perfect waves. "You attended business school with John, right? He talks about you a lot."

"Does he?"

"Oh, yes. He's always going on and on about how his old college buddy went on to become the CEO of CyberFort. If I didn't know any better, I'd say he idolizes you."

John chuckles. "Come on, babe, you're embarrassing me."

"That's very flattering, but John was the one to admire. Always hardworking and top of his class. He was the one I aspired to beat."

Michelle grins at her new husband, resting her head lovingly on his shoulder. Seeing them together like this stirs something strange within me. Their joy is almost infectious, the love clear in their eyes. I take in my surroundings with an bittersweet air. I never got this. Alina and I didn't get a wedding. No party, no pretty wedding dress, no cake. Seeing how happy John and Michelle are together makes my heart twist in jealousy.

Alina deserved so much more. *Deserves* so much more.

"So, how did you two meet?" I ask, making friendly conversation.

"We met through a friend of a friend," Michelle says sweetly. "I think it was at some charity gala a few years ago."

"I saw her from across the room," John says, no longer looking at me, but at his darling wife. I don't think I've ever seen a man more in love. "She had a whole line of guys waiting to ask her to dance, but I sauntered up and skipped the queue."

Michelle laughs. "He kept asking me for dance after dance so nobody else could ask me. And before we knew it, the night was over. I haven't been able to get rid of him ever since."

John kisses her cheek. "You're the only dancing partner I need, babe."

"Oh, stop it. Why are you always such a sap?" Michelle winks at me. "You're more than welcome to stick around, if you'd like. There's an open bar and everything thanks to my Uncle Richard."

At first, her comment goes straight over my head. Plenty of people are named Richard. It's a very common name. But then I see him from the other side of the reception.

Richard *Eaton Jones*.

Fuck, what are the chances?

He eyes me like a fat tiger ready to pounce on his third meal of the evening. His nostrils flare and his face turns red, but Richard thankfully doesn't make a scene. Now's as good a time as any to dip out.

"I'd better get going," I say quickly. "I just wanted to stop by in person and give you my best wishes."

"Are you sure you have to go?" John asks me. "I'd love to catch up."

"Maybe another time. If you're ever in the area, pop by the office and I'll take you out to lunch."

"I'll hold you to it. Thanks again for coming, Pyotr."

As quickly and discreetly as possible, I leave the area and start toward the car. Thank God I told the driver to keep the engine running. Of all the people who could have possibly been at this event, Richard is the last person I wanted to see. I have too much going on right now, and I'd rather not deal with his pain in the ass.

"Peter!" he shouts after me.

I'm tempted to ignore him, but he catches up to me. "I'm just leaving."

"Talk about a small world," he says. "We run in some pretty tight circles, hm?"

"Good night, Richard."

"Where's that pretty woman of yours?"

The hairs on the back of my neck stand on end. I don't like his tone. "None of your business."

"You have her hidden away, I see. I don't blame you. Not after those pictures leaked." Richard throws his head back and laughs. It's an ugly, choked off sound that pisses me off. "You should've known to keep a tight leash, Peter. A pretty young thing like her was bound to get bored of you sooner or later—"

Something inside me snaps. I don't know what it is. The way he addresses Alina so casually. His disrespect. The implication that she's something to control. I won't stand for it.

My body moves on its own. I snatch him up by the jacket lapels and get right up in his face. "Don't talk about my wife that way. I know you had something to do with it."

Richard shoves at my chest, pushing me back, and I release his jacket. "What the fuck are you talking about?"

"You think I wouldn't put it together? You tried to make a scene at the gala, but it didn't work, so you had to think of another way to try and embarrass us. Embarrass *her*. You sent that fucking drone to take pictures of her!"

"I don't know what you're talking about."

"Bullshit!" I hiss.

"You shouldn't go around accusing people of things they didn't do."

"That's rich, coming from you." I growl through clenched teeth. "You made Alina feel unsafe in her own home, asshole. I'm going to make sure you pay."

"Seriously, Peter, what the fuck? Why would I send drones to pap your girl? That makes no fucking sense."

"I know all about the dirty tricks you get up to in order to tank companies. That's when you swoop in and take them over. Don't stand there and look at me like I'm an idiot."

"You *are* an idiot," Richard seethes. "If there really was a drone, it wasn't mine."

"Then who—"

I cut myself off. I see absolutely zero recognition in Richard's eyes. He really doesn't know what I'm talking about. I've never known him to be a particularly good liar, but I can tell he's being truthful. Unfortunately, this is cause for even more alarm.

If Richard isn't the one behind trying to sabotage me through Alina, then who *is*? Is there another player trying to bring me down a peg? Who could it be? And more importantly, who stands to gain something if our marriage falls apart?

I've wasted too much time on Richard already. Without another word, I head straight for the car.

"Take me home," I tell the driver. "And make it snappy."

CHAPTER 29

ALINA

I t's official. I think I'm sick.

My stomach won't stop lurching. My limbs feel heavy and there's a heavy fog over my brain, making it difficult to think. I'm not coughing or sneezing, and I'm pretty sure I don't have a fever, but I'm nonetheless dizzy and nauseated.

I roll over in bed. It's a little after ten in the evening. I think I dozed off shortly after Pyotr left, but now I'm awake and can't get back to sleep. My eyes are scratchy and my face is all puffy from crying. I contemplate getting out of bed to grab a glass of water, but the thought of keeping anything down makes my stomach queasy.

I'm *definitely* sick.

With a shaky hand, I reach for my phone. Instinctually, I punch in Pyotr's number. He's really the first and only person who comes to mind. I hesitate, though, my thumb hovering over the screen. Maybe I shouldn't call him. I'm pretty sure he's still out, and given our awkward conversation earlier, I don't have the strength to face him just yet.

I call Ben, instead.

"Alina?" he answers. I can hear the familiar piano music they play downstairs in the building's lobby. "Is everything alright?"

"I think..." My stomach gurgles, and not in hunger. "I think I need to see a doctor."

"Oh, goodness. I'll come up right away and escort you to the car. Would you like me to call Mr. Antonov—"

"No," I rasp quickly. "No, it's alright. I'm sure it's nothing serious. I'll get dressed and meet you in the elevator."

"Sounds good," he says before hanging up.

It takes a surprising amount of effort on my part to drag myself out of bed and throw on some clothes. Just a pair of jogging pants and a loose grey shirt. I'm sweaty. Shaky on my feet. I'm sure whatever I have isn't too serious, but it can't hurt to be careful. Hopefully the doctor will be able to prescribe something to help settle my stomach.

By the time I get downstairs and meet Ben in the lobby, I'm a mess. He frowns when he sees me.

"I really should call Mr. Antonov."

"Don't trouble him," I insist. "It's just a little stomach bug. Besides, he's busy."

Ben presses his lips into a thin line, clearly unconvinced. He guides me out to the car regardless, shutting the door behind me as I slip into the backseat.

"Here," Ben says, twisting in the driver's seat to pass me a water bottle. "Have something to drink. I'll get us to the hospital."

"Thank you," I manage weakly as I twist open the cap and take a few sips. It doesn't really help settle my stomach, but I continue to drink anyway.

But it tastes *strange*.

As Ben pulls into late-night traffic, I find my senses slowly dulling. I'm exhausted, but I chalk it up to being ill. I take another sip of water, then another, frowning slightly as I detect a bitter note coating my tongue. It's mild and impossible to pin down. A bit like plastic, only it the inside of my mouth feels a little numb.

I'm not sure how long we've been driving. The bright lights of the city are mesmerizing, lighting up the inside of the car like stars. Everything gets blurry. Noises seem to drown out. Apart from the low rumble of the car's engine, I can't hear the rest of New York. Weird, considering the noises of the urban landscape are usually loud and clear, even this late at night.

My body feels light, like I'm floating. I think Ben takes a hard right around a corner, but I barely feel it. I'm not sure what's happening to me. It's like I'm two inches to the right of my body, watching listlessly as the rest of the world marches forward. The edges of my vision grow blurry, and my eyelids suddenly become too heavy to keep open.

"What..." I mumble. I barely recognize the sound of my own voice. "Ben, I think... I think something's wrong."

He glances at me in the reflection of the rearview mirror, hushing me softly. "It's all going to be okay, Alina. It's all going to be okay. Just close your eyes... We'll be there soon."

I like how Ben talks. Always so gentle and kind. I'm sure a quick nap won't hurt.

When my eyes start drifting shut, I spot something peculiar on the floor just in front of the passenger seat. A white plastic bag, a small box of sleep aids crammed inside. The box has been torn open, several tablets already missing from the package.

The world around me swirls and evaporates into nothing.

My vision goes black, my conscious mind dragged under.

I wake in a state of confusion.

The car has stopped. It's dark outside. The familiar bright lights of the city are nowhere to be found. My body feels too heavy to move, muscles cramped up from the awkward position I'd fallen asleep in across the backseat. A terrible throbbing sensation radiates from behind my eyes. I struggle to sit up, but when I do, I have to cling to the car door to peer out the window.

We're at an airport. A private landing strip with a jet on the tarmac, its engines roaring and ready to go.

I shake my head. I don't understand what's going on.

And then it hits me all at once.

The water. The sleeping pills...

"Ben?" I croak.

When I turn to look, I realize he isn't in the front seat. The keys are still in the ignition. I'm in the car alone, but I don't think he could have gone very far. Shivering, I summon the strength to open the door. My legs are still numb and useless, so I end up falling out of the car onto the hard pavement.

A strong hand grips me by the upper arm and hoists me to my feet. It's a cold, boney hand—one I would recognize anywhere by the sharp bite of nails into my flesh.

"Did you have a nice nap?" Mother asks me.

I blink at her. To say I'm confused is an understatement. "W-what are you... What's going on?"

She starts to drag me toward the jet. I'm still loopy from the drugs in my system; I have no energy to fight. "We're going home."

I struggle against her vice grip. "Home? N-no. Where's—"

Ben comes into view, a hard edge to his face, a facet of him I've never seen before. But he won't look at me.

"Where's my payment?" he asks my mother.

She snaps her fingers. One of her guards approaches with a heavy briefcase. He pops the top open, exposing rows upon rows of crisp hundred-dollar bills. My brain is still too hazy, but it looks like perhaps a hundred thousand dollars or so—peanuts where the Salkov accounts are concerned.

My heart sinks. "You... You betrayed me?"

"I'm sorry, Alina," he says, and he sounds like he means it. But he also doesn't do anything to help me.

"Were you working for her this whole time?" Anger simmers in my veins, threatening to boil over. I'm utterly blindsided.

"She approached me a few weeks ago," Ben says, not making eye contact. "All I had to do was deliver you to her and she'd take care of the rest."

"You sold me out? How could you?"

"I don't want to be a bodyguard forever, Alina," he tells me, a slight whine in his voice. "With this money, I can finally do something of value with my life."

"But I thought you said Merrybell stuck her neck out for you!"

Mother yanks on my arm, preventing him from answering. "Come, Alina. We've already wasted too much time."

I don't stop struggling against her. I'm not going without a fight. "But *why*? If Pyotr finds out you've taken me, this'll mean war between our families."

"I said come!" She lifts a hand to strike me across the face, but just enough feeling returns to my body that I'm able to slap her away.

"Don't fucking touch me!" I shriek.

"Insolent girl! Don't you understand? You're finally free of him."

I stare at her blankly. I'm missing something here, a part of the puzzle I don't yet have. "You... *want* me to leave him? But what about the treaty?"

"On the plane. Now."

"No!" I scream. "Tell me what the hell is going on!"

Mother huffs, her eyes cold and unfeeling. "You think I would ever willingly make peace with the Antonovs? You're a damn fool, Alina. Your marriage was supposed to be temporary to buy me enough time to gather my troops."

My throat closes. Oh, *God*.

"You used me to buy yourself time?" I say around a sob.

Mother's face twists into a sneer. "I tried to get you out sooner. I thought those pictures I had taken of you and leaked to the press would have driven Pyotr to end the marriage, but it seems your husband's far more understanding than I first thought."

"*You* sent the drone?" I don't know whether to scream or cry. "You're the fucking devil. I'm not going anywhere with you."

"You don't have a choice, Alina. Now get your ass on the plane, or I'll have my guards drag you on."

"No!"

I break away, Mother's nails shredding my skin. I make a mad dash for the car. Two of her guards try to grab me, but I manage to slip their grasp. I yank open the car door and throw myself behind the wheel, my hands shaking so badly I can barely shift gears.

Outside, I hear Mother screech my name, but I don't listen. I have to get back to Pyotr. I have to warn him that this was Mother's plan all along. I should have known peace between our families couldn't be so easily brokered. Mother is too proud, too stubborn. She's a disease, one that wants to claim anything and everything in her path. If I can get back to Pyotr, maybe he can warn his brothers before it's too late.

I slam my foot against the gas pedal and veer off—

But not before the guards start shooting.

One bullet. Two. Three.

The fourth pierces the back window, sending little shards of glass flying everywhere. I try to keep low to avoid being hit, but my view is limited because of it. I try to drive away, but the harsh *bang* of a tire bursting sends the car into a tailspin. Are they trying to fucking *kill* me?

Bang! Another one of my tires goes out. I'm riding on rims now, the angry screech of metal against the pavement screaming in my ears. I lose control of the car, the front-end crunching into a metal lamp post. I haven't given up hope yet. If Mother wants to take me back to Russia, it's going to have to be in a body bag because there's no way in hell I'd ever let her take me alive.

I've had enough of her manipulation. Her cruelty. She sees me as nothing more than an object to use and discard at will.

Pyotr and I may not have a perfect marriage, but at least he cared for me. Before he came into my life, arranged or otherwise, I never knew kindness. When I'm with Pyotr, I know I'm safe. Mother means to cut me off from the one shining ray of hope in my life. I'd rather die than let her lock me away again.

I throw the car into reverse. The engine starts smoking. Thick black plumes rise from the crushed hood of the car. No matter how many times I rev the engine, the vehicle won't respond. I think the transmission is totaled.

One of Mother's guards yanks open the door and drags me out of my seat by the hair. I scream, clawing at his hands.

"Fuck you!" I seethe. "Fucking let go of me! You can't do this!" When Mother is—unsurprisingly—unmoved by my pleas, I turn to Ben. "Please, help me! It's not too late. I won't tell Pyotr, just get me out of here!"

Ben shakes his head, looking sick. "I'm sorry, Alina. Your mother pays way better than Pyotr does."

I scream at the top of my lungs. I kick and I scratch—all to no avail. I'm thrown over one of the guard's shoulders like I'm nothing more than a sack of flour and dragged onto the plane. As I'm carried on, I watch as Mother approaches Ben.

"A pleasure doing business with you," she says sweetly. *Too* sweetly.

"Yes, thank you—"

Mother draws a gun from her pocket and aims it directly at Ben's chest. Before he has the chance to react, Mother pulls the trigger. The loud flash and bang fills me with dread. Ben slumps to the ground, red blooming across his chest as his shirt stains with blood. Without remorse, Mother tucks her gun away and bends down to pick up the briefcase full of money. I scream. At least, I think I do. He might have betrayed me, but he didn't deserve to be murdered so cold-heartedly.

I'm indignantly shoved into a seat and forcefully restrained. They use layer upon layer of duct tape to bind me to the chair. For good measure, Mother walks straight up and slaps a thick piece over my lips, but I scream anyway.

I'm going to make this the worst fucking flight she's ever had.

CHAPTER 30

PYOTR

"Alina?"

None of the lights are on when I enter the living room. It's perfectly still. Not unusual, given the late hour, but something doesn't sit right with me. It's *too* still.

"Alina!"

I check her bedroom. She's not there. Same with the kitchen and the living room. Alina is nowhere to be found.

Fuck.

It's not clear what hits me first—panic or confusion. I race upstairs and pound on Luka's door. He emerges from his room like a bat in a cave, bleary-eyed and pissed.

"Dude, what the fuck?"

"Where's Alina?"

"How should I know?"

"You've been home all day."

"I didn't get up until a couple of hours ago."

"And what have you been doing in the meantime?"

"Working on CyberFort's annual server updates."

"And you haven't left your room once?"

"Nope. I've got a bathroom and a mini fridge in here. I only leave to do my laundry."

"God, you're a fucking animal," I hiss under my breath as I pull out my phone.

I immediately dial Ben's number. He should have been posted in the lobby to keep an eye on things. I took Alina at her word when she promised not to run away again. I'm worried our argument might have upset her enough to try—and this time, successfully. Unfortunately, the call goes straight to voicemail. I try again, but I'm no luckier the second time.

Double fuck. Something definitely isn't right.

I scroll through my phone until I locate the tracking app I installed. It's been a while since I've had to use it. I don't *want* to have to use it again, but the feeling in my gut tells me something terrible is happening. If Alina's phone is on, I should be able to locate her within a few seconds. I press the button and activate the app.

A map pulls up on the screen, zooming in bit by bit as the device triangulates her exact coordinates. For a moment, I think the app is glitching out. Her little icon pops up, but it's traveling at an inhumanly fast speed over the Atlantic Ocean. Did she manage to sneak onto a boat? No, this is much faster. A plane, then?

"Luka, can you get me a list of chartered flights scheduled for takeoff in the last hour?"

My brother nods, slipping back into his cave of a room. He plops down in his chair and rolls up to his impressive desktop setup. He has three different screens, one of which is an ultra-wide with the other two mounted vertically for the sake of programming. His fingers fly over the keyboard, the rapid *click-click-click* like heavy rain on a metal rooftop.

He pulls up a website called Flight Radar, a free global flight tracking service that provides real-time information all over the world. It's kind of astounding how detailed the map is, thousands of little yellow plane icons littering the map of the world. Luka scrolls in to get a better look at New York and the East Coast.

Luka taps the screen. "This one just left. A private jet. Country of registration is Russia. Headed directly to Moscow."

I glance down at my tracking app and cross reference it with the plane symbol on Luka's screen. They match. Alina is on that plane.

I'm at a loss. What am I supposed to do? Should I go after her? Do I call Mikhail and Dimitri and let them know to intercept? Did she really run away, or is something more nefarious going on?

"I need you to locate Ben for me," I order Luka. "Can you hack into his phone?"

Luka snorts. "Is water wet?"

"Just do it, little brother. Quickly."

While he works his magic, I pace anxiously around the room. This whole time, I thought Richard was the one trying to sabotage us, but now I realize there's another player on the scene. Alina could very well have been in real danger all along. She knows as well as I do what will happen if this marriage falls apart. Alina doesn't have a malicious bone in her body, which is why I know she would never leave me like this. The only conclusion I can draw is that somebody took her. How else would she have been able to charter a plane? I'm not sure if she even knows how to do that.

"Got it," Luka announces, pulling up a digital copy of Ben's phone. We can see every single app, phone call, email, and text message mirrored onto our screen.

"Pull up his most recent messages," I order.

What I see makes my stomach flip.

VS: Bring the girl tonight.

Ben: That'll be difficult. Pyotr's been keeping her close.

. . .

VS: *I don't care. Drug her and bring her here.*
   [Location Pin.]

Ben: *You have my money?*

VS: *Yes.*

Ben: *I want half now, half after I've delivered her to you.*

VS: *No. If you want to get paid, you'll bring my daughter to me. Don't keep me waiting. The jet's ready to leave.*

My jaw ticks. VS—*Violetta Salkov.*

That manipulative bitch. What game is she playing here? What reason could she possibly have to take her daughter back after forcing her to marry me in the first place? What was the point if—

It hits me like a runaway train.

Violetta never intended for this union to be permanent, which means she was buying herself time. Time for what exactly...

"Call Mikhail," I tell Luka as I start the door. "Tell him to prepare his men and be on guard. The Salkovs are going to attack, and soon. It's going to get bloody."

I drive like a madman to Ben's last known location: a private landing strip that's closed to the public. If Luka's sleuthing is correct, Ben should still be in the area. His phone hasn't moved in almost thirty minutes, which means he either ditched the device to throw me off his trail, or he's stuck around.

I stomp on the brakes and immediately get out of my car, running toward him. Ben is lying on the cold, hard pavement, nothing but the headlights of my vehicle to illuminate his pained face. He's pale and barely breathing, a pool of his own blood under his inert body. I kneel at his side and apply pressure to his wound. He's in rough shape. I'm not sure if he's going to make it.

"Just... leave me," he croaks, choking on a mouthful of blood.

I don't say anything, moving instead to pull out my phone and call 911.

"Am I going to die?" Ben whimpers.

"Probably," I snap bluntly. I'm not exactly known for my bedside manner, and even if I was, I don't feel like sparing this traitor a lick of my sympathy.

"I'm sorry," Ben rasps. "She offered me so much money."

I almost roll my eyes. What a fucking disappointment. Men used to have honor and unshakeable loyalty. Now everyone and everything can be bought for a high enough price.

"I didn't... mean for this to happen. You d-don't think... Do you think she'll hurt her?"

At this moment, Ben looks so much like a little boy. Afraid and guilty and ashamed. I offer him no comfort. He's *not* a little boy. These are the consequences of his actions.

"Violetta abused Alina all her life," I say flatly. "And you gave Alina back for nothing more than your greed. If anything happens to her, it's *your* fault."

"I didn't think—"

"Yes, that's abundantly clear."

"Please, I don't want to die. Mr. Antonov."

"Save your breath," I grumble, snatching up Ben's hand to place over his chest. "Apply pressure. The ambulance will be here soon."

"Don't leave me alone."

"Your fate is in God's hands now."

"W-where are you going?"

I rise to my feet, my heart lodged in my throat. "I'm going to get my wife back."

CHAPTER 31

ALINA

"The cuffs are a little much, don't you think?"

I've been struggling against my restraints for so long the skin around my ankle has been chafed raw. It's been roughly three weeks since Mother kidnapped me. I've been confined to my room ever since, bound to my bed by a long metal chain wrapped around the baseboard. There's enough slack to let me move about and get to the bathroom, but not enough so I can reach the windows or the door.

"I heard about your little escape attempts," Mother scoffs. "You won't be getting away that easily from me."

"I like a challenge."

"Don't get any ideas, you little brat. You're not going anywhere. Now—*eat*."

I glare at the tray of food one of the maids set on the nearby table for me. I'm sure it's all perfectly edible, but I'm on a hunger strike. I don't care how much the plate of fresh fruit makes my mouth water, or how fluffy the chocolate croissants look. "I'm not eating until you let me go."

Mother sneers. "Fine. Starve for all I care. Who knew letting you go with that bastard would turn you into such a spoiled bitch."

She doesn't mention him by name, but just the thought of Pyotr makes my heart hurt. I'm desperate to get back to him. What if he thinks I ran away? Surely, he has to know I wouldn't go back on my promise, right? The thought of him alone at home, wondering what happened to me... I can't stand it.

"Please," I mutter. "Please, just let me make a phone call. I just want to tell him I'm okay."

"Absolutely not."

"Mother—"

"I have more important things to take care of," she snaps. "Eat or don't eat. It doesn't make a difference to me. Just remember whose side you're on, Alina."

Mother storms out of my room, slamming my door behind her. It's so loud and violent it shakes the entire room, rattling everything from my bones to my eardrums.

I immediately get to work on my restraints. There *must* be something I can do to get out of this stupid cuff around my ankle. For a brief moment, I contemplate cutting my own foot off, but I doubt I'll get very far hopping about with a trail of blood behind me.

My stomach cramps. I can't tell if I'm hungry or nauseated. My symptoms have worsened since I returned to Russia. But no matter how many times I ask Mother to let me see a doctor, she outright refuses.

Her paranoia is through the roof. None of the guards are allowed to talk to me, and the only human interaction I've had is either when she comes in to scream at me, or when the maids drop off my food. I've been cut off from the rest of the world. Someone needs to warn the Antonovs, and right now, the only person who can do it is me.

I have to get out of here. People are going to die if I can't warn Pyotr in time. There's always a chance he's figured out what's happened, but I have no way of knowing.

The walls feel like they're closing in. My options are limited. I'm trapped and I have no one to turn to.

Keep your eyes on me and breathe.

I can hear Pyotr's voice in my ear. The last thing I need right now is to freak out and panic. I just need to stay calm and clear-headed.

In and out, just like that. Repeat after me: everything's fine.

"Everything's fine," I murmur aloud.

It takes a few more minutes of heavy breathing, but I eventually get my heart rate under control. I look around the room again, searching for a way out. I'll have to get creative. There are guards just outside my door, and even more patrolling the estate grounds. My best shot is to leave under the cover of night, but first things first: getting free of the chain.

I close my eyes and try to think. What would Pyotr do if he were in my shoes? Probably brute force his way out of them. I'm nowhere near as strong, but it looks like one of the links in the chain is starting to pry open. It's only a couple of centimeters, but it might just be enough.

Moving quickly, I take my flat bed sheet and carefully slip it between the cuff and my skin. I manage to create a barrier—as thin as it may be—to protect my raw ankle. Taking a deep breath I walk away from the bed until the chain is taut, the cuff biting painfully.

I lean as far as possible, pushing against the floor with the balls of my feet. The bed is thankfully heavy enough to anchor me. I start bouncing my weight, hoping the movement will eventually weaken the link. A thrill shoots through me when I look back and see it's starting to give. I just need to give it a few more hefty tugs and—

The chain breaks.

I fall to the floor with an unceremonious *thud*, landing awkwardly on my face. I don't even care how badly my nose stings because *holy shit I did it!* Unfortunately, there isn't any time to celebrate. I need to get the hell out of here. The only question is *how?* It's not like I can just waltz straight out the front door. I need to be smart about this.

I stare down at the chain. An idea pops into my head.

Quickly, I gather the length of metal and set it on my lap as I take a seat on the edge of the bed. As long as I cover the broken link with my hands and forearms, it *looks* as though I'm still restrained. Perfect. The only advantage I have right now is surprise. I've got one shot at this. Failure just isn't an option.

"Guards!" I scream at the top of my lungs, sounding as frantic as possible. "Guards, please, come quick!"

Right on cue, the guard posted just outside of my door barges in. I may be Mother's prisoner, but I'm still technically a Salkov princess. He can't afford to let anything happen to me. It also looks like he's totally alone. Excellent.

"What's wrong?" he asks.

"My stomach…" I wheeze, clenching my middle. "Please, it hurts so much—"

The guard approaches. "Let me see."

I groan loudly, folding over as I let out an anguished scream. "What's happening?"

"Let me see," he says, quickly trying to move my hands out of the way.

That's when I strike.

Chain in hand, I jump up from the edge of the bed and swing behind him, wrapping the metal around his throat. I squeeze my eyes shut, doing my best to not freak out. I don't want to hurt him, but I have no choice. Desperate times call for desperate measures, and right now, I'm as desperate as can be. Using all my weight, I hang from the chain to apply even more pressure against his neck. The guard gasps and wheezes, arms flailing about as he struggles to free himself.

"Just close your eyes," I pray aloud. "Go to sleep. Just go to sleep…"

I thank the Heavens when he finally stops moving, slumping to the floor like a ragdoll. He's out cold. I hurry to the open door and throw a cautious glance out and strain to listen. It doesn't sound like anyone's coming, but I've been keeping careful watch of how the guards rotate. Someone will be along shortly to switch places with him, so I need to move quickly.

I waste no time and immediately get to work searching his pockets. I find a carabiner with several keys dangling from it strapped to his belt loop. It takes me a couple of tries, but I finally find the key that undoes the cuff around my ankle. When the metal finally comes loose, I breathe a sigh of relief. Damn. Now that I can feel the blood rushing back to my toes, I finally realize how tight it was.

I'm not in the clear yet, though. I keep searching his pockets and locate his wallet, his phone, a pair of car keys...

And a gun.

I gulp. I don't want to hurt anybody, but I will if I have to. Whatever Mother's planning, I have no doubt violence will occur—if it hasn't already. Who knows what havoc she's managed to wreak in the three weeks I've been locked up in here?

I have to be at the top of my game. Escaping Mother means leaving the Salkovs behind, but it doesn't mean the Antonovs will welcome me with open arms. Betraying one family for the other... It's bound to spell disaster. It can't hurt to have a little firepower on my side.

Before I leave, I drag the guard to my bathroom and lock him inside.

I poke my head out into the hallway. The coast is clear. For how long, it's too hard to tell.

As quiet as a mouse, I make my way through the estate, making sure to move slowly so the creaky floorboards don't give me away. I just need to make it to the garage. There I can find a car and get the hell out of here. I'm not entirely sure how to find the Antonovs, but that's a problem for Future Me to deal with. Right now, survival is my only objective.

I manage to make my way down the winding steps in the east wing. When I get to the ground floor, I hear a gaggle of voices. One of the most recognizable is my mother's.

"We strike at midnight," she says firmly. "Understood?"

"Yes, ma'am," a booming chorus of men answer.

With my back pressed against the wall, I remain perfectly still.

Dammit. It looks like Mother is in the middle of a strategy meeting with her most trusted lieutenants in her office. What are the chances I can get past them without anybody noticing?

"We outnumber the Antonovs three to one," Mother continues. "And we have the element of surprise. We'll go in and take the targets here and here. It'll cut them off from their allies and leave the rest of their territory for us to take. Now, get a move on. All hands on deck. I don't want any witnesses and *definitely* no survivors."

"Yes, ma'am!"

There's movement out of the corner of my eye. A fleet of men are leaving. I shrink into myself, sticking to the shadows. Mercifully, nobody looks in my direction.

My ears are still ringing. She means to attack them tonight? I have to warn Pyotr and his brothers.

Only once the house has stilled and I'm sure I'm alone, I slip into the hall and carefully peek into Mother's office space. There's no one in sight. On the table in the middle of the room are an assortment of maps and dossiers. At first glance, it's all very confusing. Curiosity gets the better of me. I step into the office to look.

Several locations have been circled in bright red markings. They're targets, I realize, the ones Mother wants her men to hit. I count five different spots all over Moscow, but what concerns me most are the areas that have been completely crossed out. By the looks of it, Mother has been carving up the city for a while now. I shudder to think how many lives have already been lost.

Credit where credit is due, Mother is frightfully efficient. Nearly the entire map has been claimed in the name of the Salkovs. At this rate, she'll have conquered all of Moscow by the end of the week—and I have no doubt she's willing to get her hands bloody to see it through. There has to be something I can do to warn the Antonovs. If I can save even one life, it'll be worth it.

I fish out the guard's phone and take as many pictures of the maps as possible. The first number I punch in is Pyotr's, but the guard I knocked out doesn't have an international texting plan. I immediately get an error message telling me it failed to send. I doubt I'd be able to get through to him if I called, either.

"Oh, come *on*," I hiss under my breath. "You couldn't spring for a better phone package?"

When I hear voices down the hall, I know it's time to leave. Thinking on my feet, I decide to send the images to Pyotr in an email. Something tells me it'll go straight to his spam folder, but I have to try. I don't even have the chance to type in a message telling him I'm alright. I attach the pictures of Mother's plans and send them off.

"Hey!" a man shouts. A guard stands in the doorway, a darkness in his eyes as he reaches for his weapon. "What do you think you're doing in here, you little rat?"

Shit.

I pull the gun I swiped early and aim it directly at the man's head. My finger's on the trigger, but the last thing I want to do is pull. I'm no killer—but *he* doesn't know that.

"Let me go!" I scream. "Let me go, or I'll blow your fucking head off!"

He raises his hands in surrender. "Easy, Ms. Salkov. Don't do anything rash."

"Step aside!"

"Alright, alright. Just take it easy."

"What's going on?" Mother's shrill voice reaches my ear.

My feet carry me forward. In a flash, I have my arm locked around her neck, choking the air out of her as I jab the tip of my gun against her temple. Her guards have all arrived, their weapons drawn and aimed at us.

"Don't shoot!" Mother screams. "Don't shoot, you might hit me!"

I drag her back, keeping my eyes on her men. One step at a time, we begin to retreat down the hall toward the garage. I just need to get to a car in one piece.

"You know," I growl against my mother's ear. "I'm not even surprised you aren't concerned they might hurt *me*, too. You really are such a shitty mother."

"What are you going to do?" Violetta hisses at me. "If you're going to shoot me, then shoot me."

"Don't try me!"

"You're not going to do it." She cackles. "You're too much of a coward—"

I fire a single shot into the air, the bullet going straight through the ceiling. Plaster dust crumbles down, showering our hair and faces. "Like I said, *don't try me.*"

Stumbling into the garage fills me with a spark of hope. I'm one step closer to getting out of here. Surviving on my own remains to be seen.

"You're a traitor to your family," Violetta seethes. "Do you really think you can get away with this? The Antonovs will kill you on the spot because of your last name alone. Your loyalty to them is pointless."

"I'm not loyal to the Antonovs," I snap. I'm a few inches away from the nearest car. "I don't give a shit about the Bratvas or your pointless need for power. All I want is to get back to Pyotr."

"Why?" Violetta says with a sneer. "Why him?"

Because he's the only one in the world who has ever shown me an ounce of kindness, I want to tell her. But I don't. I'm pretty sure Violetta doesn't even understand the word.

In a world that's cold and bleak, Pyotr is my safe haven. His endless patience, his sweet smiles... I'd choose him over the family who never wanted me every day of the week. He may not love me, but *I* love him, and that's why I'd rather die trying than sit back and watch my mother go after him and his family. Love is selfless, unconditional. I'll do everything in my power to protect him.

I keep my arm locked around Violetta's throat until I manage to get behind the wheel. The second I've got the keys shoved into the ignition and the engine roaring to life, I shove Violetta away. She falls to the ground, smacking her head on the pavement. I don't even feel bad about it.

I stomp my foot onto the gas pedal, tires screeching behind me as

I make a break for it. This time, I'm prepared for the ensuing chaos. They managed to stop me from getting away at the airport, but now I'm armed, too.

Bullets fly. They shoot at me, but I return fire. Violetta's guards have no choice but to scramble for cover, giving me ample opportunity to peel out of there and leave them in my dust.

CHAPTER 32

PYOTR

I probably look like hell.

I haven't slept in three weeks. It's impossible. Every waking moment, I'm plagued with worry. And when I try to get some shut eye, I'm rewarded with endless nightmares. Alina is out there somewhere, but I don't know whether she's dead or alive. Shortly after I'd located her phone signal, it had gone dead. Likely, her mother discovered it and had it destroyed. I'm not a praying man, but I find myself praying for Violetta to show her daughter mercy. I know what that woman is capable of, and that's exactly why I'm afraid for Alina's life.

"Another one of our warehouses was hit last night," Mikhail informs us as he walks into the room. We're gathered at his place. The kids are upstairs, fast asleep and none the wiser of the turmoil our family's been going through for the past few weeks.

"How many did we lose?" Dimitri asks severely. There's a hard edge to his tone which tells me the stress is getting to him. My twin is normally much better at letting things slide right off this back.

"All of them," Mikhail says gravely.

I'm more than aware of the gravity of the situation. I stand at the back of the room, arms folded across my chest as I listen to the bad news rolling in. Our Bratva is losing territory and manpower faster than we can blink. The Salkovs have been hitting us hard and fast, working so efficiently we haven't been able to retaliate.

I can't help but feel guilty.

None of this would be happening if I hadn't left Alina alone. I should never have gone to the wedding. If I'd been there to protect her... Alina was the only thing standing in the way of the Salkovs making their move, and now that Violetta has Alina in her grasp, there's nothing to keep that madwoman from going after us.

"I want us to remove our remaining men to protect the last bit of our territory," Mikhail says. "If we lose our remaining businesses, we'll lose our foothold in Moscow for good."

"Remaining men," Dimitri echoes, sounding almost incredulous. "Mikhail, we *have* no remaining men."

"What of our allies?"

"They want nothing to do with this conflict."

"Those fucking bastards *owe* us."

"I'll make a few calls and see what I can do, but it's starting to look hopeless. We had a good run. Maybe we should cut our losses and get our families the hell out of here before it's too late."

Mikhail sneers. "Don't let me hear you say that again, Dima."

"I'm trying to be pragmatic here, that's all."

They bicker back and forth. I'm with Dimitri on this. It really is starting to look helpless, but defeat isn't a concept we Antonovs understand. We've worked too hard for too long to see our efforts dashed, but if I'm being frank, there's something far more pressing on my mind.

"I'm going out to look for her," I announce. "This is your business, not mine."

Mikhail gives me a hard look. "It's *family* business. You're as involved as any of us."

I shake my head. "No. I never agreed to be a part of the Bratva. You chose to return to this life and I'm not going to judge you for it.

But it's not what *I* want. I need to find Alina. That's the only reason I'm even here."

Dimitri regards me with much more obvious sympathy. "I know you're worried about her, but now is not a good time for an Antonov to be wandering around in the streets. Violetta Salkov has amassed an army—"

"All while under your nose," I snap. I don't mean to, but my nerves are fried. The longer I sit around doing nothing, the more anxious I become. "How could you have let her get the upper hand?"

"Mistakes happen," Dimitri says with a shrug. "We thought your marriage would be the end of things."

"Turns out, Violetta Salkov is a woman without honor," Mikhail mutters bitterly.

"I have to get out there," I insist. "Can't you spare any of your men to help me search?"

"The Salkovs are picking us off left, right, and center. It would be unwise to go out right now."

"Then *when*?" I snap. "After Violetta has run us out of town? When we're all six feet under?"

"Mind your tone, Pyotr," Mikhail warns darkly. "I know you're worried, but we can't afford to lose focus."

Dimitri walks over and pats me on the back. "Let's take a walk in the gardens. You need some fresh air."

For what it's worth, Mikhail has a lovely garden in his backyard. It's littered with my nieces and nephew's toys. There's a sandbox and a swing set just off to the side, sheltered beneath the shade of a tall tree at the very corner of the property. At first glance, Mikhail's home in the Russian suburbs feels incredibly ordinary. On closer inspection, however, that's simply not the case.

It doesn't take an eagle eye to notice the plethora of cameras posted around the perimeter. One's hidden away in a fake birdhouse, another drilled up high near the apex of the house's roof to provide a wide field of vision. I'm convinced there's no place safer in all of Russia than my brother's home.

I pace the garden planters. Aurora's flowers are in full bloom, but they do little to calm my nerves.

"Deep breaths, Pyotr," Dimitri says firmly. "You need to be patient."

"Don't tell me what to do, Dima."

"All I'm trying to say is you need a clear head. We all do. If we fall apart, the Salkovs win."

I feel sick. I'm a man of action. The fact that I can't do anything makes my insides boil. I understand why Mikhail doesn't want to throw us head-first into battle, but I see no sense in being sitting ducks, either. With every passing second, Violetta grows closer to smothering us to death. The Antonovs have little territory left, and what ground we've managed to keep likely won't last another onslaught. Our numbers are dwindling, our allies have all turned tail, and somewhere in the middle of all that chaos, my wife is likely being held against her will.

The guilt has been eating me alive. The last time I saw Alina, she was upset and vulnerable... and I didn't do a damn thing about it. I regret the way I left things, and I regret it even more with every passing day. The cold, bitter anguish festers inside, destroying me bit by bit. The *what ifs* haunt me day and night.

What if I'd given her my answer? What if I hadn't left her alone? What if I wasn't such a coward and told her how I feel?

It's enough to drive a man insane.

My phone goes off, but I ignore it, too busy with my furious pacing to bother checking. Business can wait. CyberFort is the last thing on my mind right now.

"What is Misha even waiting for?" I grumble.

"You know our brother. He's too proud to surrender."

"And risk losing it all? What of his family?"

"I've got a plane at the ready," Dimitri assures. "If things go tits up, I can get everyone to the States before Violetta can get her hands on us. But we're not going to admit defeat until there's no other option."

"I don't understand you two. What's more important—your families or the Bratva?"

Dimitri gives me a sympathetic smile. "I don't expect you to understand. To us, they're one and the same." My phone goes off again. While I'm inclined to ignore it, Dimitri tosses his chin toward me. "Aren't you going to get that?"

With a sigh, I dig my phone out of my pocket. It's an email from an address I've never seen with several images attached. My first and immediate thought is to send the email to my spam folder. As the head of a cybersecurity company, I'd be a fool to open any attachment from an unknown sender. Who knows what viruses could be lurking in its code?

But something in my gut tells me to give it a look. The email address ends with a *.ru*, meaning the email likely originated from right here in Russia. It feels a little too conspicuous to be random, so despite my better judgment, I click on the image.

My eyes widen in shock.

"Holy shit. Dima, look at this."

My brother hurries to my side, peering over my shoulder as I zoom in on the picture. Maps. Not just any maps, either, but ones designed to track Bratva territory, army positions, and the Salkov's plan of attack.

"Who sent this?" Dimitri asks, understandably suspicious.

"I'm not sure."

"Could it be fake?"

"What if it's not?" I ask. I tap the screen. "According to this, the Salkovs are going to move in to the last of Antonov territory."

"You need to show this to Mikhail. This could help us turn the tides."

"Do we have an informant amongst the Salkovs?"

"I have no idea," Dimitri confesses. "But if this is real, it means Violetta has a traitor in her ranks."

A tiny spark of hope ignites in my chest. Who could it be? Who within the Salkov Bratva would be willing to risk their life sending us this information? I have an idea who it might be, but the odds seem insurmountable.

Dimitri quickly reaches into his own pocket and pulls out his phone. "Natalya," Dimitri says. "I need you to close up early. Yes, I know the clinic's supposed to be open for another two hours, but something's going down. I need you to go home and take care of the children. Yes, I'll explain everything, just go straight home."

He hangs up and gives me a nod.

We both head inside. The winds might finally be blowing in our favor.

CHAPTER 33

ALINA

I trip into the nearest convenience store, clutching my bloody shoulder.

I thought I made a pretty clean getaway. When I had to pull over to ditch the car at a gas station at the edge of the city, I realized I was wrong. In all the chaos, I didn't realize that one of their bullets managed to pierce the back window and hit me in the back of the shoulder. I was so hopped up on adrenaline I didn't realize until at least twenty minutes later when I felt the wet, sticky sensation of my blood soaking into my shirt and dripping down my back.

My vision is getting blurry. My muscles are strained and weak. I'm so hungry and tired and in so much pain I can barely see straight as I stumble into a nearby store. It's empty in here, soft Russian pop music playing over the speakers. I quickly meander over to the nearest shelf, searching for a bottle of ibuprofen.

"Goodness!" an old woman, one of the employees judging by her green work vest and nametag, gasps when she sees me. She was in the middle of mopping in the next aisle over. Olga, according to her nametag. "Miss, are you okay?"

"I'm fine," I rasp. "Pretend you didn't see me. Sorry for bleeding all over your floors."

"You need to go to the hospital."

"No," I say quickly, shaking my head. "No, I'm just grabbing a few things and I'll get out of your hair."

Olga bites her lip in concern, her wrinkled face twisting up in worry. "You're one of them, yes?"

"What?"

"One of *them*."

I furrow my brows. "I have no idea what you're talking about."

She presses a finger to her lips. "It's a secret, I get it."

"Seriously, lady—"

"There's a doctor near here. A few blocks that way. She treats your kind, no questions asked."

Realization dawns. "You think I'm a gangster?"

"You were shot, yes? Can't get the police involved."

I swallow, my mouth terribly dry. I'm so delirious at this point I can barely make sense of what she's saying. Have I accidentally walked into a Bratva's territory? How else would she know so much?

Olga quickly shrugs off her vest and throws it over my shoulder. "You must go quickly. Lots of violence out there. It's not safe to be in public."

"I don't understand..."

"Have you been living under a rock? Gang violence, my dear. Lots of innocent people are getting hurt. The police can barely get a lid on the situation."

"I'm sorry, but... Whose territory am I in?"

The woman blinks at me, suddenly suspicious. "This business is under the protection of the Antonovs. You *are* with the Antonovs, are you not?"

I nod furiously, hope blooming within me. "Yes. Yes, I am!"

"Come," she says hastily. "I will take you to see Dr. Chekov."

She moves quickly, closing the front door to the convenience store and locking it. Olga flicks off the light and flips the sign to *Sorry,*

We're Closed. She ushers me to the back entrance. "Move, move! There's no time."

It's honestly a miracle I don't pass out on her. I've pushed myself to the limit. Between the blood loss and the hunger, I'm surprised my legs haven't folded out from under me.

As we make our way through the cramped streets, I'm recognize the havoc around me. The blaring wail of sirens are never ending. There's a noticeably jittery quality to all the pedestrians we pass. Several shop windows have been shattered, a few of them boarded up, while others have been left in shambles. It's a war zone, nothing but destruction and chaos.

"Here it is," Olga says, waving me over. The two of us stand outside a small clinic, its outsides painted a dull grey. It doesn't exactly strike me as a doctor's office. If I'd been passing by on my own, I'm sure I would have missed this place entirely.

I knock on the glass of the door, huffing and puffing. I can barely see straight. "H-hello?" I call out. No answer.

Olgra frowns. "How strange. She's not supposed to be closed for another two hours."

"Is the doctor still here?" I try again.

"I'm sorry, I'm closed!" I hear a woman's muffled voice from the inside.

"Please, I... I really need to see a doctor. It's an emergency."

I'm not sure how long it takes, but the door eventually opens. A woman with light blonde hair and dazzling blue eyes peeks out, her brows knitted together into a frown. "I'm sorry, but if you need medical attention, you'll have to—" She spots my bloody shoulder, the messy state I'm in. "Good God, what happened?"

"I need... Please, I just need..."

She ushers me in hurriedly, supporting my good arm. "It's going to be okay. Let's get you to the exam room. Just keep breathing slowly for me, alright?"

"Alright."

"This is where I leave you," Olga says. "Good luck, my dear."

"Thank you so much. I won't forget this kindness."

"What's your name?" the doctor asks me as she helps me inside.

"Alina."

"Nice to meet you, Alina. I'm Dr. Chekov. Natalya."

"Pretty," I mumble, so loopy my voice sounds foreign to my own ears.

I let out a massive sigh of relief when I'm finally able to lie down. The examination table is covered in some sort of foam, a thin sheet of paper rolled over the top for sanitary purposes.

"I need you to take your shirt off, Alina," Natalya says. "So I can take a better look at the wound."

I do as she asks. I don't have the energy to argue or worry about looking suspicious. She helps me peel my shirt up and over my head, the fabric sticking to my shoulder.

"How did this happen?" Natalya asks me.

I chew on the inside of my cheek. I'm not sure what I can and cannot tell her. "Olga said you don't ask questions."

"I don't talk to the *police*," she corrects. "I still need to know what happened to inform my decisions."

"The Salkovs," I mumble.

"They shot you?"

"I was... trying to get away."

Dr. Chekov nods gravely. "You're not the first person Olga's helped. All this senseless violence... I'm sorry you got caught up in it."

I wince when she begins to wipe the dried blood off my shoulder and applies a disinfectant. The sting is unbearable, like a million little needles digging under my skin.

"It looks like you were shot twice," the doctor informs me. "One of them is just a flesh wound, but I think the second bullet might be lodged in your shoulder. I need to get it out. I don't have strong enough anesthetics on hand, so we'll have to do this with you awake."

I groan. Could this day get any worse? "Do whatever you have to, just... give me a second."

"Take all the time you need."

I close my eyes and think of Pyotr. I have to get back to him, no matter what obstacles might stand in my way.

Keep your eyes on me.

Just breathe.

"O-okay," I mumble. "Let's get this over with."

"I'll try to be as gentle as I can."

Pain washes over me in waves. Sometimes it's too much to bear, and other times it's nothing more than a dull ache. Natalya has incredibly deft hands, skillfully removing the bullet lodged in my shoulder. I block out the sounds, the sensations, holding back my tears. I can do this. Not just for Pytor, but for me, too.

It's almost fitting, in a way, that Violetta would have me shot in the back. All the years I endured beneath her reign of terror are finally at an end. There's no need to talk of loyalties when she never did anything to earn my loyalty to begin with. I know where I stand and who I stand with—and Violetta certainly isn't it. Whatever doubts shackled me to her are no more. We may share the same blood, but she's in no way family. Now that I've finally managed to escape—and hopefully for the last time—I'm done with her.

The Salkov Bratva can burn to the ground for all I care. I relinquish my name and my association with them. I'm leaving the Bratva and this mad, crazy underground world behind. I'd gladly trade it all for the safety of Pyotr's arms a thousand times over without a single regret.

Dr. Chekov finishes stitching me up, working quickly to apply fresh bandages to my shoulder. "There," she says, sounding rather triumphant. "That wasn't so bad, was it?"

"You weren't the one under the knife."

She laughs. "No, I suppose not. Does anything else hurt?"

"My stomach feels terrible," I confess. "And I'm really nauseous. I've been feeling like this for weeks, though."

"May I ask when you last had your period?"

I arch a brow. "Um..." I struggle to do the mental math. "Gosh, I... Over a month ago, I think?"

"Have you been sexually active?"

I'm surprised I have enough blood left to blush, but the telltale heat in my cheeks tells me I'm as red as a tomato. "Yes, actually. My husband... You don't think I'm pregnant, do you?"

"There's only one way to find out. Wait right here, I'll grab you a pregnancy test."

I nod numbly. "Thank you, Doctor."

She smiles. "Please, just call me Nat."

The doctor leaves and returns a few minutes later, dropping off a pregnancy test and directing me to the bathroom. I walk to the bathroom in a strange, dream-like trance. Is this really happening? How many curveballs does the universe plan on throwing my way today? I suppose peeing on a stick is the easiest thing I've had to do today.

While I wait for the minutes to pass, my mind swirls. I need to figure out how to contact Pyotr. With any luck, he's seen Violetta's battle plan and forwarded the information to his brothers. I just want this madness to end. I never understood Violetta's need to consume everything in her path, claiming all the wealth and power as her own. Can she not see the harm she's doing? How many people are getting hurt because of her greed? If she does, it means she must not care—a truly chilling thought.

When the two minutes are up, I look down at the pregnancy test.

I can hardly believe my eyes. Two solid blue lines.

Pregnant.

I leave the bathroom in a hurry, Natalya waiting just outside.

"I need to call my husband. He doesn't know where I am."

Natalya frowns in concern. I'm sure she must be very confused, but I'm afraid I might scare her if I go into further detail. "You can use my phone."

"He's in America. Are you able to call long distance? I'm so sorry for the trouble."

"That's no problem, Alina. What's your husband's name?"

"Pyotr," I say, unable to help my smile. "Pyotr Antonov."

Natalya's face blanks. "Did you say Pytor Antonov?"

"Yes?"

"Do the names Mikhail and Dimitri Antonov mean anything to you?"

My heart shoots up into my throat. "Who are you? How do you—"

Natalya laughs softly. "Dima is my husband. Pytor and Mikhail are my brothers-in-law. We're family, Alina." She grasps my hand. "Pyotr's here in Moscow. He's been looking for you everywhere!"

Tears sting my eyes. "I can't believe it."

She seems to be in just as much disbelief. "This is nothing short of a miracle. I'll call him for you right now, okay? He's going to be so happy. Just take it easy, and make sure not to agitate that shoulder. I'll be two minutes."

All I can do is nod as a relieved sob bubbles past my lips. I don't know if there's a God above, but I'm eternally grateful we've finally managed to catch a break.

CHAPTER 34

PYOTR

"Out of my fucking way!" I snap as the car rolls up the driveway. "Let me through. Let me see my—"

The passenger door opens, revealing the woman seated inside. Carefully, Alina steps out of the vehicle and I'm suddenly overwhelmed.

She's still as beautiful as the day I met her, but it's clear Violetta must have put her through hell. Not only does my wife look thinner than I remember, but she's sporting a bloody shoulder.

The sudden rage surging through me nearly tears me apart. I'm going to kill Violetta for what she's done. How dare she harm my woman—her own *daughter*.

"Pytor..." Her name falls from her lips in a breathless whisper. The sound of her voice soothes my nerves better than a salve.

I rush to her, tender as can be as I take in the extent of her injuries. I must look like something frightful because Alina reaches up and smooths the space between my brows with the tips of her fingers.

"It's okay, Pyotr. I'm okay."

Except I don't believe her. I gingerly cup her face in my palms and dip down to kiss her. God, I didn't realize how much I missed the feel of her lips until this moment. I comb my fingers through her hair, trace my fingers over her cheeks, kiss her again—almost like I'm trying to convince myself she's real and not a dream that will slip away at any given moment.

I know I should probably say something, but I'm at a loss for words. There aren't enough words in either the English or Russian dictionary to describe just how much I've missed her. I can't tell her how sorry I am for letting Ben take her away, that she fell into her mother's clutches because I was careless. How can I possibly tell her how happy she makes my heart? How when I hold her in my arms, she feels better than home.

"Did you get the email?" Alina asks hastily.

"That was *you*?" I don't think I've ever been prouder.

"I overheard Violetta talking to her lieutenants. They're going to strike at midnight—"

"You let us take care of it from here," I tell her. "You've done more than enough."

"She needs rest," Natalya tells me. "A good night's sleep and a light painkiller should do the trick. Doctor's orders."

"Let's get you inside," I say to Alina before scooping her up in my arms.

She's light. She really has lost a lot of weight. It's concerning as hell and triggers something in my hindbrain. The first thing I'm going to do is get her tucked into bed and then make her something to eat. I need to protect her, provide for her. Who better suited to tend to her needs than her husband?

Mikhail's guest room is already made up for her. I lay her down on the bed, mindful of her shoulder as I diligently cover her up with the softest of blankets. I go so far as to fluff her pillow and adjust the thermostat so the temperature in the room is a touch on the warm side.

"I'm going to get you something to eat," I say dutifully.

"Pyotr, wait..."

When she reaches out to me, I'm at her side in an instant, kneeling at her bedside. I take her hand and lace her fingers through mine, relishing the way she squeezes it lightly.

"Stay with me for a moment," she says softly. "Please. I promise I'll eat, just... I want to be with you."

I nod. I feel the exact same way. "I'm here, Alina."

The corner of her lip curls up into a weary smile. "I missed you."

"I missed you, too. More than you know."

She stiffens. "Is Ben... Mother shot him as we were leaving. Is he—"

"He'll be fine. It'll take him some time to recover, but he's in stable condition. Once he's well enough, the police will be questioning him. He's facing several charges, including accessory to kidnapping."

Alina chews on the inside of her cheek. "Pyotr?"

"Yes, lyubimaya?"

"About that night... I'm sorry we fought. I dumped a lot on you all at once. It wasn't fair of me to put you on the spot."

I shake my head. "You have nothing to apologize for, Alina. I'm sorry I was such a repressed asshole that I couldn't tell you how I truly feel."

Her eyes are droopy with sleep, but she still manages to arch a curious brow. "How you truly feel?"

Bringing her hand to my lips, I kiss the back of her fingers. "Alina, these past few weeks have been hell for me. I was worried sick about you. You were on my mind morning, noon, and night. It killed me not knowing where you were or if you were okay, and seeing what Violetta's done to you..." My rage bubbles to the surface, the muscles in my jaw ticking. "I'm not good with words, Alina. Sometimes I don't know how to... express myself."

Alina smiles gently. "You don't have to, Pyotr. I get it."

"When you told me you were falling in love with me, I was over the moon. You took me by surprise, is all. I wasn't ready to tell you then, but I am now. I'm in love with you too, Alina Antonov. I would do anything to keep you, if you're still willing to be mine."

She gently caresses my cheek and smiles, the corners of her eyes crinkling as she does. "That sounds a lot like a wedding vow."

"Is that a yes?"

"Come here, silly. Of course I'll be yours."

I rise to my feet and climb onto the bed with her, cradling her as gently as I can. Our lips come together carefully, every kiss tender and true. This time when I kiss her, I take my time savoring the taste of her lips and tongue. I commit to memory her soft sighs and sweet touches. I'm not the type of man who gets nervous easily, but I'm nervous now. I'm worried I'm going to hurt her, that I'll move too fast or take too selfishly.

My Alina deserves so much more than that. She needs to know just how much she's cherished and adored. So I kiss her slowly, the rest of the world fading away as an afterthought. Now that I finally have her in my arms again, nothing else truly matters.

"My beautiful wife," I murmur against her mouth.

"My handsome husband," she says with a quiet giggle.

A low moan rises out of me. "Call me that again."

"Husband... *My* husband..."

The sound of her voice goes straight to my cock. I can feel my arousal hardening in the front of my pants. I mentally scold myself. Now isn't the time to be feeling my tired, injured wife up.

"I really should get you something to eat," I tell her.

"There's just one more thing I have to tell you," she says.

"What?"

Alina's pretty green eyes lock onto mine as she nibbles on her bottom lip. "It's a really big deal. You have to promise not to freak out."

My heart pounds. "Telling me not to freak out is a sure-fire way to make sure I freak out."

"When I was at Natalya's office, I mentioned I was feeling nauseated. It was actually the reason I left with Ben that night. I asked him to take me to see a doctor."

I frown, sitting up a bit straighter in my growing alarm. "O—*kay*?" I answer slowly.

She takes a deep breath. "Natalya had me take a test. I'm pregnant, Pyotr."

The air rushes out of my lungs. I stare at her in disbelief. My eyes flit down to her belly as a warm sense of pride and excitement swirls in my chest. Instinctively, my hand slips down to rest over her stomach.

"Our baby…"

"The first of six," she teases lightly.

I don't think my heart has ever felt fuller. Whatever troubles I thought I had suddenly vanish into thin air. Nothing else matters except for the little family I now hold in my arms.

"I want to make love to you, but I'll just have to wait," I tell her as I pull the comforter over her battered body.

Her smile is everything. Sweeter than candy, brighter than the sun, more brilliant than the stars above. She wraps her arms around me and kisses me softly. "It'll be worth it."

"Mother of my child," I murmur into our next kiss. "God, I can't believe it."

She laughs as I kiss her again. "Are you happy?"

"So happy. Unbelievably happy. We're going to fill that penthouse full of kids."

"We're going to have to kick Luka out to make space."

"It's about time he got his own place anyway."

She laughs quietly, a laugh that causes a grimace of pain. But her smile is breathtaking.

No matter what tomorrow has in store for us—either our downfall or our unlikely triumph—I'm content as long as I have her.

We stare deeply into each other's eyes, not a word exchanged. I explore the pretty green of her irises while she traces the line of my jaw with the tip of her finger. I'd gladly trade the remaining years of my life for each and every one of her soft giggles and shy smiles.

When her stomach grumbles loudly, I sit up. "Something to eat," I say, getting out of bed in a hurry. "You stay right here."

"Pyotr..."

"I'll take care of everything, my beautiful wife. Just relax and take it easy."

Alina smiles sleepily. "Thank you, husband."

CHAPTER 35

PYOTR

Within the hour, Mikhail's home transforms into our new base of operations. What few men we still have are busy preparing for tonight's onslaught. While Dimitri reviews the maps, Mikhail gives the orders.

"Violetta plans on swarming us on all sides," Mikhail says. "No matter what, we're facing heavy casualties."

"Misha," I grumble, "you need to throw in the towel. Dimitri has organized a flight out of here. We could be gone twenty minutes."

"I'm not letting that woman defeat me."

I gesture to the images Alina risked her life to take. We've printed them out and arranged them on the table, recreating the exact layout Violetta had in her war room. "This is the last of your territory, Mikhail. It's as you said, we'll be swarmed. Is it really worth losing our lives defending what little we have left?"

"You don't understand, Pyotr. We will never surrender."

I pinch the bridge of my nose and pray my headache away. I love my brother, truly, but sometimes it's like I'm talking to a wall. "Mikhail... You have to listen to reason."

"This—" he motions to the map, "is *ours*, Pyotr. Our kingdom, our land. You don't get it because you're not Bratva. Not really."

"That's *why* I'm the one you should be listening to. You're too close to this. This is personal for you and you're not thinking clearly. Your wife and kids are upstairs. Just for a moment, think about what's at risk."

Mikhail's nostrils flare. "Don't bring them into this, Pytor."

"I have to. I've seen Violetta's cruelty on my wife's marred skin. You think she'll spare your children? She's already proven she has no honor by using my marriage as a diversion while she gathered her troops. That witch will kill every single one of us without hesitation—the children included."

My brother's jaw ticks in frustration, a good sign as far as I'm concerned. It means he's actually listening to me.

"Misha?" his wife speaks. Aurora pokes her head out from around the corner and peers into the room, worry etched into her soft features.

Just like that, everything about Mikhail's normally domineering energy softens. "What's wrong, kisa?"

"We couldn't help but overhear," she says, entering with my other sister-in-law, Natalya, hot on her tail.

"This is turning into quite the family meeting," Dimitri comments lightly as his wife joins him at his side. I think he's trying to lighten the mood, but it doesn't land. We're all more than a little aware of the corner the Salkovs have backed us into.

"How much of that did you hear?" I ask the women.

"Almost all of it," Natalya informs. "None of you are particularly quiet. Your voices tend to carry."

Mikhail regards his wife with the utmost adoration, the softness in his gaze reserved only for her. "What do you think we should do?"

Aurora sidles up to him, one hand pressed to his chest while she rests her head against his shoulder. "I want whatever option ensures we all get out alive."

He sighs. "I gave up everything to bring this family back from the pits our uncle dragged it into."

"But look what you gained," Natalya points out. "There is no shame in a strategic retreat. It doesn't mean surrender, just that you're regrouping until you can figure things out."

Dimitri's face lights up as he listens to her talk. "She has a point. We faced greater odds when we were up against Konstantin and Levitsky."

"But our reputation will never recover," Mikhail argues. "No one will ever take us seriously if we back off now."

"Maybe you just have to *look* like you're backing off," comes a familiarly soft voice.

I'm the first to react, turning to find Alina slowly rounding the corner. She's got a little more color in her cheeks, and while the dark circles beneath her eyes are still present, she's looking much better now that she's had a well-deserved nap and a belly full of food.

"You should be in bed," I tell her, though I certainly don't complain when she wraps her good arm around my waist.

"What do you mean?" Dimitri asks. "Look like you're giving up?"

"I know my mother," she says. "Violetta will stop at nothing until she gets what she wants. And what she wants right now is the last of your territory. She's pulling out all the stops. In a couple hours, she'll have hundreds of men spread out across Moscow to eradicate what remains of your Bratva. But her pride has always been her downfall. She has a one-track mind. We know her game plan, so what's to stop us from coming in behind her and taking them by surprise?"

Mikhail frowns. "Why should we trust you?"

I set my jaw, a protective arm around Alina's waist. "*I* trust her. That should be good enough for you."

"You'll have to forgive me for not jumping off the deep end just because she asks me to."

"Misha," I growl. "Alina escaped that woman to warn us. She risked her life to get these pictures. She's on our side—her last name be damned."

"Believe me, there's no love lost between Violetta and me. I might be your best shot at getting a glimpse into her mind. She never involved me in Bratva business, but I know how she thinks better than anyone in this room." Alina points at the map, tapping one of the red X's. "Clear out your men. Have them hold back while the Salkovs storm the place. They'll think it an easy victory, that you're running scared. Then you come from behind them and strike. If you're smart about this, I'm confident you can take them out. *All* of them."

I glance at Dimitri, then to Mikhail. I can practically see the gears turning in their heads. It's a sound strategy, though it's not without risks. We're still outnumbered and outgunned, but if we play our cards right...

"Does your mother know you sent us these pictures?" Mikhail asks.

"I don't think so."

"What are the chances she changes her plan of attack?" Dimitri adds. "She could pick another day, another time."

Alina shakes her head. "No. Violetta has been planning this for weeks. She's spent lots of time and money moving everyone into position. She'll attack tonight, of that I'm sure."

I glance at my wristwatch. "We have four hours. What's your call, Misha?"

People say I'm hard to read, and even harder to crack, a trait I probably learned from my eldest brother, because right now, his face is impassable. His whole body is rigid and impossibly still. His mind is either completely blank, or he's formulating a hundred different plans all at once. My money is on the latter.

Mikhail's eyes flick up to meet mine. "You *do* trust her?"

"With my life," I answer firmly.

"Then this is what we're going to do," he says, no longer speaking as my brother, but the head of the Antonov Bratva. "Aurora, you'll stay here with the children. If things go south, I want you to take them on the next plane to New York. Natalya, you'll be our field medic. You'll be far from enemy lines taking care of our injured.

"Dimitri, you'll be with me on the ground with the rest of our men. We'll divide ourselves into two groups, an east flank and a west flank. If we can sneak up behind the Salkovs on either side, we'll be able to cut them off with a pincer maneuver. Pyotr, how's your aim?"

I shrug my shoulder. "I'm a decent shot, but it's been a long time since I had any practice."

"That'll have to do. We're short on firepower, so it's all hands on deck. You'll be stationed here." Mikhail taps the map, indicating a tall high rise a few blocks away from an important storage warehouse that belongs to the Antonovs. "You can pick them off from afar and call out movements. You'll be our eyes out there."

"You got it."

"What can I do to help?" Alina asks. She stands her ground when Mikhail casts her a scrutinizing look.

"You're with me," I tell her. "If I'm going to be sniping our enemies, I'll need a spotter. Plus, I'd rather you stay away from the majority of the action. You'll be safe at my side."

She nods. "Alright then."

"Let's move out," Mikhail says. "Everyone get ready. This is going to get messy. Pyotr, Alina... You two come with me."

I'm not sure what my brother has in mind for us, but we follow his orders regardless. He takes us down the hall and down the stairs to his basement. The door is locked, but he has a key in his pocket to grant him access.

"I tell the kids it's just storage down here," he says.

When we descend the stairs and see what he has hidden away, everything suddenly becomes clear. He's got a bunker down here, practically a private armory full of a wide range of weapons. Everything is securely mounted on the walls—machine guns, pistoles, rifles. There's also a little security station set up, several monitors hooked up to show the live feeds from all the security cameras posted around his property. It's no wonder he doesn't let his kids down here. Mikhail turns to Alina.

"You're going to be Pyotr's eyes and ears. He may be able to see and help us from afar, but his own view of his surroundings will be narrow when he's looking down the scope." Mikhail hands her a pair of binoculars. "You must protect him. I would do it myself, but I'm needed on the ground. I'm trusting you with a very important job, do you understand?"

Alina nods, holding the binoculars tightly to her chest. "I understand."

"And you," he says, turning to pick a rifle from its mount. Mikhail hands it to me but says nothing. A silent conversation passes between us, his message conveyed in a single look. *Be careful.*

I take the weapon from him with a nod. This is it, the moment of truth.

There's no going back now.

CHAPTER 36

PYOTR

Moscow from above is an intimidating sight. The buildings are tightly compact, the streets organized in neat rows and columns. The urban density makes for a challenging landscape, but we've thankfully chosen a vantage point that gives me a wide depth of field. I can see the warehouse clearly from here, and thanks to the scope attached to the rifle, I can clearly make out the movement of not only the Salkovs, but our own men.

The wind is harsh tonight, bringing with it an abnormal chill. I'm lying down with the rifle braced against my shoulder, trigger finger at the ready. My heart beats steadily, and my breathing is even. I'm surprisingly calm, all things considered. After our showdown with Konstantin all those years ago, I thought for sure my fighting days were over. I don't like the thought of having to take a life, but I know for a fact the Salkovs have no qualms about killing my family.

It may be harsh, but it has to be done.

Beside me, Alina shifts. The gravel covering the rooftop crunches beneath her boots. She has a pair of binoculars up to her eyes as she scans the horizon, looking for anything suspicious that could thwart our plans. What we're doing here is risky, but my faith in Alina is unshakeable. If she says Violetta will follow through with her plan of action, then I believe her. We can't afford to back out now.

"There's a whole fleet of cars coming," she says breathlessly. "Hold your fire, though. Mother's cars are all bulletproof. You'd be wasting ammo."

"Copy that," I mumble. "How many do you count?"

"Three groups, each with roughly fifteen cars. They're getting out now."

"Stay low, lyubimaya. Be mindful of the glint of your binoculars."

Alina settles beside me on her knees, peeking over the edge. Even though she hasn't said anything, I can sense her unease in the way her body trembles and her voice hitches in the back of her throat. I can't blame her. Tensions are high. If one thing goes wrong, it could be the end of the Antonovs once and for all.

I exist in a heightened state of being. Like I'm watching everything unfold from outside of my body. The adrenaline coursing through my veins leaves the tips of my fingers and toes tingling. I'm hyper aware of the sound of my breath over the distant wail of police sirens. It's all winding down to this exact moment. The odds are against us, but if there's one thing to be said about the Antonovs, it's that we're fighters. We'll go out kicking and screaming if we have to.

"They're moving in," Alina says on an exhale.

"Steady," I tell her.

It plays out in slow motion. Through my scope, I can see the Salkov men getting out of their vehicles. They're all heavily armed and dressed in thick protective gear. These aren't just gangsters—they're a fucking militia. It's unsurprising given Violetta's resources and seemingly endless finances. They've got rifles and pistols and knives tucked into their boots.

But my family knows how to give as good as we can get. We've faced worse odds. It's time to show the Salkovs we're not to be trifled with.

They move as a coordinated unit, quickly approaching the front gates of the warehouse. They're speedy and efficient, but in their haste to claim the territory, they fail to realize that we've spent the last hour rigging the place to blow. It was a no-brainer to sacrifice the building. We can rebuild a warehouse; we can't bring good men back from the dead.

The moment the first few men try to enter the warehouse, a bomb goes off—courtesy of Natalya Chekov. It was only a few years ago when she tried to kill Dimitri with a car bomb. Her unique skill set has proved useful. The first explosion triggers a chain reaction. Once one bomb goes off, so do the next eight around the property.

It's carnage.

At least half of Violetta's private army is killed or severely maimed in one fell swoop. A pity for them, but a much-needed win for us.

"Your brothers are moving in," Alina informs me.

That's my cue to get ready. While Mikhail, Dimitri, and their few surviving loyalists come in from behind, I've got their backs.

It's difficult to keep track of everyone. There's too much movement, too many gun flashes. I have to remind myself not to panic. The only way I can help my brothers is if I keep a clear head.

Mikhail is pinned down behind an armored vehicle, crouched down low while he shoots blindly around the bend. He doesn't see the Salkov merc coming around from the other side. Mikhail probably can't hear him, so I ready my rifle and breathe in, setting my sights on his attacker.

I pull the trigger.

The violent sound of the gunshot is muffled in my ear. Disorienting. I've managed to take him out. Mikhail keeps moving, making his way to Dimitri a few yards away.

"Two men at one o'clock," Alina informs me.

I adjust my position and find two Salkov soldiers quickly approaching. I tap the trigger once, reload, and shoot again. Both fall, slumping to the cold, hard ground. With the coast clear, Dimitri and Mikhail are able to push forward. I have to remind myself not to celebrate until the war is won, but the hope rising in my chest makes it difficult to do.

This is all working so well...

Too well.

"There's only a handful left," Alina informs me. "We might actually—Pyotr, look out!"

Before I have the chance to react, something hard and heavy is suddenly on top of me. I barely have enough time to blink before a furious fist comes flying down to pummel my face. A mercenary dressed in all black attacks me from above, reaching for the blade attached to his utility belt.

"You motherfucker!" he hisses at me. "I'm going to enjoy gouging your eyes out."

He brings his knife down, but I manage to squirm out of the way just in time. Summoning every ounce of my strength, I throw him off me and scramble to get on top. Our positions are reversed now. He's at my mercy, but not for long. He swings at me, the edge of his blade slicing across my chest, blood dripping from my opened skin.

Damn him. I didn't even hear him coming. Had it not been for Alina, I'd probably be dead.

"Pyotr!" she screams. "Duck!"

I don't hesitate. I roll out of the way just in time to see Alina whip out a gun. She fires two shots, both of which hit our attacker square in the chest. She trembles but keeps a brave face. Staggering to my feet, I approach her carefully, placing my hand over hers to lower the gun. I know that couldn't have been easy for her.

"Are you okay?" she asks, sniffling back her tears.

"Yes, all thanks to you—"

All of a sudden, five more Salkov soldiers storm through the building's roof entrance, their weapons drawn and ready to fire. I'm running purely on instincts now. I snatch Alina's hand and drag her behind the building's water tank. A series of pipes and large ventilation fans are close to take cover behind, but we won't be able to hide forever. The Salkovs must have realized there was a sniper picking them off from afar and have come to deal with the problem.

Alina's eyes are wide and full of fear. "What are we going to do?"

It's five on two, though I'm not going to risk putting Alina in a head-to-head fight, so it's more like five on one. Our priority is to escape. If I can clear the way, maybe Alina can make it out of here in one piece. At this point, I don't even care if something happens to me as long as my wife and the child she's carrying make it out alive.

"Wait for my signal," I whisper to her. "And no matter what, know that I love you."

She frowns. "Don't say that like it's a goodbye."

I kiss her on the lips quickly before getting up and rounding the corner, leaving her well-hidden and out of the way.

The Salkovs are still searching for us, but they're not doing as thorough a job as they could be. I remind myself that these aren't actually well-trained soldiers. They're just run-of-the-mill gangsters running around with their overpowered toys. They know nothing about strategy, only point and shoot—something I can take advantage of.

Keeping low, I take stock of their weapons. They're all armed with Makarov pistols. I have one of my own in New York. It's a common weapon, and the magazines hold twelve bullets—and maybe one in the spout. What this really is, is a numbers game. If I can get them to waste their bullets, then maybe I'll have bought us enough time to get out of here.

Crouching down, I gather a handful of gravel. The pebbles are cold and damp against my palm. From my hiding spot, I pick up a single pebble and toss it as hard as I can toward the other side of the roof. It clinks off a ventilation hood, drawing the Salkovs' attention.

Two of them fire blindly, wasting up to five shots before they realize nobody's there.

"Hold your fire, idiot!" one of them snaps.

They're all skittish. Good. This will work in my favor.

I pick another pebble and toss it elsewhere. Again, they fire in the same direction as the sound. While they freak out, I'm mentally counting the number of bullets remaining.

"Where the fuck are you?" one of the Salkov soldiers screams.

"Come out, you fucking cowards!"

"I knew it. The Antonovs are fucking pussies!"

I let their insults wash right off my back. I won't be goaded into making a mistake. This time, I let them stew in their own uncomfortable silence. I can tell they're getting agitated because their insults become much more colorful and vile. They fan out, searching the area slowly with their weapons drawn. They've left the rooftop entrance wide open—perfect.

From where I'm hidden, I catch Alina's eye. I point to the door, a silent signal to run. She nods, albeit hesitantly, before moving toward the exit as quiet as a mouse. Only once she makes it do I start to follow.

The cold, hard tip of a gun jams into the base of my skull.

"Nice try, Antonov."

Fuck.

Slowly, I rise with my hands up in surrender. That's the second time tonight I've allowed myself to be snuck up on. If only my hearing were better, I would have heard the guy coming.

"Any last words?" the Salkov brute asks me.

I take a deep breath. I don't see Alina. All I can do is pray she has enough sense to leave me behind. "I sure as hell wouldn't waste them on the likes of you."

"Fine by me, asshole."

I hear the cocking of his gun, the pull of the pistol's hammer. This is it. My only regret is that I didn't get to spend the rest of my days with Alina and our child. I could have given our family a good life, full of laughter and love. What I wouldn't give to hold her in my arms one last time...

"Do svidaniya, Antonov."

I squeeze my eyes shut and wait for the inevitable pain. The nothingness that follows.

It never comes.

"Get your fucking hands off my husband!" Alina screams, as she raises her pistol and points it at his chest.

CHAPTER 37

ALINA

It was a shitty idea and an even shittier plan, but I wasn't about to watch him blow my husband's brain out.

I pray the man can't see how shaky my hand is, the gun heavy. My finger is on the trigger, and I will pull it if he makes me.

"Listen," he begins, a smarmy smile on his face as he raises his hands. "I'm going to turn and walk away. I won't turn back, and I won't tell the others where you are."

I sense a trick, but before he can do whatever he's thinking about doing, Pytor rushes at him, slams into his body, and tosses him over the ledge. He almost goes with him, flailing his arms to keep his balance. I race over and grab his shirt, yanking him backwards. We both hit the ground hard.

The solider screams as he falls over the edge of the building. He screams and screams and screams until—he comes to an abrupt stop.

Several gunshots rip through the air, and luckily Pyotr and I are huddled on the ground. He quickly asks if I'm alright, I nod, and we get back in the fight. We dispatch with the few men on the roof. I feel sickened and guilty, but I know it's us or them. I can't lost Pyotr or the baby inside me, so I push the guilt away.

We stand together, panting, thinking the situation is over for the moment, when a lone gunman rushes out from behind where he'd been hiding, bullets flying as he shoots wildly. Pyotr pushes me behind a wall, his arm lifted as he squeezes the trigger. The man falls with one shot.

"Alina, are you alright?"

My heart is pounding as I run my hands over his chest. Nodding, the relief I feel is overwhelming, manifesting itself in shoulder-shaking sobs. I cry his name, clutching his bloody shirt. He wraps his arms around me, my own personal safety blanket as he peppers my face and hair with kisses.

"Fuck," he grumbles.

"He was going to kill you!" I counter.

"I love you, Alina. So fucking much."

I'm not sure whether I laugh or cry or if the sound out of my mouth is an odd combination of both. "I love you, too, Pyotr."

There's no telling how much time passes. It all seems rather moot at this point. All I care about is the fact that we're both alive—albeit battered and traumatized. As I look around the rooftop, I see the four remaining Salkov thugs still and unconscious. We won our little battle.

"Any news from your brothers?" I ask shakily.

"No."

We struggle to our feet. My legs are jelly. I think it's going to take me a while to come down from this particular thrill ride. Only a few seconds ago, I was about to make peace with my own death.

I stumble over and pick up the binoculars I dropped. My hands won't stop trembling, which makes it difficult to gather my bearings. Once I have the warehouse in view, I take in the chaos. The building is up in smoke. Bodies litter the ground. The flash of red and blue lights and the wail of sirens draws ever nearer.

"I don't see Mikhail or Dimitri anywhere," I squeak. "You don't think they—"

"Fuck," Pyotr hisses. "We need to get out of here. We agreed to rendezvous at our checkpoint. We have to go right now."

I nod numbly. My heart is beating so hard and fast I can feel my pulse vibrating my teeth. "Right," I mutter breathless. "Can we please get off this damn roof?"

Pyotr takes my hand. "Let's go."

"Wait!" I say hastily, spotting something strange out of the corner of my binoculars. "Is that..."

A black SUV is parked about a block away from the warehouse. It hasn't moved since arriving, and now I see why. I spot a familiar figure standing just outside the car door, screaming her head off at a few of her guards. She looks *pissed*.

Violetta.

"What is it?" Pyotr asks.

"It's my mother. I think she knows she's lost."

"What is she doing?"

"Getting in her car. I think she's going to try and get away."

She slips into the car, and I can see her frantic gesturing through the windows. Her driver peels away in a hurry, tires likely screeching as they make their quick getaway. The look on her face is priceless. It's the look of a woman who thought herself indestructible only to crumble into a heap. Her hubris landed her in this situation. She never saw me as a threat, and that was her mistake. All it took was a little outmaneuvering, and her entire operation has fallen apart.

"We can't let her escape," Pyotr says. "The only way to end this once and for all is to capture her."

I gulp. "And then what?"

The question hangs in the air like an ax waiting to drop. I'm not an idiot. I know what my husband is implying. Violetta can't get away, but if we capture her... the Antonovs will likely want her dead. I'm pretty sure they'll want to put a bullet between her eyes themselves to be doubly sure she's no longer a threat.

I do not love my mother. All my life, she's tormented me. I hate the woman with every fiber of my being... But do I want her dead?

"We'll worry about it after, Alina," Pyotr tells me. "Right now, we need to go after her. The car's still downstairs."

"Okay," I mumble. "Let's go."

CHAPTER 38

PYOTR

Driving through Moscow is already a pain and a half on a good day. Driving through Moscow after a massive shootout between two rival Bratvas is understandably next to impossible.

The cops are everywhere, along with ambulances and fire trucks. The streets are congested, impossible to navigate. It feels like a warzone. Violetta really picked the perfect time for a car chase. She's only a few cars ahead, her driver weaving in and out haphazardly. I'm not sure if she knows we're tailing her, but we're going to lose her at this rate. Too many cars are in the way, too many panicked bystanders. If only we could predict where she's going...

A lightbulb goes off in my head.

I hand Alina my phone. She's seated in the passenger seat. "Call Luka."

She does as I ask, putting the call on speaker so I can focus on barreling through the streets at top speed. Violetta's vehicle is really legging it. They must know they're in deep shit.

My little brother answers on the second dial tone. "Dude, it's four in the afternoon, I'm *sleeping*."

"Then wake up!" I snap. "It's life or death over here. I need you to track a car for me."

"Hold on, hold on." There's some shuffling in the background, probably Luka rolling out of bed. I hear the telltale sign of his computer whirring to life. "Okay, I've got the grid up on my computer. It's going to take me a second to access the network."

"Make it quick. We're running out of time."

"Do you know if the target has a phone on them? It might be easier to triangulate their exact location."

"Yes, it's my mother's phone," Alina says before promptly giving the number. "I didn't know you could track them in real time."

"All in a day's work," Luka replies. I can practically hear the smug grin he's wearing. "Alright, I'm locked on and I'm in the grid network, too."

"I need you to give us all greens," I tell him, laying onto the gas pedal. "Clear the way for us until we're out of the city."

I hear the *click click clack* of his keyboard in the background. "You've got about thirty seconds before the system boots me out. You should be free and clear once you're outside the city limits and on the highway."

"Thanks, Luka," Alina says.

"Good luck."

Just like that, every intersection ahead of us suddenly turns from red to green. Cars move forward freely like an unstoppable current. I've got my eyes trained on Violetta's car. It's really flying now, but I'm as determined as ever to catch up. I'm not going to let that woman get away. After everything she's done, I'll make sure she faces justice.

By the time we get to the outer limits of the city, there's no question we're following them. We're the only other vehicle on the road chasing them down at top speed. When I see one of the men roll down their window and stick a gun out to fire at us, I have to swerve to the right to avoid taking a bullet head on.

"They're shooting at us!" Alina screams.

"Shoot back!" I tell her over the roaring engine.

This is nuts. Crazy. We've only got a quarter of a tank of gas left. If we don't put an end to this soon, Violetta will get away. We can't afford to lose her. If she manages to slip through our fingers, there's no telling what kind of havoc she'll wreak upon us in her revenge.

I keep the car steady, narrowly missing bullets as Alina sticks her arm out of the window and fires the gun. She's out of practice, something that shouldn't matter, and won't ever matter again. I'll keep her out of this life after this is all over.

As we speed down the road, she shoots a few more times, which does deter the man from shooting at us. Luck is on our side when a car pulls out in front of Violetta's forcing the SUV to jerk to the right.

The driver loses control, and they hit a pothole, which sends the vehicle careening off the road and into a ditch. It flips onto its roof, the windows breaking and showering its occupants with shards of glass. The engine smokes and sputters out, hazard lights blinking on and off uselessly.

I bring our own car to the side of the road and come to a stop. I look at Alina and say, "Stay here."

"I'm going with you," she answers defiantly. Her stubbornness is both endearing and maddening.

We get out of the car together and approach carefully. The wreckage is horrifying. The driver is dead, eyes still open in shock. Two guards sit in the back, both breathing but unconscious. Even from this distance, I can see bones sticking out in various spots. And Violetta...

The woman coughs and groans as she undoes her seatbelt, body slumping onto the roof of the overturned car. She crawls out of the broken window, glass piercing her palms and knees. She doesn't notice us in her disorientation, so she struggles for a few feet to get away from the scene of the accident.

Her eyes are bloodshot. Her hair is stringy with sweat and blood. It's an incredibly dark night, but the dim silver moonlight gives away the broken bridge of her nose and her shattered teeth. Violetta barely has enough strength to stand on her own two feet. Instead, she collapses onto her back, lying helplessly in the muddy roadside ditch.

She notices us then, her face twisting with hate. "*You.*"

Alina remains at my side, her own expression impassable. "Hello, Mother."

The tables have turned; victory has never been more delicious.

Violetta looks like a kicked dog. Defeated, alone, and scared. I can't speak on Alina's behalf, but damn if it isn't time for this woman's comeuppance.

"Little bitch" she seethes, her words slurred by broken teeth. "I should have known you'd side with them. How could you betray your own family?"

"You're one to talk. How could you treat your own family like shit?"

Violetta cackles. It's a truly awful, wet sound from the back of her throat. "Because you're not mine."

I look at Alina; her eyes are wide with shock. "What?"

The woman tries to roll her eyes but winces in pain instead. "Your father had a mistress. You're a bastard. I would have put you out of my house when he died, but he'd made provisions against that in his will."

Alina takes a deep breath, her lips curling into disgust. "So that's why you were so cruel? Because I wasn't your child?"

"You were in the way."

Alina's green eyes turn glossy with the threat of tears. "You're a monster."

"And you're a waste of fucking oxygen!" Violetta screeches, though there is little power in it. "It would have been better if you'd never been born in the first place."

I take a step forward, gun at the ready. I've heard more than enough. "You will never speak to my wife like that again."

"What are you going to do, Pyotr? I thought you didn't dirty your hands with Bratva business."

I cock my pistol. "I can make an exception."

Alina reaches out and sets her hand over my own, lowering the gun. "Don't, Pyotr. She's not worth it."

"I'd let him shoot me, if I were you," Violetta cackles. "If you don't kill me now, I'm only going to come back and make your life a living hell. This won't be the last you hear of the Salkovs. As long as I live and breathe, you'll never know a moment's rest."

I regard Alina carefully. I can see how brave my wife is being despite everything. The anger, the hurt, the anguish I feel is all on her behalf. "She's right, Alina," I say softly. "If we let her live, she'll only come back to haunt us."

Her brows knit together into a steep frown. "I hate her, I do. But I can't kill her, either."

"Even after all the pain she's put you through?"

Alina shakes her head. "Violence breeds violence, Pyotr. Let it end here. If we kill her, she wins."

My hand falls to my wife's belly. "Think of our future, lyubimaya. All it would cost is a bullet to ensure our family's safety."

"There has to be another way."

I sigh. I can't argue with my wife's soft heart. Perhaps she's right. We can't allow Violetta to force our hand and turn us into willing murderers.

"I'm all ears, Alina. If you can think of something, then it's up to you."

Alina is quiet for a very long time. She disappears within herself, within her own thoughts. "I heard a rumor a long time ago," she says slowly, staring at her mother as she speaks. "Tell me more about The Pit."

CHAPTER 39

ALINA

The Pit is a lot brighter and more welcoming than I imagined. Growing up, I'd heard the most horrific stories about this place. I imagined it to be a dirty, grimy, dark place with rusted metal bars for cells, rats sneaking around corners, and the constant smell of mold and damp.

Imagine my surprise when I walk into a building so clean and white it feels like I've walked into a high-tech facility. That's what it is, I suppose, a fancy prison meant for the criminally insane—and the Antonovs most notorious enemies. Often, they are one and the same.

I lose count of how many floors we descend. The elevator takes us deep into the earth, far enough down there's next to no cell phone signal. The walls are a pristine white, the floors are polished white linoleum, and the ceiling is a seemingly endless sea of fluorescent light panels. It's abnormally quiet here, nothing but the hum of the ventilation and the dull buzz of the lights. I feel like I've walked into an alternate dimension, completely cut off from the outside world and where time stands perfectly still.

The Antonov brothers don't utter a word as we take the elevator down. Mikhail and Dimitri keep their eyes forward. They managed to make it out of the battle unscathed thanks to Pyotr's sniping efforts. Beside me, my husband has a protective hand on the small of my back. He's rigid, a sign he's more nervous than he lets on. I suppose I can't blame him. It was my idea to see Violetta one last time before we fly back to New York.

I'm not here to rub it in her face or to hope for an apology. Violetta isn't the kind of woman to ask for forgiveness, so I don't plan to give her any. The reason I'm here is for some closure, to see her safely locked away for my own peace of mind.

We finally arrive at her floor. My ears pop due to the difference in air pressure. I can't believe this place is even real. It makes me wonder what other tricks the Antonovs have up their sleeves. We step onto the floor and make our way down the hall. A series of cameras are mounted to the ceiling, watching and recording our every move. When we reach Violetta's door, it takes both Mikhail and Dimitri to unlock it, each inputting their own codes into a number pad to my right.

We enter without pomp or circumstance.

A thick glass wall separates me from Violetta's chamber. Holes are drilled into the glass, not just for air flow, but so we can speak freely. While comfortable, her cell is a far cry from the luxuries she's so used to at home. No fancy clothes, no luxurious four-post bed, no bathtub to soak in.

Violetta's been forced into a plain white shirt and paper-thin pants. Her bed is nothing more than a raised mattress in the corner. And her bathroom facilities are out in the open, toilet and shower visible from all angles of the room. It's a prison cell befitting a megalomaniac like her.

"Come to gloat?" she hisses at me.

"Yes," I answer coldly.

"I'm going to get out of here one day, you know. And when that day comes, you're all going to regret it."

I must look worried because Pyotr dips down to murmur in my

ear. "There's no way out of this place. She's all talk. No one has ever escaped the Pit before, and that'll never change."

The warmth and proximity of his body fills me with relief. I don't know what I did to deserve a man like Pyotr, but I'm glad I have him. In a world that has been nothing but cold to me, he is my one and only protector. In many ways, I'm strangely thankful to Violetta. Arranging my marriage to Pyotr was ultimately the kindest thing she ever did for me.

"You can tell yourself whatever you want," I say calmly. I'm emboldened by the thick sheet of bulletproof glass between us. Violetta will never get her hands on me again, and that thought alone is truly liberating. "I just wanted to take one last look at you before I go home."

"Home," Violetta scoffs. "What home?"

"To New York with my husband. While you're in here rotting away, I'll be far, far away and thriving."

"You little bitch. You think you can get away from me that easily?"

"I *know* I can."

"Mark my words, Alina, I'll be your worst fucking nightmare."

I shrug my shoulders. "Save your breath, Violetta. You don't scare me anymore." The corners of my lips tug up into a confident smile. "Goodbye and good riddance," I say, before turning on my heel and walking out the way I came.

I adore my nieces and nephews. They're all energetic balls of energy, chaos incarnate, and I love it.

We're gathered in Mikhail's backyard, enjoying the sunshine and warm weather. It's almost hard to believe only a week ago, we thought we were in for the fight of our lives. There's no talk about the Bratva war, no discussion about how the Antonovs were not only able to take back the territory they'd lost, but the glorious addition of Salkov territory, as well. The Antonov Bratva have taken over Moscow completely but talk of rebuilding can wait until tomorrow.

For now, we celebrate.

"I know it's a little early for a baby shower," Aurora says as she hands me a gift wrapped box, "but I want you and Pyotr to have this."

I can't stop smiling. In the little time I've gotten to know them, Aurora and Natalya have become more like sisters than my actual sisters. Well, half-sisters, it would seem. I wonder if Oksana, Nikita, and Yasemin know the truth, that we didn't share a mother. It would certainly explain why they never came to my defense or treated me with much kindness. I push them out of my thoughts. That's all in the past now. What matters is what's ahead of me.

I open the box and find a baby mobile inside. It's beautifully crafted and designed in the shape of stars and planets. When the mobile rotates, it plays the soft notes of *Twinkle Twinkle Little Star*.

"It's beautiful," I say. "Thank you so much."

"Open mine next!" Natalya says excitedly, handing me a present of her own.

I tear into the gift wrap and pull out several pairs of little baby shoes in a wide range of sizes. "They're so cute!"

"Babies grow *really* fast, so here's hoping there's a pair for each stage of their development. Most of your money is probably going to go toward diapers and clothes, so I figured I could help you get a head start."

"Thank you both so much. This is amazing."

"We'll make sure to visit once the baby arrives," Aurora says. "I can't wait for another niece or nephew to spoil."

"Have you thought of names yet?" Natalya asks. "I have a book full of baby names lying around somewhere."

I laugh. "I don't even know if it's a boy or a girl yet. I'm sure Pyotr and I will think of something soon, though."

My gaze naturally finds Pyotr standing with his brothers by the deck. They've got a barbecue going, roasting burgers and hotdogs over a hot grill. I find him watching me with nothing but adoration in his eyes.

"God, that's so weird," Aurora comments with a laugh.

"What?" I ask.

"Seeing Pyotr smile. In all the years I've known him, I didn't think it was possible."

A giggle bubbles past my lips. "I must bring it out of him."

"Boy, I'll say."

"Are you sure the two of you can't stay a while longer?" Natalya asks.

I nod. "You know Pyotr. Always down to business. It's a miracle he's lasted this long being away from CyberFort. I'm sure he's eager to get back to work. Luka's been managing things in his place, but I'm sure my husband would much rather be running things himself."

As if on cue, Pyotr arrives with a plate full of fresh fruit for me. He sits on the wooden arm of the chair I'm in, leaning down to press a kiss to the top of my head.

"I just got a call," he informs me. "Our flight is scheduled for first thing in the morning."

I smile up at him, my heart full and my soul soothed. "I can't wait," I tell him.

CHAPTER 40

PYOTR

"This feels familiar," I mumble as we board my private jet. The last time Alina and I were on this plane was the day we were leaving Moscow after our rushed wedding at city hall.

Alina laughs as she takes her seat. "Do you think we'll have to deal with turbulence this time?"

"Probably."

"I guess you'll have to hold me tight."

"With pleasure, wife."

It isn't long before we take off. The jet engines roar to life as we go speeding down the runaway. Alina excitedly watches out the window as we take off, Moscow becoming smaller and smaller the higher we ascend. We're well above the clouds now. There's something almost wistful in her green eyes, a look of bittersweet contemplation.

"Are you going to miss it?" I ask her. "Maybe get a little homesick?"

She shakes her head. "No. My home is with you."

I can't help but chuckle. "Come here, lyubimaya."

Alina undoes her seatbelt and crosses the short distance between our seats, settling onto my lap with a kittenish smile. I cradle her in my arms, breathing in the wonderful scent of lavender I've come to know and love.

"What's going to happen now?" she asks, resting her cheek against my shoulder.

"Now, I'm going to take you back to New York. I'm going to love you and our child with every ounce of my being. You two are my only priority."

I adore the way her face turns pink. There's honestly nothing cuter than when she blushes. I think it's the way her nose scrunches up when she's embarrassed, or the way Alina can barely look me in the eye when I shower her with compliments. She's just so precious, my gorgeous wife. I'll happily spend the rest of my life finding new ways to make her blush.

"So," she says, nibbling on her bottom lip. "We have ten hours to kill. I wonder how we should pass the time."

My eyes flit down to her lips. She's deliberately baiting me, but I don't care. I don't think I can keep my hands off her for a second longer.

"Have you ever heard of the mile high club?" I ask her suggestively.

Alina giggles, her cheeks turning an even brighter red. "Oh, Pyotr..."

"Is that a no?"

She circles her arms around my neck and presses her lips to mine. "I had no idea my husband was such a daredevil," she says, smiling into our kiss. "How exactly do we join?"

I grip her hungrily by the hips, helping her get settled on my lap. "Just like this."

We quickly devolve into a tangle of arms and legs. The high altitude and thin oxygen make for a surprisingly delightful experience. I'm delightfully dizzy, totally consumed by my craving for her.

"Thank God I can afford a private jet," I grumble against the crook of her neck, my hands slipping beneath her shirt hastily.

"Why?" she asks breathlessly, rolling her hips against my growing erection.

"Because I want my pretty wife naked and riding my cock, and I'm grateful for the privacy."

The smile she gives me is downright mischievous. "Are you ready to roll about my cabin?"

I throw my head back and laugh. It's so cheesy and awful it's hilarious. "Fuck, I love you."

She laughs with me. "I love you, too."

After that, it's all blur. All I care about is taking off her clothes and putting my lips on her. I toss her shirt to the floor, unhook bra, and immediately dive in to mouth at her perfect breasts. I tease her nipples with my tongue, sucking hard enough to leave marks all over her skin. I'm consumed by my need for her. She tastes so sweet, is so addicting. How I managed to survive this long without her is a mystery to me.

Her jeans and underwear go next. She straddles my thighs, completely naked. My eyes drink in every inch of her delicate body, every wondrous curve of exposed skin. I grab her ass, grip her thighs. When I slip a hand between her folds, my fingers come away wet with her desire.

"Pyotr..."

"So fucking beautiful. It's enough to drive me crazy."

She grinds against my hand, seeking her own pleasure. Her movements are incredibly sexy, and it drives me crazy how sensitive she is to my touch. "Oh, that feels good. Take your clothes off, Pyotr, I want to feel you against me."

"You've got two working hands," I say, nipping at her collarbone as she continues to gyrate her hips. "Get to work, wife. These buttons aren't going to undo themselves."

She groans but doesn't complain. With trembling fingers, she starts at the very top and undoes my first button. She's about to move onto the one just below, but I slide my fingers over her clit, teasing her sensitive bud.

"*Oh!*"

"Did I tell you to stop, wife?"

She laughs lightly. "You're such a tease, husband."

"Is that so? Well, let's see how you fair when I do *this*." I slip my hand down and slide a finger into her, gesturing in a beckoning motion so I can seek out her sweet spot. I'm pretty sure I find it because Alina all but jumps off my lap with a languid moan. I wrap my free arm around her waist and hold her against me, relishing the way her body trembles with pleasure.

"Pyotr, *fuck—*"

"That's the idea, lyubimaya. Keep at it. This shirt isn't going to undo itself."

Alina tries, *really* tries. My sweet girl manages to work her way down, clumsily shoving my shirt open with a deep moan. I insert another finger, adoring the way her pussy clenches around me, her walls fluttering around my knuckles.

"Pyotr, *please...*" She grips my shoulders for support. "Please, I need you inside me."

"I *am* inside you. I don't understand what you mean."

"Your cock—" she gasps, moans, whines. "I want your cock inside me."

"Then undo my belt and take it out yourself. I'm enjoying your pussy too much to do anything."

Alina huffs, fumbling with my belt and zipper. I'm so hard it's bordering on painful, but relief is instant the moment she wraps her fingers around my erection and frees me from the confines of my pants.

"Move your fingers," she demands, her desperation causing her voice to go high and squeaky. "I want to ride you."

I click my tongue. "What happened to your manners, Alina? What's the magic word?"

"Please! Please move your hand I need to—"

I remove my fingers and bring them to her lips. "Open."

She does as I ask, parting her lips so I can run my fingers over her tongue. She moans as she sucks, tongue flicking over my digits hungrily.

"Do you like how you taste?" I grin at her. "Such a good girl. Go on, Alina. Ride my cock while you suck on my fingers."

The sound that escapes her is enough to make me feral. It's a cross between a moan and a gasp, so delightfully sexy it sends a shiver down my spine. Alina spreads her legs for me and lowers herself onto my cock, her slick heat surrounding me as I bury myself deeper and deeper inside.

My wife truly is a sight to behold. Never in a million years did I think I'd need another person this badly. I know Alina and I didn't have the most conventional of starts, but I wouldn't have had it any other way. Because now she is mine and I am hers, and when I'm with her, I have everything I need.

She rises and falls, seeking her pleasure. Her moans are enough to shake the entire cabin. I'd gladly drown in the sounds she makes, basking in the brilliance of her smile until I no longer have the strength to do so.

"Pyotr, I'm gonna—I think I'm going to come."

"Go ahead, my darling. Let me feel that tight pussy."

Alina screams my name as she reaches her climax, her eyes screwing shut as wave after wave of ecstasy wracks her body. Her pussy clenches around me, gripping me tight. It's almost enough to send me flying right after her, but I'm nowhere near done with her.

All it takes is a press of a button to make the seat I'm in recline. It's not nearly as comfortable as a bed, but considering where we are, it's the next best thing. I grip Alina tight against me and roll, switching our positions so I'm on top. She laughs softly as she reaches for me, cupping my face to drag me down for a kiss.

It's my turn to set the pace, my hips snapping against her in search of that sweet friction. She takes me so well, our bodies intertwined like two pieces of a puzzle. I can't remember what life was like without her. Did I ever truly know happiness until I found her?

"You feel so good, Alina. It's like you were made for me."

"Pyotr," she whines my name. "Pyotr, I'm going to come again."

I smile into our next kiss. It's bruising and possessive, like it's the only way we know how to exist. Before long, I feel her walls flutter around my shaft. Her breathing quickens and becomes shallow. The moan that rips from her lungs sends me spiraling after her.

In this moment, everything makes sense. Every decision I made, every step I took... it was all meant to lead me to her. Alina—my wife, the mother of my child, the only woman I've ever truly loved. She completes me in ways I didn't think were possible. She keeps me grounded, brings a lightness to my life I didn't know was missing.

We lie there together, curled up in each other's arms, smiling and giggling like naughty school children.

"That was exhilarating," she admits.

"If that's the case, I've got good news."

"Oh?"

"We have nine more hours until we arrive in New York."

She beams at me, her smile so radiant it's almost blinding. "I love the sound of that."

CHAPTER 41

ALINA

I'm so nervous I think I might be sick.

I fiddle with the hem of my dress. Adjust my hair. Take a deep breath. Then start all over again. I don't know how Pyotr is able to stay so calm. He sits beside me, totally unfazed, as he scrolls through his phone and checks his various emails. Meanwhile, I feel like I'm about to fly out of my seat, leaving nothing but a gross puddle of sweat where I once was.

"Should we run over our practice questions again?" I ask under my breath.

Pyotr reaches up to adjust the volume on his hearing aid. "What did you say, lyubimaya?"

"I asked if we should go over our practice questions. You know, just to be sure?"

He chuckles softly, reaching over to take my hand. He threads his fingers between mine and squeezes lightly. "Relax, Alina. We've got this."

"How can you be so sure?"

"Because I know you and you know me, and we love each other.

There isn't a thing I don't know about you and vice versa. You have nothing to worry about, my love."

I shift uncomfortably. "No, I know, but what if the interrogator gives us a trick question or something? What if I remember incorrectly? I don't want to go back to Russia, Pyotr."

He lifts my hand to his lips and kisses the back of my fingers. "If they deport you back to Moscow, then I'll drop everything to be with you. We can live our lives there if we have to."

My cheeks warm. "You'd really do that for me?"

"Without question. Now, *breathe*. You won't be able to answer any questions if you're passed out on the floor."

I suck in a slow, deep breath, exhaling only once my lungs begin to burn. It helps, but only a little.

My eyes scan the waiting room. The immigration office downtown is kind of plain. Grey walls, ugly brown carpet, panel lighting above our heads that sort of makes my head hurt. The plants are all made of fake plastic. There's a water cooler in one corner, but the blue water jug is pretty much empty. I don't think any of the staff feel particularly inclined to change it.

There's a whole wall full of informational pamphlets featuring smiling faces and a series of happy couples and families. Most of them have faded from extended exposure to sunlight. Something tells me they don't make for very popular reads.

Outside, the sounds of New York filter in through the small gap in the window. I've grown used to the constant symphony of traffic and the distant rumble of the subway system a few yards below our feet. It's a sunny day, which I'll admit is the only thing keeping my mood from dipping into the realm of sullen. It'll be a nice reward to go for a walk around Central Park after this interview is over.

Provided we pass, of course.

"Mr. and Mrs. Antonov?" calls one of the office assistants.

"That's us," I say, rising to my feet. Pyotr joins me, his hand falling to the small of my back.

We make our way down the hall toward the immigration officer's office. His name is Archie Jenkins, and he looks kind of like a squirrel with glasses. His cheeks are chubby, and his eyes are big and cute. He doesn't seem *too* terrifying, but his chipper appearance does little to settle my nerves.

"Ah, please take a seat," he says, shaking our hands. "I'm sure you're excited to get this interview underway."

I gulp. "Y-yes, we are."

Mr. Jenkins pauses when he looks at Pyotr. "Oh, my! I know you. Weren't you on the cover of *Forbes* last month?"

Pyotr grins, which I've come to learn is his version of blushing. "Yes, that was me."

"I use CyberFort antivirus software on all of my home computers," Archie says proudly. "I've never had a virus in all the years I've been using it."

"I'm glad to hear it," Pyotr says easily, confidently.

We take our seats. I'm even more nervous now than when I was in the waiting room. My heart skips a beat and my stomach flutters when Archie pulls out a file full of documents. He's already received my green card application form and is dutifully scanning over the details.

"This is how this is going to work," he says kindly. "I'm going to ask you both a couple of routine questions. It looks like all your forms have been filled out thoroughly, so I don't suspect we'll run into any trouble."

I smile and nod, waiting on bated breath.

"So, tell me, Alina... Where were you born?"

I clear my throat. "In Moscow."

"And where was your husband born?" he asks me.

"Pyotr was actually born in a city called Kazan, but his family moved to Moscow shortly after. That's where he lived until he moved to America when he was a boy."

"Ah, very interesting. Does your husband have any siblings?"

"Yes. Three brothers. Mikhail's the oldest, Dimitri is Pyotr's fraternal twin, and then there's Luka, the youngest. He actually lives with us."

Pyotr chuckles. "Rent in New York, am I right?"

Archie laughs. "Tell me about it." He shifts through a couple of his papers, taking notes with a ballpoint pen. "So, tell me, how did the two of you meet?"

"Through a family friend," I answer. "My mother set us up, actually. She thought we might make a good match. Turns out, she was right. I think it surprised her, how well we got along."

"And is your mother still in Russia?"

I nod. "Oh, yes. She's not much of an international traveler."

"And how does she feel about you moving away?"

"Disappointed," I answer honestly, but not for the reasons he might think. "But that's how all mothers feel, I'm sure. My older sisters had to move away when they got married, so I'm sure this is nothing new."

Archie looks at Pyotr. "And how many siblings does your wife have, Mr. Antonov."

"Three, as well. Oksana is the eldest, and she lives in Colombia. Nikita is the second eldest, she lives in France. And then there's Yasemin, who lives in Moscow still."

"My, you two have very large families."

I smile. "That we do. And we're starting one of our own."

"Well, congratulations."

I rub my belly instinctively, practically bursting with maternal pride. "Thank you very much. We're very excited."

"How far along are you, if I may ask?"

"A little over four months," Pyotr says. "But we'd like to keep it under wraps. We're not ready for the public to know quite yet."

Archie nods understandingly. "I totally get it, though… I have to bring it up because it's my job, but… those pictures circulating a little while ago. The ones with you and another man in your penthouse—"

"That was an invasion of privacy," Pyotr snaps. "And taken out of context."

I place my hand on his lap, calming him. "Please forgive my husband. He's very protective of me." I take a deep breath. "The truth of the matter is the man I was seen with in those photos was my bodyguard. He was delivering flowers sent to me from Pyotr. Unfortunately, someone decided to cross a line and spread a false narrative to harm our relationship and Pyotr's reputation."

Archie's brow furrows. "How terrible. I guess it's true what they say, you can never believe what you read online."

The tension in my shoulders melt. I feel like the hard part is over. I knew that question would likely come up, so it's a good thing Pyotr and I came prepared. The remainder of Archie's questions are a breeze.

"How many children do you plan on having?"

"Six," I answer.

"Or more," Pyotr adds.

"Who does most of the cooking?"

"I do," I answer. "But when I'm feeling lazy, we just order in."

"Which side of the bed do you sleep on?"

"I sleep on the left," I say. "That way he can hear me."

"Mr. Antonov, does your wife have any allergies?"

"Cat hair."

"And do you know her blood type?"

"O negative."

The next hour is a breeze. There are no more curveballs, just straightforward questions about our daily routines, our habits, our home. By the end of it, I'm feeling as confident as ever. The entire time, Pyotr holds my hand, brushing the pad of his thumb lovingly over my knuckles. His soothing touch is the only thing that keeps me from flying out of my seat when Archie announces we're finally finished.

"Thank you for your time," he says. "You know, I see a lot of couples in the run of the day, but I can tell you without a doubt the two of you seem like a perfect pair."

"Thank you so much." I smile wide. "Uh, what happens now?"

"I'm going to send your forms off for processing. You should receive a follow-up letter and your green card in the coming weeks."

I have to hold back my squeal of excitement. We did it!

Walking out of the building feels like I'm skipping over clouds. The hard part is finally over.

"Let's go get lunch to celebrate," Pyotr says. "What are you hungry for, wife?"

"I have a craving for pickles and ice cream." I laugh at the way my husband's face curls up. "I'm *joking*, Pyotr. How about that pizza place around the corner from us? The one with the brick ovens. We can bring Luka back a few slices."

He wraps an arm around my waist and dips down to kiss me. I'm pretty sure that's a *yes*.

CHAPTER 42

PYOTR

"Have you heard?" Merrybell asks, strolling into my office with purpose. "It's all over the news."

I arch a brow, though I don't look up from my computer screen. I've been buried in paperwork for days, doing my best to keep on top of a new product launch. We have a new antivirus product set to release in the coming days and I need to ensure everything goes smoothly. It's going to be a massive, world-wide update—and I'll frankly be lucky if I only have to deal with a hiccup or three.

"Richard Eaton Jones was arrested today."

That catches my attention. I look up from my screen, trying to force away my smile. "Oh? What a shame."

"Aren't you going to ask what they got him for?"

"I have a pretty good idea, but I have a feeling you're going to tell me anyway."

"They got him on blackmail charges!" she tells me excitedly. "They found hard evidence in his inbox linking him to several hostile takeovers. The DA has everything they need to put him away for many, many years, provided his lawyers don't figure out a way to get them to drop the case, of course."

As happy as I am to hear the news, I don't want to get my hopes up. Richard Eaton Jones is a slimy bastard. I'm sure he'll find a way to weasel his way out of any serious charges, but I find some comfort in the fact his reputation will never recover from a scandal of this size. Will he lose it all? Probably not, but he'll have a hell of a time showing his face in public again. I suppose I'll take a win wherever I can get it.

Merrybell shakes her head in disapproval. "I never liked that man."

"Believe me, nobody does."

"Aren't you running late?" she asks, checking her watch. "Your appointment is in an hour."

"I promised to meet Alina there. I just need to send one more email, and then I'm taking the rest of the day off."

"You must be very excited. You may get to find out what you're having!" My personal assistant looks almost as overjoyed as I feel. "You must tell me how everything goes."

"I will," I promise. "What are you going to do with the rest of the afternoon?"

Merrybell shrugs. "I'm probably going to pop by Ben's apartment to check on him. I really can't thank Alina enough. Please do give her my thanks again, okay?"

I press my lips into a thin line but nod anyway. After Ben was released from the hospital, the police were there to pick him up immediately after. Thankfully for him, Alina changed her story, telling the authorities that instead of helping Violetta kidnap her, Ben tried to protect her and was shot.

I personally wouldn't have stuck my neck out for him. I'm livid just thinking about it, but my wife and her soft heart didn't want to see Ben behind bars. He's still young with the rest of his life ahead of him. Since she wasn't hurt and he was shot in the chest, she figured he's more than learned his lesson.

"You tell him to be on his best behavior," I tell Merrybell.

She gives me a knowing smile. "Believe me, I will."

The first and only question I ask when I get to the doctor's office is, "Where's my wife?"

The nurse gestures down the hall. "I can take you right this way, Mr. Antonov. We've taken her to Exam Room C."

When I enter, Alina greets me with the biggest smile I've ever seen. She's already seated on the exam table, dressed in a paper gown provided to her. We're long overdue for this checkup, which is why I can practically feel her excitement buzzing in the air like an electric current.

"How was work?" she asks me as I step into the room.

I quickly make my way to her side and kiss her tenderly. "It was fine. Numbers, meetings, phone calls. Boring stuff."

She giggles. "Well then, you're in for a real treat."

"I thought our appointment was at two. I didn't want you to be alone."

"They had a last-minute schedule change, so they bumped me up. Don't worry, I wasn't alone for long. You got here ten minutes after I did."

"Still," I mumble.

"If you're so worried about me, maybe you should take a page out of Luka's book and start working from home."

It's definitely a tempting thought. I have a home office I rarely use. It'd be an easy enough transition to make, moving all my important company documents to the penthouse and video calling in for any important meetings. Now that Alina is five months pregnant, I really want to be around in case she needs me. She has an independent streak, always wanting to do things for herself, but I'm incredibly protective of her and our little one. Maybe to a fault, but Alina certainly doesn't seem to have any complaints.

"I'll make it happen," I decide aloud. "Starting Monday, I'll have everything moved."

"Really?" she squeals in delight. "Oh, that makes me so happy!"

I reflect her smile. God, I adore this woman. "It makes me happy, too."

Three soft knocks sound at the door. A short woman with a pink streak in her hair enters with a smile. Dr. Thorne is one of the best OB/GYNs in all of New York. Getting Alina on her list of patients was no easy feat, but I spared no expense and exhausted every contact I had to make sure Alina got in to see her.

"How's Mom feeling today?" Dr. Thorne asks as she makes her way over to the ultrasound machine. "Any discomfort or nausea?"

Alina shakes her head. "It's been smooth sailing."

"That's a lie," I say. "She's been having trouble sleeping."

"Pyotr, I said it wasn't a big deal."

"It's a big deal to me, my love. And she's also been complaining about joint pains."

Dr. Thorne nods knowingly. "Let me guess, trouble staying asleep because of frequent bathroom trips?"

Alina nods bashfully. "I'm convinced the baby thinks my bladder's a trampoline."

"That's perfectly normal. The baby is currently positioned right over that particular area, so I recommend avoiding lots of fluids before bed. As for your joints, that's also perfectly normal since your ligaments are stretching and your bones are moving to prepare for baby to grow. You can take Tylenol if it gets particularly bad."

I nod as I listen, taking careful mental notes.

"Now, let's take a peek, shall we?" The doctor presses a series of buttons on the ultrasound machine, the low *thwub-thwub-thwub* of the device filling the room. After applying a bit of lubrication to Alina's belly, Dr. Thorne presses the wand to her stomach.

I watch in quiet anticipation, almost too afraid to move. I can't make sense of the black and white image on the screen, the shapes too difficult for me to decipher. After moving the wand for a little bit, the doctor settles on a single spot.

"How are things looking?" Alina asks, her voice soft and nervous.

"Perfectly healthy! I count ten fingers and ten toes." The doctor gives us both a coy look. "Are Mom and Dad interested in learning the gender?"

I look at Alina. We've talked about this at length, many sleepless nights spent wondering about whether we're going to have a boy or a girl. My elder brothers all knew ahead of time what their wives were expecting, but a part of me has always liked the idea of waiting it out. I'd be happy with either a boy or a girl, it makes no difference to me. All I care about is that they're happy and healthy, and that I'm there to welcome them into the world.

"We want it to be a surprise," Alina says with a giddy laugh. "It's more fun that way."

The doctor nods. "Well, if that's the case, Baby Antonov is developing very nicely. I'll step out for you to get changed, Alina, and on you way out, you can schedule your appointment for next month. If you change your mind about knowing the gender, just give me a call."

"Thank you, doctor," we say together.

"Well?" Luka asks us the moment we step out of the elevator. "Come on, don't keep me hanging. I bet Dimitri a hundred bucks it's going to be a boy."

Alina laughs. "We didn't ask."

"Are you kidding me?" Luka sighs. "I don't want to wait that long to find out."

I roll my eyes. "Are you hurting for cash?"

"No, I'm just trying to spice my life up."

"You better not let this turn into a gambling habit."

My little brother snorts. "Oh, please. I have more self-control than that. I just want to rub the fact that I'm right in Dima's face."

"I'm going to change into something a little more comfortable," Alina tells me, hopping up on her toes to give me a kiss on the cheek. "But then I can play some piano for you while you cook dinner?"

I kiss her back. "I'd love that. How does chicken fried rice sound?"

She smacks her lips. "*Yum.*"

Alina disappears down the hall, humming contentedly to herself as she leaves my line of sight. I turn to Luka, who's casually leaning against the back of the couch.

"Since I have you," I say, "there's something we need to discuss."

"Uh oh. Am I in trouble?"

I chuckle. "No, Luka, you're not in trouble."

"Then why did you just name drop me? You only ever name drop me when I'm in trouble."

I give him a gentle smile. "Listen, kid... With the baby on the way, I've been thinking..."

"You want me to move out, don't you?" he says, finishing my thought for me.

"There's no rush, of course."

"Nah, it's cool. I've already got a place."

I arch a brow. "You do?"

"Yeah," my brother says, crossing his arms casually over his chest. "I thought it was high time I found a place of my own to get away from all your, uh, *vocal* lovemaking."

I bristle. "I wasn't aware you could hear us."

"Unfortunately, sound carries easily in this place. That's why I signed the lease a month ago."

"Then why are you still living here?"

"What kind of a brother would I be if I didn't mooch off you for the free food?"

I ruffle his hair with a laugh. What would I do without my family?

CHAPTER 43

ALINA

"No peeking."

I sigh. "For the hundredth time, Pyotr, I'm not going to peek."

He knows as well as I do I can't see anything with his big hands covering my eyes. We've been walking for a couple of minutes. I've never had a particularly keen sense of direction, so I'm as lost as can be. The only clues I have to work with are the distant sounds of barnyard animals, the cool evening air as the breeze whistles past, and the lovely scent of roses...

Lots of roses, if I had to guess.

"Pyotr," I say around a light laugh. "Come on, where are you taking me?"

"Just a few more steps," he promises me, his voice a low chuckle in my ear.

"This isn't going to end up being a hike, is it? It'd be cruel to force your pregnant wife to march a long distance when she's only a few weeks away from her due date."

"Trust me, lyubimaya. I would never do that to you."

"Are we there yet?"

"Yes, we are."

I have to blink a few times once his hands fall away, too stunned at what lies before us for my brain to comprehend what's going on. We're facing a field under a pergola in which every square inch is covered in vases full of freshly cut roses. It's practically a sea of red petals, the sweet floral scent filling my nose.

But what captures my attention isn't the thoughtful display, but the grey Trakehner waiting patiently by a nearby post. My eyes immediately swell with tears, my elated heart practically seizing in my chest.

"Polina!" I all but shriek, rushing over to my long-lost mare.

I pat her nuzzle and stroke her mane. I honestly never thought I'd see her again. It's been almost a year since I was forced to leave her. I'm so grateful Violetta didn't go through with her promise to sell Polina for horse meat.

I turn back to Pyotr and find him smiling. "How did you... When did... *Oh my God!*"

"Are you happy?"

"Happy? Pyotr, I'm over the moon!"

"I'm sorry it took so long," he says. "I wanted to surprise you earlier, but it turns out there's a lot of paperwork when it comes to transporting animals of the equine variety."

I can't stop myself from smiling. "I'm really curious to know what your search history looks like."

He chuckles. "Don't ask."

"Do you want to pet her?"

Pyotr steps forward cautiously, eyeing Polina suspiciously. "She's not going to bite my fingers off, is she?"

I throw my head back and laugh. "Not as long as you're careful." I take my husband's hand and bring it up to Polina's neck, showing him how to pet her just the way she likes. "Thank you, Pyotr. This is honestly so amazing."

"Don't thank me just yet. I have something else planned for you."

"You mean there's *more?*"

He gestures behind him toward a table I hadn't noticed. It's covered in little tea lights, their flames flickering against the inky black of the evening sky. A bottle of sparkling apple juice and two dinner plates have been set on the table.

Like a gentleman, Pyotr pulls out my chair and helps me take a seat. I'm smiling so hard my cheeks are starting to hurt.

As he pours me a glass of apple juice, I ask, "So, what's the occasion?"

"Do I need an occasion to spoil my wife?"

"I suppose not. It's just that it's so out of the blue."

"Once the baby arrives, we won't have a lot of time with just the two of us," he says gently. "So I figured why not?"

"Well, consider me pleasantly surprised."

When he smiles at me, there's nothing but adoration in his dark eyes. I wish I never had to blink so I could savor his expression forever. Pyotr is the only man I've ever loved, and grand gestures like these remind me he's not all scowls and business. My husband is a loving man, and I have no doubt he'll also be a doting father. I savor every single one of his smiles, especially the ones for me and me alone.

"Hungry?" he asks me as he takes his seat across from me.

"Famished."

All it takes is a quick glance over his shoulder and someone steps out from the nearby farmhouse. Merrybell hurries over with a tray balanced in her hand, our meals still steaming because they're so fresh. The scent of rosemary and garlic fills my nose, causing my stomach to grumble eagerly in response. Merrybell sets our meals down with a flourish of her hand.

"I hope you enjoy," she says with a big grin.

I giggle. "Did he rope you into this, too?"

"Are you kidding? I *volunteered*. He was going to need all the help he could get to pull this off. Who do you think took care of Polina's transfer?"

"I should have known."

"Merrybell," my husband groans.

"I'll leave you two lovebirds to it."

"You're not going to stay?" I ask.

"Oh, no. It's quite alright. I've got a hot chocolate waiting for me inside, and I'm sure Mr. Antonov has a pressing question to ask you."

Pyotr clears his throat. "Thank you, Merrybell."

I glance at him. "Question? What question?"

Merrybell scurries off with a quick *oops*, but Pyotr doesn't explain further. Instead, he tells me, "Please, enjoy your meal."

I eye him suspiciously. "I'm not going to stop asking until you answer me."

"It's nothing, Alina."

"Then why are you blushing?"

Pyotr huffs. "I'm not blushing."

It's true, he's not. I just wanted to see if I could fluster an explanation out of him. I smirk at him. "What are you hiding?"

Finally, he sighs. "I was hoping we could enjoy dinner first, but I guess this is as good a time as any."

"What are you talking ab—"

Before I can my sentence, Pyotr vacates his chair and gets down on his knee beside me. He reaches into the inside pocket of his suit blazer and pulls out a small, navy-blue ring box covered in soft velvet. He pries the box open to reveal—

Nothing.

To say I'm confused is an understatement. A bemused laugh bubbles past my lips. "I don't understand. What's going on?"

"You're already wearing the ring," he points out, but then his expression suddenly turns grave. "I never got the chance to propose to you, Alina, so I wanted to do it now."

"We're already married, silly."

"That's true, but it wasn't on our own terms. We're about to start a family together… I want us to be able to look back one day and not have any regrets."

I hold my breath. I understand what he means perfectly. Our choice to wed was stripped from us, but now we're calling the shots. Yes, we're already husband and wife, and this proposal is largely symbolic, but that's why it's so important to me. How can I ever begin to describe the love I have for this man? How could I have ever known that the day we got married would be the first step to the rest of my life?

"Alina," he begins, "from the moment I laid eyes on you, I was stunned by your beauty."

"Really?" I ask with a light laugh. "You looked half as terrified as I was."

Pyotr grins. "No, I was mesmerized. There's a difference. I couldn't stop staring at you because I didn't know what I was getting myself into. I thought you deserved so much better." I shake my head, but he continues. "You're smart, you're brave, and you're selfless. When you walk into a room, my whole day immediately gets ten times better. I look forward to every morning I get to wake up beside you, and every evening holding you in my arms. So I'm asking you for real this time. No deals to be made, no peace treaties to uphold... Alina Salkov, I love you. Will you marry me?"

Happy tears well up in my eyes. I'm practically bouncing out of my chair with pure, giddy excitement.

"Yes!" I exclaim, throwing my arms around him.

The momentum throws him off balance and he stumbles back with a hearty laugh. I kiss him, tender and true. When our lips finally break apart, Pyotr takes my hand and kisses the ring already on my finger.

"I love you," he tells me with the biggest smile I've ever seen.

"I love you, too."

I stop, a sudden pain radiating from my stomach. It's not terrible, but certainly unpleasant. Pyotr's face goes blank as he grasps me by the shoulders.

"Alina? What's wrong?"

The voice in the back of my head figures out what's happening before the rest of my body can. "I think... I think my water just broke."

Pyotr's eyes widen. "Are you serious?"

"The baby's coming!"

He laughs and kisses me at the same time, quickly scrambling to his feet and offering me a helping hand. "Merrybell!" he shouts. "Merrybell, the baby's coming!"

The door to the farmhouse bursts open. Merrybell looks like a woman on a mission, car keys already in hand. "Get in the car! I'll call the hospital on the way and the bags are already loaded in the trunk. Let's move, move, *move!*"

If I didn't know any better, I'd say she's more excited than I am.

Pyotr takes my hand and gives me an encouraging nod. "Are you ready, wife?"

I nod back, happy as can be. "I'm ready, husband."

CHAPTER 44

PYOTR

Luka thought it was a little ridiculous. Why hold a wedding ceremony when we're already married? He just doesn't get it.

It's a small ceremony, only a handful of guests—mainly consisting of my family. Regardless, I spare no expense. The location, the flowers, the lights. I want today to be perfect because Alina, frankly, deserves no less.

I stand at the altar, Dimitri at my side. It wasn't hard picking him to be my best man. As my twin, it was an obvious choice.

Merrybell, Aurora, and Natalya are all fawning over my daughter, Ava. She's as cute as a peach. Dare I say it, I think she might be the most beautiful baby in the world. My brothers will likely argue with me if I ever say that out loud, but I know the truth. Nobody can hold a candle to my darling girl.

"Would you relax?" Dimitri says as he claps me on the shoulder. "Why are you more nervous now than when you did this the first time?"

"I just want everything to be perfect," I answer, smoothing out the non-existent wrinkles of my tuxedo. "I want to make sure it lives up to her expectations."

He gives me a knowing smile. "I'm sure it will, Pyotr. Seriously, relax a little. You're supposed to enjoy your wedding day, not end up in the back of an ambulance because you've given yourself a stroke."

I take a deep breath. Always with the dramatics, Dimitri—but I know he's right. I've been so focused on making sure Alina has a good time I've forgotten this is *my* wedding day, too.

When the string quartet I hired switches seamlessly into the bridal march, I tense up. This is it. The moment I've been waiting for since I don't know how long. Alina rounds the corner on Mikhail's arm. The moment I set eyes on her, I can't look away.

She's so beautiful, I want to savor every last gorgeous detail and burn it into my mind so I can think back on this day for the rest of my life.

Her wedding dress hugs her waist and plumes out into a long train, delicate beadwork making the front shimmer in the gentle chapel lighting. The sweetheart neckline accents her delicately long neck and the shape of her face, the cropped sleeves adding to her elegant air. Her locks are done up in graceful spirals, the lace veil sitting atop her head fluttering behind her as she walks.

A literal angel on Earth.

She blushes as she smiles at me. I can practically feel her giddiness radiating off her as she makes her way to the altar. Mikhail graciously kisses her cheek, a gesture of good will.

"Welcome to our family," he says kindly.

"Thank you," she responds before stepping up to take her place across from me. I offer her my hand and guide her onto the small platform, unable and unwilling to take my eyes off her.

"You look stunning," I murmur.

"You're pretty dashing yourself," she teases.

Already, this ceremony is leagues above our first one. There are no startled faces, no obvious signs of distress. We're both here of our own volition to celebrate the love we found in one another. When the officiant steps forward, nobody tells him to cut to the chase, I certainly don't cut him off when he asks if we have vows to exchange.

I was unprepared before, but this is different. This time, I have plenty of promises to make when it comes to the love of my life.

I take her hands and begin. "Alina, I vow to be a good husband to you. I will care for you and I will treasure you, come what may. I hope to spend the rest of my days striving to make you as happy as you do me."

It's Alina's turn. She smiles up at me sweetly, her eyes brimming with tears. "Pyotr, in every sense of the word, you are my savior and protector. I vow to be a good wife to you. I will support you and love you, through thick and thin. I love you so much, and I can't wait to begin the rest of our lives together."

In the front row, Merrybell wipes her eyes. My sisters-in-law also look incredibly misty.

"Now, the exchanging of rings?" the officiant asks.

I slip a new wedding band onto her finger. It's far nicer than the first one I gave her, this one made of white gold and encrusted with a row of delicate little diamonds around the top. This time, she has a ring to give me, too. She takes my hand and slips a matching band of thick white gold around my finger. It feels like a far bigger promise than any oath I could ever utter. The weight of it takes some getting used to, but it also feels great. It's a physical reminder that we belong to each other, no matter what.

"With that," the officiant says, "it's my honor to pronounce you husband and wife. You may kiss your—"

He doesn't even get the chance to finish before I step forward, wrap my arms around Alina's body, and pull her into a bruising kiss. I denied her the first time, but now I'm ready to practically throw myself at her. Nothing tastes sweeter than her lips, nothing makes my heart beat faster than the soft moan escaping her. The rest of the world falls away. I don't hear my family clapping and cheering, I don't care that we've probably been kissing for far too long. I'm going to savor every last moment of our special day, and nobody is going to stop me.

"I love you," I murmur against her lips.

She grins up at me. "I love you, too, Pytor."

"What do you say? Ready for our honeymoon?"

"We're getting a honeymoon? What about the baby?"

I chuckle. "I hired Merrybell to be our nanny. She'll be coming with us to look after Ava, so we won't have to be very far from her."

"Where are we going?" my beautiful wife asks me curiously.

"Wherever you want," I state. "Someplace tropical? Someplace up in the mountains? It's all up to you, lyubimaya."

"Up to me? Goodness, you're spoiling me."

I smirk. "Well, you'd better get used to it."

EPILOGUE

ALINA

I can't remember the last time I was this nervous. My fingers are so cold they're too stiff to move, yet the rest of my body feels like it's hot enough to rival the sun. Peering out from the wing into the crowd is a grave mistake. At least three hundred guests are in attendance tonight, most of them important business and political figures. I heard there were even a couple of bonafide A-list celebrities in attendance. Pyotr's connections are certainly impressive?

Closing my eyes and taking a deep breath, I have to remind myself this is for the greater good. Tonight's charity concert has already raised over a hundred thousand dollars based on ticket sales alone, and every single cent will be put toward CyberFort's educational initiative for inner city youth. We're doing good things here today, and I can't allow my nerves to keep me from stepping onto that stage.

I can't see Pyotr or our little Ava from where I'm standing. The stage lights are too bright, and the rest of the music hall only has floor lights to illuminate the way, so it's difficult to make out any faces. I know they're out there, though. Pyotr promised me he would be front and center, cheering me on.

There's no putting it off any longer. It's my time to shine.

A thunderous applause shakes the room as I walk out onto the stage. It's surprisingly warm under the spotlights, which makes my overheating situation that much more daunting. My palms are clammy, but all it takes is one look out into the crowd—and I see him, front and center.

My husband is only a few feet away, seated comfortably in the first row with our infant daughter in his arms. The stage is elevated by a few feet, so he has to tilt his head up to look me in the eye. He wears a small smile upon his lips, as encouraging as it is sweet. He gives me the smallest, almost imperceptible nod as if he's trying to say *you've got this*.

Our daughter is bundled up in a blanket her aunts, Aurora and Natalya, had made special and sent to us directly from Moscow. She has a full head of dark brown hair courtesy of her father, but she has my big green eyes. She's incredibly well behaved, making only the softest coos, but she's starting to get a little restless based on the way she squirms in Pyotr's arms.

Maybe a little night's music will help soothe her to sleep.

I take a seat in front of the Steinway and allow my hands to hover over the keys, taking in the pattern of white and black just beneath my fingertips. It's not as nerve wracking now that I'm here and facing away from the crowd. I've prepared for this moment for months, and I refuse to let Pyotr down.

I begin to play.

Muscle memory quickly takes over. My fingers know where to go before my brain has a chance to think about it. I've got an entire repertoire lined up, every note memorized and every phrase perfected. Before long, I'm genuinely enjoying myself. I'd almost forgotten the joy playing the piano used to bring me. It's such a universal thing, music. You don't have to be from the same place or speak the same language to understand what it is or appreciate it, and I think that's really beautiful.

The audience seems enraptured, some of them swaying with the beat of the music in the corner of my periphery. Everything is going swimmingly until my mind blanks. I play the wrong note and my hands suddenly freeze up.

My cheeks immediately pool with heat. *Oh, please no. This can't be happening.*

I try to remain calm and try to keep playing, hoping muscle memory will see me out of this little stumble, but now my heart is beating loud and fast and the panic is setting in. I hear murmurs rise from the crowd. Nothing malicious, more like pity. Either way, the perfectionist in me is having a full-on meltdown.

I take a deep breath and try the bar again, but the same thing happens. Of *course* this had to happen to me on the last song of the evening. I try to restart again and again, until finally...

I turn to the crowd and laugh. "And this, kids, is what happens when you don't practice!"

The crowd laughs *with* me, not at me, breaking out into amused applause. They erupt into a roar as I stand up from the bench and take a bow, smiling bashfully as I chuckle the whole experience off as gracefully as I can. I'm not going to beat myself up about it. Overall, I think tonight was a grand success and a huge accomplishment.

Pyotr rises from his seat and climbs the few steps leading onto the stage, joining me at my side as easily as breathing. He kisses me on the lips in front of everyone without a care in the world, little Ava reaching for me with a happy laugh.

"That was amazing," he murmurs in my ear.

"Really? Even that last bit."

"I thought it was incredibly charming. Everyone does."

"Go on, give your speech so we can go to the afterparty."

Pyotr smirks as he turns to face the crowd. While he thanks everyone for coming and informs them there are complimentary drinks and hors d'oeuvres in the main hall, I stare up at him. I love the way he addresses the room with such ease and confidence. All eyes are on him, but then he turns and his eyes on me. It's hard to ignore the glint in his eye, the one he only gets when he sees me.

When he dips down again and kisses me, I know without a shadow of a doubt that he's my everything.

The End

Made in the USA
Columbia, SC
03 June 2023